5 AUTHOR ANTHOLOGY

EVERNIGHT PUBLISHING ®

www.evernightpublishing.com

Copyright© 2017

Evernight Publishing

Editor: CA Clauson

Proofreader: Laurie White

Cover Artist: Jay Aheer

ISBN: 978-1-77339-507-4

5 AUTHOR ANTHOLOGY

5-Author Erotic Contemporary Romance Anthology

Meet the hardcore heroes of LAWLESS! They're fearless, dangerous, big on revenge, and defiantly walk on the wrong side of the law. Although their morals may be compromised, their loyalty to that one man is never in question.

Our five hand-picked novellas are dark, dirty, and will make you see bad boys in a whole new light. From bikers to hitmen, these dangerous men won't be satisfied until they have everything they came for— until they have him.

Table of Contents

MONSTERS

A Club Cox Story

James Cox

Copyright © 2017

Chapter One

There's this feeling after a really good date, like you had a good orgasm after a month of abstaining. It's adrenaline and happiness. Rainbows and unicorns. That kind of cheesy shit. Anyway, that's how I felt right now. Last night had been my third date with Mr. Sexy, aka, Sebastian. We went to the beach of all things. The beach at the end of fall. The crisp, cool air made me shiver, but I quickly warmed up when Sebastian held my hand. We should have looked ridiculous. Two men walking down the beach holding hands and carrying their shoes. Seb didn't seem like the type to flaunt our virgin relationship, but he did. I loved it. He was ten years older than me and, being twenty, it was a bit of a gamble to see if we'd work out together. Best part of the night? That kiss. Damn! That kiss was crazy. I've been kissed a thousand times. Okay, maybe not exactly that many. It's not like I'm a virgin or that I've counted how many times my lips have locked with another guy's. But never have I experienced a kiss like that.

That should explain why I was sitting in my

father's house smiling. I never smiled when I was here. I loved him, don't get me wrong, but once my mother passed away we both just drifted apart. His house was filled with stuffy old furniture and perfectly neat rooms with nothing out of its place. Ever. It drove mom and me nuts. Anyway, here I was with his two brothers, triplets, talking about updating wills. No, I still couldn't tell them apart and yes, they were all disappointed in me. My father was the only one who ever got married or had a kid. These were literally the only Millers left in the world. Which is why we were here talking about my inheritance. They all made me want to roll my eyes and drop dead. Okay, that was a bit harsh, but they were stuffy and old-fashioned. They looked down on me because I was gay. These guys were making me grouchy. Fortunately, at that moment my cell phone rang.

"Really, Mickey?" My father's deep voice was filled with annoyance and disappointment. No one can put that type of feeling into a tone like he did.

"Sorry, dad." I glanced at the phone. *Sebastian!* "Oh, it's work. I have to take this."

"Work? What exactly is a bartender needed for at," He glanced at the Rolex on his wrist. "Ten in the morning? Is there an emergency drunk that needs to be escorted home?"

"Funny, dad." Yeah, he was still bitter about me not going to medical school. "I'll be right back." Hey, I loved bartending and I was saving up money to open my own place. It was all I wanted to do and he would never respect that. My grandfather ran a bar and his father and his father going back generations. My father and his two brothers were the only ones who broke the tradition and went into the medical field. I stood up and moved to the hallway where the front door was closed to the world outside. Although I could hear the horns honking and people yelling. This was New York City, after all. "Hello?"

"Hey, Mickey."

"Hello there." I grinned, thinking about our kiss. He had tugged on my hair and taken my breath away. Even now, despite my surroundings, my cock began to harden. "How are you?"

"I have to see you."

Yeah, I wanted to see him, too. "Sure. When?" I licked my lower lip, practically drooling at the thought of seeing Sebastian again.

"Now."

"Now?" It was ten in the morning. That was early for a date unless he planned on having sex for a few hours. Oh, that sounded fun.

"Yes. Right now." His voice was urgent, nervous almost.

"I want to. Really, I do but I can't right now. Tomorrow…"

"No!" He shouted.

Okay, this was getting creepy. "Um, Sebastian."

"Please. Listen to me. You have to leave that apartment, right now."

How the fuck did he know I was in an apartment? Well, this was the city. "What? Leave?" I was so confused.

"I don't care if you think I sound crazy. Leave that house. Right now. Meet me at the north corner. Now. Right now. Start moving!"

"Okay. Okay." What the fuck was going on? "Dad, I'll be right back."

"We're in the middle of the wills, Mickey." He sounded pissed. "Must you leave this moment? Is my death that much of a nuisance to you?"

"Dad, you're in better health than I am. I'll be

back in five minutes." I hoped. This was weird. With the phone still on, I opened the door to the streets of the city. People jogged past and a few taxis went by as I moved down the front steps. Which way was north? Oh, there was a street to my left that had north in the name. Maybe that's what Sebastian meant. I started walking and thinking, then doubting. If it was an emergency, why the hell would he call the guy he'd only been on three dates with? This didn't make sense. I arrived at the corner and stood there. A middle-aged lady glanced at me and grabbed her purse. Yeah, thanks, because I looked like a mugger in blue jeans and a suit jacket. I wrapped my arms around my body as the chill in the air made me shiver. Where the hell was he? This was crazy. He was crazy. How did he even know where I was? Stalker and nut flashed through my mind. "Screw this shit." I turned around to go back.

That was when the apartment exploded.

Chapter Two

I was blown back by the intense heat and wind. My ass hit the ground first, and then my back. I managed to close my eyes sometime during that, because I found myself opening my eyelids and seeing chaos. Horrible, terrible, chilling chaos. Glass and bricks littered the street. There was no sound. Shouldn't there be sounds? Screaming, for instance. "Oh, my God." I said the words, but couldn't hear them.

The apartment just exploded.

My father's apartment.

"Oh, my God!" I shoved to my knees and heard an intense ringing. No, not a ring, a scream. "Dad!" I shouted, not sure how loud or if anyone heard. There was a taxi flipped over. The driver crawled through the broken window. It didn't seem like anyone was too badly hurt, but I didn't stop to find out. "Dad!" The stone stairs were surprisingly intact and I fumbled up them. "Uncle Clide?" Jesus, the front door was gone. There was just a big hole there. "Uncle Chris?" I could see the hall as I stood outside. The wall to the kitchen was gone. Bricks were in pieces and picture frames crunched under my feet. "Dad?" The living room was a complete loss. The ceiling had collapsed. The four-poster guest bed with cherubs carved into the wood was on top of crushed couches. "Damn it, Dad. Answer me!" I shouted. Was that sirens? I gave a deep bellow of a shout and the dresser fell through the hole in the ceiling. It slammed against the wall which caused the entire thing to collapse. I leaped back as bricks tumbled down into the street.

"Mick…"

"I hear you! I hear you!" I shoved past the elaborate wooden staircase that was no longer attached to the second floor. "Where are you?" I didn't know who it was, but there was someone in the study. The door was blown off the hinges and the window was shattered on the opposite wall. A bookshelf had been knocked over. "Fuck." There were legs sticking out from under the eighteenth century overturned desk.

"Mickey?" The voice was so weak. My foot slid on a book and I fell to one knee. The pain reverberated up my back, but was quickly dulled by adrenaline. I knew that sweater vest! "Dad." I don't know where I found the strength, but I pushed that desk off him and it fell over with a loud thud.

"Mickey? Mickey, what happened?" He had a cut on his jaw and a dark bruise forming around his eye.

"I'm here. I'm here. Anything broken? Ribs? Legs?" Where the hell were the ambulances or the fire engines? There was smoke coming from the corner of the room and I wasn't sure if it was debris from the blast or an actual fire.

"Nothing broken," he answered.

My father suddenly looked older. I mean, I know he was in his sixties, but now he really looked it. His hair was splattered with plaster and his vest had a huge hole in it. He stayed in shape, so his muscles bunched under my palms as he fought to get up.

"Clide? Chris?" My father reached out and used me to help get to his feet.

"Where were they, Dad?" I shifted my arm around his back to support him walking.

"Living room."

"Shit."

"What?" My father must have hit his head because he didn't immediately yell about my vulgar language. "Where are they?" We came through the hall and he paused. His mouth fell open. "Oh, no." His bottom lip actually trembled.

"This is the FDNY," a firefighter yelled as he entered what was left of my childhood home.

"Here! We're here." I waved at him, but quickly needed both hands to hold my father upright.

"You have to leave. The building could collapse. Anyone else unaccounted for?"

"My two uncles." I nodded my head toward the devastated living room then started toward the door ... or where the door had been. Three cop cars wailed down the street. A fire engine blocked my car in and EMTs were already circulating. "Hey. I need help here!" A blonde raised her head and rushed toward us with a medical bag. "Please. Help him. He was in the explosion."

"Explosion?" my father roared.

Another EMT with a stretcher jogged over and I helped my father to it.

"An explosion?" he asked again, shock written all over his face.

Yes, an explosion that would have killed me if I hadn't left the apartment. An explosion that probably killed my uncles and wounded my father. My hand actually shook as I pulled my phone out of my pocket. The glass was cracked, but my last caller was still on the screen.

Sebastian.

****

"So he told you to leave just before the explosion?"

"Yes."

"But he didn't tell you why he wanted you to leave or what he wanted from you?" The detective gave me a bushy eyebrow raise as he asked the question.

I didn't even blame him. "I thought maybe he was in trouble or something but he never showed. When

I went to go back to the apartment that's when it … it…"
Fuck, I couldn't even say it.

"And the full name is Sebastian Graves?"

"That's what he told me. I haven't been to his house, but maybe the restaurant we went to would have his information. He paid with a credit card."

"That's good." The detective nodded and jotted down in his notepad.

Honestly, he looked like a guy that would be extremely judgmental and homophobic. White guy, big mustache—the older generation tended to be more conservative in my opinion, but the cop had been completely professional with the exception of that one eyebrow lift. If I heard this crazy-ass story I'd have done a lot more than that.

"We'll call you if we find him or need any other information." He tucked his writing pad in his front jacket pocket. "Um, I'm sorry about your uncles. I heard your father's going to pull through and, well, I hope he's okay."

"Thank you, detective." I stuck out my hand and we shook. He turned to leave and I straightened in the waiting room seat trying to keep myself together. My father was in there with the doctors now. A few minutes ago, that detective had confirmed that they found my uncles in the house. Deceased, he said. Such a simple way of saying their lives were gone.

"Mr. Miller?" The man in the doctor's coat smiled. "Good news. Your father's going to be okay."

I think my chest collapsed. I fell back and took the deepest breath of my life.

"Bruises. Stitches on his jaw. No concussion, no internal bleeding, no broken bones. He's very lucky."

"Thank you. Thank you so much!"

"We're going to keep him overnight to keep an

eye on him, but you can take him home tomorrow."

Except that he didn't have a home to go to. "Thanks." Fuck. I had to plan funerals. They'd be pretty empty because there was no one else in our family and now it was just the two of us. How fucking depressing. "Can I see him?"

"We gave him some pretty powerful pain medication. He'll be sleeping most of the night."

"Oh, okay. Well, thanks. I'll see you tomorrow." God, I felt drained. I dragged myself out of the waiting room and down the back stairwell where I took a taxi home. There were reporters lingering near the front when the taxi passed and I ducked down a bit. The explosion was being investigated, but so far, they ruled out a gas leak. Considering his home hadn't used gas, I could have told them that wasn't it. A fucking explosion. My eyelids were beginning to droop as we pulled in front of my better-than-modest apartment. The only reason I didn't live in a cardboard box was because my father agreed to pay my rent until I turned twenty-five. Only five years left.

I paid the cabbie. When I opened my door, I paused and listened for the ticking of a bomb. Stupid, I know, but it had been a fucked-up day and I was exhausted. I closed the door, kicked off my shoes, and collapsed onto the nearest couch.

"Don't yell."

Sebastian's voice made me jerk to my feet and face him. He was nothing but a shadow in the hallway, tall and menacing. "Hey." What the hell did I say? Do I demand to know what the hell happened? Do I try to call the cops?

He took a step forward and came into view. God, he was gorgeous with shoulder-length black hair, deep brown eyes, and a chiseled jaw. Sebastian filled out clothes like they were a second fucking skin. My feelings took second place to the shit that happened today. "I don't know what to say." Cops? Run? Ask him? I took a soft, subtle step toward the right. My cell phone was on the table and the door with all those potential witnesses was beyond that. At least I had a backup plan.

"Will you hear me out?"

"Okay." *Shit. Fuck. Hell.*

"It's not what you think." He paused. "Or it is what you think, but not the reason you think." He winced. His lips pressed together in a firm line. "I'm not explaining this right."

"Explaining?" I snapped. "You want to explain what the fuck happened? You tell me to leave the apartment and then it fucking explodes." I shut my mouth after the outburst. *Damn it.*

"I couldn't…" He took another step forward. Suddenly that six feet of sexy looked extremely dangerous. "I couldn't let you die in there."

He knew! "You killed my uncles. You nearly killed my father." I swiped the cell off the table and held it like a weapon. "The cops are looking for you."

"I know. I'll have an iron-clad alibi."

The fuck? "But you're admitting to me you did it?" Oh, God, he did it. Why was he telling me? I'd be a fucking witness. Witnesses didn't survive. They were always casualties.

"You don't understand."

"Understand? Understand? No, I don't understand how you can set off a bomb in my father's house!" I shouted, my voice wavering in pitch. "There is no fucking understanding." I dialed 9-1-1 as I yelled. "Nothing could explain why that would be okay or why you'd think I'd ever, ever, ever fucking see you again."

"He's a serial killer."

Random sounds popped out of my mouth as I sputtered. "What the fuck?"

"Your father. He's a serial killer." Sebastian took a step toward me. He was getting closer and closer. "I'm sorry to tell you like this. I didn't want you to know, but you arrived at his house and there wasn't time to save you without exposing myself." He threw his hands up. "Mickey, I've been hunting them for years. Years! And I've never once made a mistake like this. I never get attached and in three fucking dates you had me. The second I saw you go into that building I couldn't catch my breath and I thought I would fucking pass out from my heart beating so fast."

"So you what? You fucking love me? After three dates?" I scoffed. "You're insane. Leave it to me to go on a date with a guy who should be in a mental institution!"

"I'm not crazy. Your father was…"

"Is."

"Is?"

Fuck. I think I just admitted he survived. "He's not a killer. He's my father. He's a normal guy, a doctor, for fuck's sake." The soft ringing stopped and a 9-1-1 dispatcher mumbled something into the phone. "So, you admit. You blew up my father's house."

Sebastian paused and his eyes darted to the phone discreetly curled in my hand.

Shit. "Sebastian."

He shook his head, looking sad and alone. Then he turned on his heel and walked toward the front door.

"Sebastian!" He didn't say a fucking word. I didn't even hear the door open or close, but when I ran around the wall, the main hall was empty. "Fuck you, too." I fell back against the wall and couldn't catch my breath. Explosions. Serial killers. What the fuck was going on?

Chapter Three

After a restless night and a fruitless trip to the precinct, I took a taxi to my father's house, or rather what was left of it. There was no merit whatsoever to what Sebastian was saying. Apparently, he had an iron-clad alibi for the explosion. He was on camera walking into a spa to get a massage and the camera was trained on the only door in or out. Half an hour later the same camera showed him leaving and giving the sexy masseur a generous tip. The detectives considered him a dead end even thought I tried to persuade them otherwise.

The house still had crime scene tape around it. Scorch marks stained the sidewalk and street. According to the firefighters and the inspector, the house was still stable despite losing so much. No load baring walls were damaged and there was zero percent chance of collapse. Hey, that was good news. I knew the insurance company was coming by in a few days—I made the phone call this morning between the shitty sleep and talking to the cops. Then I went to see my father who was still out from the drugs. I planned on gathering a few things I knew he couldn't live without, his phone, a few literary classics he read over and over. He needed some clothes, and of course, pictures of mom. Shit, I still had to deal with my uncles' funerals. I sighed as the cabbie pulled up. After I paid him, I trudged up the stairs.

"Excuse me, sir. This is an active crime scene." A cop was standing beside the large hole. I hadn't even realized he was there.

"Oh. Yeah, I know." I pulled out my license. "My father lives … lived here. I just wanted to grab some of his stuff for the hospital."

"The guy that survived? God bless him." He took

a second to confirm that I was allowed inside. "I have to check the stuff before you leave."

I didn't have anything to hide. "You got it." I tiptoed my way down the hall and avoided looking into the living room. Water dripped from somewhere in the kitchen, I heard the rhythmic tapping as I passed. Luckily, my father's room was connected to the study. Upstairs was the main bedroom he shared with my mother. Once she passed away, he moved down here and used that as a guest room. I stepped into the untouched room and grabbed what I needed. I shoved it all into a pillowcase which would have pissed my father off to no end. Not that I was going to tell him how I transported all his shit to the hospital or my apartment because I had no doubt I was stuck with him. Wouldn't that be fun? We didn't exactly mesh well.

The living room floor had caved in some, leaving a bunch of boards warped. They curved downward into the small basement where I heard more trickling water. Was there a pipe leaking or something? That would ruin whatever storage he was keeping down there. Sebastian's accusation kept replaying in my head. Well, I could check this basement out just to prove that he was batshit crazy, too. My father wasn't a fucking serial killer. I rolled my eyes at the thought. I dropped the sack and then made my way down the stairs by the kitchen.

The horrific smells that drifted up my nostrils made me cough. Water had leaked from a pipe with a puncture. It covered the soles of my sneakers as I trudged through. "There's nothing here." I said it aloud because I felt fucking ridiculous doing this. Why the hell was I listening to some guy I'd only been on three dates with? Why? "Because I'm an idiot," I muttered and stood in the middle of the small one-roomed basement. I didn't even know what I was looking for. There was a washer, dryer, heater, and water tank here. Well, nothing screams serial killer like folded socks. I grabbed the white pair on the dryer and stuffed them in my pocket because that's the one thing I forgot to pack. "See? Nothing." I threw up my hands and turned around.

Beside the steep stairs was the end table that had once been next to the couch. My coffee cup had been on that the day of the explosion. Now, that fancy white mug was embedded into the brick wall.

Jesus, it really had been one hell of an explosion. How no one died on the street was a miracle or really fucking good planning, which was disturbing. I took a deep breath and coughed. "That smell!" I closed my nostrils with my fingers and started up the stairs.

Something clobbered to the ground and broke. I could hear it shatter, like glass or something.

When I turned around, nothing had fallen. There were no ripples in the water. Nothing down here could have made that sound without splashing water. Okay, so maybe that was a bit creepy, but serial killer creepy? Really? I stood on the bottom step, frowning, and debated with myself. It took a full thirty seconds before I sludged back through the water to the coffee cup. With my fingers on the edges, I tugged and the sucker didn't budge. Okay, so a piece of that hadn't fallen. What the hell made that sound then? Maybe it was upstairs. I couldn't believe this. Here I was searching for clues that my father might be a murderer all because some jackass said so. I slapped the mug which sent it flying through the air, against the stairs and into the water.

For a second I stared at it only to blink a few times at the hole the cup left. The brick wall should have light coming through. This was an above-ground basement and it was daylight out there. I stuck my fingers into the dark recess and frowned. "No. No. This is crazy." I turned around only to stop and fumble for my cell phone. "This is fucking insane." I turned on the flashlight option and stuck the phone over half the hole. "Oh, my God." There was another fucking room back here. What the hell? That made no sense! I could see a chair and a desk and … was that a small television with a DVD player? There were jars on the wall. That had to be what fell before.

"Mr. Miller?" The officer's voice was like a bell going off right next to my ears.

"I'm here. I'm right here." Unless I fell, hit my head and was hallucinating. "I … I think you should see this."

****

Forty DVDs. Forty lives snuffed out on those DVDs.

I heaved, but breakfast had already come up hours ago. The cops broke down the wall and found what I could only assume was a fucking hallucination. For the first half an hour I thought maybe I was caught in the blast, too, and this was all a horrible, coma-induced nightmare. That terrible thought slowly wore off to reveal an even more horrific reality. What I saw was real. Jars of … of … of souvenirs. Bracelets, necklaces, earrings, and the tapes. Jesus fucking Christ, there were tapes. The cops wouldn't let me see what was on them and I had to thank God for that. I didn't want to know what secrets were buried down there. After cleaning out my stomach, I went to the police station where I was questioned mercilessly and I couldn't process it all.

They found proof.

Real.

Fucking.

Proof.

My father, that crazy son of a bitch, had murdered

people. People! Not a person, which was bad enough, but more than one. Two hours later they sent me home with a stern warning not to leave town and that my father would have a police escort until this was all sorted out. I heaved again and held my stomach while I laid my head back against the wall.

What the fuck was there to sort out?

I dragged myself up off the bathroom floor and brushed my teeth. My head hurt, my body ached, and my chest felt heavy with … what? Emotion? Grief? Disbelief? The sun had fallen while my world shattered, so I threw on the light switch and walked into the kitchen to grab the entire bottle of wine. I didn't see the shadow standing in the corner, not until I popped the cork, took a slug, and turned around. "Fuck!" I leaped back and smashed my hip on the counter. "God damn it! Don't you use doors? Those are the things you knock on and people open to let you in, so that you don't scare the shit out of them when they see you in the shadows."

Sebastian stepped out of the darkness in black jeans and a dark gray t-shirt. "I'm sorry."

"Use the door, or the window, or a fucking bell on your neck for all I care." I placed the wine on the counter and turned to face Sebastian. He stood there, still as a fucking statue. "They found a room. In the apartment. The basement was smaller than it should have been and…" I swallowed hard. "There were things in that room. DVDs." I swallowed again, having a hard time, and then felt queasy. "You were right." I glanced at the floor. "You were fucking right. He's a … my father's a monster. We've never really been that close, but I never thought…" I shook my head. "What if I'd had a sister or nieces or…" The DVDs all had women's names written in thick black marker on the side. "How did you know, about him, about his … how?" The man I'd been on three dates with was an expert on my family and he found the worst secrets he could possibly find.

"Sebastian?"

"I've been hunting him."

I grabbed the wine and drank until I had to take a breath.

"He started when he was a teenager, but he stopped when he met your mother. When she died, he started again. Taking women, mostly prostitutes. I saw him one night. He took a blonde girl from the street and then nearly ran me over with his car. It took a while to find him."

"And when you did? You thought the best way to get to him was through me."

"Yes."

Fucking bastard! I threw the wine at the sink and watched as the bottle shattered. Dark shards and red liquid splashed on the counter.

"And then I spent time with you." Sebastian took a step forward. He dragged a hand through his black hair. "That's why I called you. I saw you go into that apartment and you were innocent in this. I … I like you. I haven't felt emotions like this for years, Mickey. I broke my own rule about not getting emotionally involved and I called you even though it would implicate me."

Because being liked by a serial killer hunter was my main priority right now. It shouldn't be, but his words made me wish I'd kept the wine. "You killed my uncles!" I couldn't forget about that. I marched into the living room. "They were all I had. My only family in the entire world."

"They helped him hide the bodies."

I fell back and landed on the couch arm. "What?" My God, there was no way this could be true. How could everyone in my family be so evil?

"They helped him hide his most recent kills in a wooded area on your uncle Clide's land."

I slid back so the couch could support me.

"I watched them with binoculars. I was following your father and was surprised when he went to his brother's house. I couldn't tell them apart at first and I wasn't sure who the real killer was, but they were all guilty."

He sounded so fucking calm. How could he be so calm? "Who the fuck are you?"

"The monster hunter." Sebastian walked slowly to the coffee table and sat down in front of me. "I'm sorry this happened to you."

"My whole world is falling apart stitch by stitch and you're sorry? What if it was genetic? Oh, my God, what if this violent, psycho behavior is in my genes?" *Wait. Wait. Calm down.* I had my mother's genes, too. She was completely innocent.

"Have you ever thought about killing someone?" Sebastian asked, leaning his elbows on his knees.

"No."

"Do you like animals? Dogs? Cats?"

"Love them. I have a cat who hates strangers. She's probably hiding under the bed."

"Ever thought about hurting her?"

"My cat?" I jerked my head up to stare at him. "Never. Ever. Ever. Times about a million."

"Do you get sexually excited at the thought of hurting or killing?"

"No! God, no. Fuck, no." I was nauseous from the thought.

"I'm pretty sure you don't have any serial killer instincts." Sebastian reached out and touched my hand. It made me flinch. "I'm so sorry about your family. Truly, I am. I had only planned on going on one date to see if you were close with your father. The other dates weren't supposed to happen, but I couldn't resist seeing you again."

"Sebastian." I wasn't sure what to say. My father was probably going on trial for more than one murder. My uncles were dead. Soon the whole world would know my family for the deepest, darkest depravity. "Who are you?"

He licked his lips. "What I told you was mostly true. Another first for me. I am an ex-marine. I am thirty and my birthday is on July twenty-ninth."

"And you don't work for the government?"

He shook is head slowly and lowered his gaze to our hands. "People, victim's families, hire me to find justice. I find the person or persons that killed their loved one and I don't use the legal system. I exact a more bloody revenge."

"You kill … killers?"

"Something like that."

"Jesus Christ. Jesus fucking Christ." I pulled my hand away. "What the fuck? What the actual fuck!" I shoved to my feet and paced to the flat screen TV then back to the couch where I plopped down in front of him. "Someone hired you to find my father?"

"Anna Carson's family. She was sixteen. Ran away from home. She was last seen in the same alley that the blonde victim was taken from."

"My father … he killed her, too."

Sebastian slowly nodded.

"I … I can't deal with this sober. Holy shit." I got back to my feet, but was quickly pulled to the couch.

"Mickey."

"No. No. My whole family are murderers! That's not something a normal man can deal with. They … they… Holy shit."

25

Sebastian slid a hand along my jaw. "Let me help you forget."

"Sex? That's your answer?" I needed a bottle of tequila and some salt.

"No. My answer is to show you that you're much more than your family." Sebastian eased closer.

"We've only known each other for three weeks."

"But it feels like I've known you forever. It feels like I've found home." Sebastian glanced away. There was so much pain in his expression. "Mickey. Let me help you forget."

I opened my mouth to protest, but he closed the distance.

Chapter Four

Sebastian didn't hesitate or go slow. His open mouth pressed against mine and his tongue instantly invaded. For all of thirty seconds, I was completely thoughtless. My mind was filled with lust and erotic images. Then he paused to tug my shirt off and sanity came crashing back. "Sebastian." His name came out in a whine.

"Don't think. Please. God, Mickey. Don't think." Seb's voice was raspy and deep. He slipped his hands up my torso and along my flat stomach. He rested his palms on my chest and snuggled his fingers in the crisp, dark hair. "Kiss me."

Was it so horrible to want to drown my emotions in sweaty sex with a hot guy? I leaned forward. Our mouths were just as wild and untamed.

"Mmm." Sebastian licked my lower lip then grabbed my wrist. He placed my hand on the back of his head. My fingers sunk into the soft strands. "Pull my hair."

"O ... okay." I tugged.

"Harder." Sebastian nipped at my chin. "Please. Mickey. Harder."

Fuck me. This sexy, six-foot god wanted me to give him pain. I pulled his hair and shivered at the deep, needy moan that came from Sebastian's mouth. Our lips met again. He softened the touch and I took control.

"Oh, yes." Sebastian slid his hands to the tops of my thighs. "Can I touch you?"

He needed to ask? "Yes." I sputtered the word and took Sebastian's earlobe between my teeth. When he cupped my crotch, I pulled his hair.

Sebastian grunted and gasped.

I let go of his hair and drew his shirt up. A hard-earned six pack greeted my vision. "Damn, you're gorgeous."

Sebastian lifted his arms to help me, but once I threw the shirt over the couch he lowered to his knees. He rubbed his hands up and down my jeans-clad thighs. The material only made me growl in frustration. I wanted skin to skin. I needed to keep my mind on sex. I leaned back and reached for my belt.

"No. Please, Mickey. Let me." Sebastian stared at me with those big brown eyes and upturned face. "Please."

I showed him my palms. "Go for it." So, he was, what? A submissive? I thought they were timid? I read BDSM books, but never experienced it with a guy before. He was more like an aggressive bottom.

"Pull my hair again." Sebastian begged as he loosened my belt and popped the button.

I was really liking this. More confident, I pulled his hair and watched him lower my zipper. My cock pressed against my white underwear.

"Can I take your pants off?"

Well I was kind of hoping that's where this was going. I nodded. Sebastian lowered to my crotch and began rubbing his face against me. "Damn, that feels great."

"Lift your hips, please."

Hearing the polite request coming from such a masculine badass made pre-cum bubble out. I lifted my hips and Sebastian heaved the jeans down. He made a production of pulling my boot off. Then he skimmed his hands along the arch of my left foot and ground his palm into my heel. I groaned. Why did that feel so good? Sebastian yanked the left pant leg off and massaged my calf muscle then kissed my knee. He dug his fingers into my thigh and made me feel like melted butter. I collapsed back to the couch while he did the same to my right side. When Sebastian finished the thigh massage he pressed kisses around my belly button. My dick was so hard I could probably chop wood with it. The pressure was almost painful.

"What would you like me to do?"

Rhetorical question? I glanced at Sebastian. He sat back on his butt with his hands idle in his lap. "Oh." He really wanted to know. "Um … suck me?" A blowjob would definitely make my night better.

"Whatever you want, Mickey."

More pre-cum bubbled out. His submission was such a fucking turn-on, and I'd never been into that kind of stuff before. I was drunk with the power of domination as he pulled my underwear off. My bare ass was nestled in the couch cushions. My thick shaft jutted from my body with a few beads of pre-cum dripping along the foreskin.

Sebastian glided his hands up my hairy thighs and his thumbs grazed my balls.

I jerked and took a deep breath. I was so ready to explode.

"Do you want me to lick your balls?" Sebastian asked as he rubbed his cheek along my thigh.

"Yes. Yes, I do." I managed to sound calm even though my heartbeat soared. Sebastian gave my balls an open-mouthed kiss and then started to lick. "Fuck!" I lifted my hips and then hefted one leg so he had full access. Never in my entire life had a lover licked my balls so thoroughly. He took his time. Sebastian tasted and savored. He slid an arm under my leg and directed it so that I rested my leg on his shoulder. "Fucking hell!" I shouted as he swirled and sucked. "Sebastian. Seriously. Can't last long with that." I wiggled my hips in anticipation and need. I couldn't stop squirming.

He kissed my inner thigh. "Do you want me to suck your cock now?"

More than my next breath seemed like a pathetic answer. "Yes." I breathed the word.

"Will you pull my hair while I deep throat you? Please?" He moaned and pressed his hips against the couch.

"Sure." I said and he gave me a smile that would have fucking melted my pants right off if I'd been wearing any.

He opened wide and grabbed my dick at the base. "Mickey?" He gave me this completely hopeful expression as he pointed to his head.

"Oh. Right." A blowjob for hair pulling seemed like a fucking fantastic deal. I tugged and Sebastian licked my slit. The sound I made was a sputter of syllables. He swirled his lips along my tip and his tongue probed my foreskin. "Sebastian!" I gasped. My hips jerked upward. He squeezed my shaft and started to take my length. "Fuck!" I had to grit my teeth to keep from screaming. Inch after inch he took into his mouth. Saliva dripped down my balls. His tongue teased the underside of my cock. The rigid roof of his mouth was amazing against my skin. He coughed and eased up. "That was great!" I squirmed. I was so close to coming I could feel the promise of orgasm.

He took a breath and then sucked on my tip.

"Fuck! Sebastian!" He started to deep throat me again. He took every inch and I wasn't a small guy. His nostrils tickled my pubic hair. Saliva dribbled from my balls to the couch. His hands squeezed my thighs. He held there and I rewarded him by jerking on his hair. On his slow way up, I came. It was a sudden burst, and cum spurted out of my slit into his throat. I kept coming as he swallowed and swirled his tongue around my foreskin. "Sebastian!" I yelled as every muscle in my body burned from tension. Then I was empty. I fell back to the couch and loosened my grip in his hair. "Wow." My eyelids closed.

Sebastian laid his cheek on my thigh. "Did I do a good job?"

Seriously? "Best. Blowjob. Ever."

He smiled against my skin and kissed my softening dick. It gave a hearty twitch, but didn't thicken. "Mickey. May I come now?"

What? He hadn't come? Fuck me, he hadn't even taken his pants off yet. "Yes. Yes, of course." I sat up. "Do you want me to touch you? Lick you?" My mouth watered in anticipation. I couldn't deep throat as well as him though.

Sebastian lifted to his impressive height. "Will you watch?"

"Absolutely!"

He hauled his pants down right in front of me.

"Oh." Well, then. Fuck, it was like a damn weapon when fully erect. I bet if I got hit in the face it would actually give me a black eye! My mouth fell open. There was no way I could deep throat that.

Sebastian sat his bare ass on my coffee table. "Do you like it?" He grabbed his shaft at the base and gave it a violent squeeze.

"Oh, yeah." I sat forward and placed my hands on his knees.

Sebastian began to stroke his cock. Each pull was rough and quick. He hissed out a breath. His eyes locked onto my limp dick dangling between my legs.

"Feel good?" Wasn't that too rough?

"So good. So, so good." He moaned. "Will you kiss me?"

I didn't hesitate. This time I locked our lips together and took control. I kissed him as Sebastian jerked his shaft up and down. "Hair?" I asked. He really seemed to like that.

"Yes. Now. Please, Mickey!"

I pulled hard on his hair, wrenched his head back and sucked on his neck.

Sebastian growled as he came. Cum gushed from his cock. It splashed my thighs, his legs, the table and when he sighed in satisfaction, I eased my grip. "Thank you." Sebastian laid his forehead against mine.

"My pleasure. Literally."

He grinned, pants around his ankles, still sitting bare-assed on my coffee table. His dick began to soften and the relaxed expression turned stoic. He shifted, stood, and dragged his pants up. Once that beast was tucked away he guided me to my feet and planted a kiss on my lips that nearly brought my erection back to life. "Can I see you tomorrow?"

"Of course." More kissing! More licking! "I'd like that." Look at me sounding all calm and cool.

Sebastian reached down and squeezed my ass cheeks. "Good night, Mickey." He let go and moved to the front door.

Why was he leaving? I wanted him to stay! If he was with me all night he'd keep my mind busy with thoughts of his thick cock and crazy, sexy submission fetish. I opened my lips to stay something, but the world around me took shape. The city was alive outside, cars, horns, shouting. Somewhere out there was my father in a hospital bed. Somewhere out there detectives were sitting down with families to tell them their little girls were dead. Being in Sebastian's arms all night would help me forget. I rushed toward the front door and wrenched it open. The street was empty. I sat naked on the couch and started thinking again. Damn it!

Chapter Five

"The insanity plea!" I screamed into my cell phone as I opened my front door. After cremating both my uncles and spreading their ashes in a stream near the cemetery. I got a call from my father's lawyer. That's right, he had a lawyer to say he was mentally insane after my mother died and they wanted me to be a character witness. *Me*. "Are you fucking serious?"

"Mr. Miller." The crisp, cold lawyer's voice came through loud and clear. "You're his son."

"Something I regret with every passing day. I can't answer my home phone because of the fucking reporters and there's been a news van following me around all day." It had been hell. Absolute hell. Everyone knew me as the son of the serial killer. Victims' families were harassing me. I got several huge offers, I'm talking in the thousands, for exclusive interviews. The shitty bar I work at put me on suspension because the bar was filled with reporters instead of drinking customers. Then there were the death threats. "First, we were never close. Second, he's a serial killer. I found the proof! Third, he's a fucking serial killer!" I screamed it into my cell phone and slammed my front door shut just as the horde of camera-clicking people charged up my stairs.

"Mr. Miller…"

"Don't call me that." I hated it. Absolutely hated it. That meant I was related to a serial killer that so far had been charged with forty counts of torture and murder. "In fact, don't call me again. I will not testify on my father's behalf."

"We can subpoena you."

"Then do it, but it won't help your case." I slammed the off button and then threw the phone across the room for good measure. It would have slammed into the wall if Sebastian hadn't reached up and grabbed it.

"Hello."

"Window or back door this time?"

The corner of his lips lifted into a grin. "Upstairs window."

"Impressive." My cell phone started ringing and he tossed it to me. "My father's lawyer." I dropped the phone on the small table near the door.

"I enjoyed last night." Sebastian said. His voice was firm and confident as he stood.

"Me, too. A lot." I swallowed hard. "I've never met anyone like you."

Sebastian grinned and the wicked look was exactly what I imaged the devil would give you before he snatches your soul.

I licked my lips. "It's like a circus out there. My father's pleading mental defect or disease and he wants me on his side."

Sebastian paused and his jaw hardened. "Are you? On his side."

"Of course not!" Was he nuts? "That stuff I found. There's no way it just got there by accident, for fuck's sake." When I woke up at about three in the morning, I had paced the apartment like a madman. The weight of everything had ground down on my shoulders. Never in the far reaches of my mind would I have thought my father was a serial killer. The small fear that it was in my genes had grown until I was sitting on the floor numb. Of course, that's when my picky cat decided to come over for a cuddle, which was rare. She was tiny, furry, and innocent. Wouldn't she be my first victim if I were like him? I spent a full hour petting her and giving her ear rubs. Even when I rubbed her belly and she attempted to bite my finger, I wasn't mad at her. I gave her a kiss and an extra midnight snack. She was my pretty girl and she gave me hope that the crazy-ass murder gene had skipped me. "Sebastian?"

He was walking toward me, his head down and his eyes locked on mine.

It reminded me of a lion stalking its prey. A shiver slithered up my spine. "How did you … how did you even start doing this job? I mean, you don't graduate high school and decide to secretly kill murderers for a living."

Sebastian stopped in front of me and frowned. "You do … if your boyfriend is taken by one."

"Oh, my God." I hadn't thought of that. Why hadn't I thought of that? "Was it…" I cleared my throat. "Was it…"

"Your father. No."

I remained silent, hoping he'd tell me what happened. How had his life led up to this? But he didn't say a word. "Sebastian."

"He died. I survived. It's not a long story." He leaned closer and sniffed my neck. His lips grazed over my jaw.

"Oh." I wanted to know more, but I didn't want to push.

"I actually haven't had a boyfriend since then. Or sex. Yeah, my right hand doesn't count as a relationship."

I snorted and gasped when his tongue glided along my lower lip.

"Nobody until you, Mickey. Three dates. Fuck me, three dates and I couldn't get enough of you."

I smiled. "That's romantic."

"Which should tell you something because I'm not normally a romantic guy." Sebastian pressed kisses along my eyebrow.

"It's okay. I can be romantic enough for the both of us." I was good at that stuff. Flowers, anniversaries, candlelit dates.

"Mickey. You make me want to be romantic." Sebastian whispered the words against my lips and then kissed me.

I slid my hands into his hair and tugged. It made Sebastian groan and I shifted our lower bodies together. I forced his mouth wider and was overly aggressive with my tongue. It felt strange to be so forward, but not a bad thing. Why did stress make sex sound so fucking perfect? My cell phone started blaring and we separated. I could hear reporters outside. Someone was knocking on the door. The phone stopped, but then started ringing again. "Damn." Reality was crashing in too fast.

Sebastian took my hand and twined our fingers. "Do you want me?"

"That should be kind of obvious." I glanced down at my tented jeans and saw Sebastian was sporting his own erection.

"I want you inside my ass so bad." He groaned. "But I want this to be about us. You and me. Not just making you forget…"

Like last night. I squeezed his hand. "The only two people in here are you and me." And the phone ringing for the third time.

Sebastian smiled then led me to the narrow stairs.

Climbing gave me a fantastic view of his ass in those jeans. There were only two rooms on this floor, my bedroom and a large bathroom. There was a third set that led to the roof, but I learned years ago that sex on a roof in the city was like inviting the freaks and voyeurs in. Me, being the curious perv with the binoculars. I did, however, leave an anonymous note to the couple the next day so they knew they weren't alone when on the roof.

Sebastian led us into the bedroom. I was slightly embarrassed by the fact that the bed was unmade and yesterday's clothes were still on the floor. Also that empty bottle of shaving cream sticking out of the overturned garbage.

Sebastian faced me. "Do you have condoms? Lube?"

"Yeah." I cleared my throat. "Yes. Nightstand."

He dropped my hand and moved to the wooden stand. I only had one because this was a small room. I opened up the bathroom for extra space so I could fit that huge jet tub in there. The light was pretty good here though. The sunlight streamed through thin curtains that occasionally billowed in the breeze. Seagulls mulled around the Hudson River, squalling.

Sebastian grinned as he held two porn magazines. "Who uses magazines anymore?"

"Porn sites have viruses," I muttered lamely.

He laughed lightly and dropped the magazines back in the drawer. He walked toward me gracefully. His hips swayed and his bare feet glided along the carpet.

When had he taken off his shoes? I was leaning forward by the time he met me and our lips found each other.

"Can I take your shirt off?"

I noticed the harder his dick got, the more submissive he became. "Yes."

Sebastian slipped his hands under my shirt and pulled it over my head. He flicked my nipples and then dragged his palms down my stomach. "Pants, too?"

I had to look up into his eyes because he was a few inches taller than me. "Yes." He unbuckled my belt, removed my boots then jeans and pushed everything to the side. My cock was well on its way to fully erect. It bounced slightly, curving to the right.

Sebastian rose to his feet. "I'd like to undress for you, Mickey."

I don't know if I'd survive that. "I'd like that, too." I sat on the bed, legs wide, dick sprung. I expected him to start with his shirt but Sebastian removed his belt first. He unbuttoned and unzipped. He tugged his pants down, but his mouthwatering shaft and balls were hidden. He turned around then slowly lifted his t-shirt. That ass was fucking perfect. It met his back in a graceful curve. When Sebastian threw his shirt, he remained standing. "Mickey. Will you spank me?"

"It'll be a first for me."

Sebastian leaned over with his hands on his knees. His balls hung beautifully between his legs.

"Do I just..." I slid my hand up the back of his thigh. "Do I just slap your ass? Do I warn you before each spank? How hard is too hard?" My fingers practically tingled. I wanted to do this. I wanted to give him pleasure. The urge was a slow simmer steadily growing.

"Whenever you want. As hard as you want. I won't say stop."

"There has to be a limit." Didn't there?

"Please!" He glanced over his shoulder. "Please, Mickey, spank me."

I skimmed my fingers across his right ass cheek. "Okay." I gave him a soft pat and then a resounding slap.

Sebastian moaned. His balls swayed on the next spank.

"Harder?"

"However you want." His voice was soft and almost dreamy.

I gave Sebastian's left ass cheek a hard slap and he flinched. I liked it, maybe a little too much. I spanked one cheek then the other and the tan skin turned red.

"Tell me if it hurts." I slammed my open palm against his flesh.

"It hurts! God, it hurts so good!"

"I'd love to suck your cock right now." That just kind of slipped out.

"Anything you want, Mickey." His thick, muscular thighs flexed.

Feeling bold and horny, I spanked Sebastian again.

And again.

And again.

His skin was a deep red and my palm actually stung when I sat back. "Was that too much?"

"Never." Sebastian moaned the word. A dribble of pre-cum slid down his balls and dangled there. "I'm a pain slut."

I licked him clean with a swipe of my tongue and Sebastian let out a shaky moan.

"Oh, please. Please, let me get myself ready for you."

The plea in his voice was intoxicating. "On the bed." I wanted to watch him spread and finger himself on my bed. Fuck, I wanted that image burned into my mind.

Sebastian crawled onto all fours then lowered so his face was against my sheets. "Like this?"

"Mmm." I rose to my feet and watched him spread his cheeks. That tight, pinkish hole winked at me.

"How many fingers do you want me to start with?" Sebastian asked as he held the lube.

I swallowed hard. "Two."

He lubed up two digits and bent so he could pierce his hole. He hissed as he plunged his fingers deep on the first shot. In and out. In and out. All the way. No hesitation.

"Three." I croaked and grabbed my cock. Damn, I

was so fucking hard. My toes were curling as I circled my dick and drew my fingers to the tip.

Sebastian uncurled another finger and from one thrust to the next, he used three fingers to open his hole. "Mickey!" He moaned. "Will you please touch me?"

The bed dipped as I knelt behind him. "Do you want me to spank you while you get that sexy hole ready for my dick?" Wow, that was dirty. I didn't usually do dirty talk.

"Yes. Please."

I glided my hand over that red patch of skin and slapped him.

Sebastian flinched and shoved three fingers as deep as they would go. "Oh, fuck." He moaned into the sheets. He lowered to his belly then stretched his arms above his head. "Will you fuck me?"

"Yes." There was no calm in that word. I sounded like an excited teenager. My body was so fucking tense. The pressure in my balls just kept mounting. I grabbed my cock at the base and slapped it against his red ass.

Sebastian gasped. "Again! Please, Mickey, please."

I slapped my dick against the raw skin of his ass then I placed the tip against his lubed-up hole. I rubbed my shaft over the puckered entrance, loving the sharp gasps coming from Sebastian.

"Do you want me to put the condom on you?"

"Next time." I was ready to burst. I seized the packet, ripped it open and rolled on the condom in record time. "More lube?" I asked as I pressed my tip against him.

"No. I like the burn."

My cock head popped inside him and we gave a mutual groan. With my hands on his hips I eased forward. "Are you sure about the lube? You're so fucking tight."

"Feels amazing."

I shifted my legs so I straddled him and pushed forward. Fuck, yes. I was afraid I would really hurt him. I started to pull out, but Sebastian clutched my thighs.

"Please. I need you inside me. I need the burn. I need to be filled. Right now, Mickey. I beg you."

Who the fuck could resist that? I dug my fingers into his ass cheeks and spread him then I pushed my dick up his ass. "Oh, fucking hell."

Sebastian cried out.

"Too much?" I was almost balls deep. My legs shook as I held myself, ready to pull out if he asked. "Sebastian?

"Don't stop!"

I slammed myself inside him in one violent thrust.

Sebastian screamed into the sheets.

I could hardly breathe as those tight, lubed-up muscles squeezed around my cock. I leaned over him, kissed his shoulder, and used my heels to increase the pressure.

"Hair!"

I shoved my hand against his head and tugged so his head arched back, exposing his neck. "Fuck!" He was squeezing around me. I pulled out and slammed back in. My balls slapped against him.

Sebastian grabbed my free hand and placed it around his arched neck. "Please."

I squeezed his neck gently, pulled his hair and thrust deep.

"Oh, God. Mickey. Mickey. Mickey."

I did it again, squeeze, pull and thrust.

Sebastian groaned and humped against the bed. "Can I come? Please, let me come."

"Come, Sebastian. Spray that cum all over my bed."

He moaned and shifted faster.

Each move sent my shaft in and out of his hole. "Tell me when." I squeezed his neck.

"Almost. Almost." He said it twice more before his whole body shivered and he screamed, "Now!"

I dropped my hold on his neck and his hair. I grasped his hips and buried my cock inside him in one violent thrust. Sebastian gasped and sputtered. He went wild underneath me, squeezing my dick so tightly that I came. Pure pleasure surged through me. I plunged hard and deep. Over and over. I couldn't breathe as my whole body focused on the climax. With a heave of breath, I collapsed on top of him. "Fuck me!"

Sebastian reached back and caressed my hips lazily.

"Am I too heavy?" I felt boneless.

"No. You're perfect." He wiggled his ass.

My shaft slid out of him. I gave his shoulder a few kisses and then rolled off him, to my back. "That was fantastic." I sounded smitten. I felt smitten.

"Yes, it was." Sebastian practically purred the words. He moved to his side, reached down and grasped my flaccid cock. The condom was rolling up on itself. He peeled it off and then used his mouth to clean me up.

I twitched and squirmed the entire time. Sebastian threw the used condom in the general direction of the overturned garbage and kissed me. My cum mingled on our probing tongues. When Sebastian laid his head on my chest I swear I heard angels singing. I'd never had a more perfect moment in my life.

"Mickey?"

"Yeah?" My voice was still hitched from trying to catch my breath.

"Can I stay?"

I wrapped my arms around Sebastian. "You're not going anywhere."

Chapter Six

I'd never actually taken a shower with a man before and it was really fucking hot. When we got out we each put pants on and then I led Sebastian to the roof. We cuddled on the floor where I laid out a blanket and watched the sun set over the Hudson River. He laid his arm over my shoulders and I hugged his waist. For a few hours I felt happy and whole. It was like the weight of the world slipped off my shoulders.

"What are you thinking?" Sebastian asked as he glanced down at me.

"That I found the perfect guy and he found out my father is a crazy killer." Sadly, when reality comes crashing back it does so brutally. There would be a trial and a jury and press coverage. My life was hectic now, but in the next few months it was just going to get worse. I wanted to just run away, anything to get the fuck out from this. My father was dead to me. I know he survived the blast, but knowing what he was, my mother would have crawled from her grave if she could have. Her memory was ruined by the blood on his hands.

"It's my job."

"I know." I wasn't really mad at Sebastian. Okay, I was at first, but that sort of faded, as seen by our recent hot encounter in the bedroom. Everyone in my family had been guilty, so fucking guilty of one of the worst sins in the world. Taking a life. I shivered and tightened my grip on him.

"Do you really think that I'm the perfect guy?" He lifted an eyebrow like I was about to yell surprise.

"Maybe. You went from a crazy motherfucker blowing up buildings to the best lover I've ever had."

"Thanks for that." Sebastian blushed. "And the

bombs didn't kill anyone innocent. I always make sure the target is hit and if someone else will get hurt then I wait for another time. However, in your case, I had all three suspects in the same area. If you hadn't gone into that apartment…" He went quiet a minute and then rubbed his thumb along my bare shoulder. "Edward."

"What?"

"His name was Edward. My boyfriend from high school. He was the first guy I ever liked, my first crush, first love, first boyfriend, first guy I ever came out to, first time for everything sex-related."

"Edward."

Sebastian nodded and removed his arm from me, then shifted to face me. "I haven't told anyone this in so long. It hurts to talk about him." He swallowed hard. "Edward had dimples and a laugh that would…" He glanced out at the sunset reflected on the water. "We went to prom together. We'd done oral before, but this night, it was both our first time having sex. In the back seat of a black pickup truck under a full moon just a few blocks from the big party."

Oh, God, this was going to take a horrible turn.

"We cleaned up in a stream that was nearby. We used to fish there all the time growing up. Edward took longer and when we got back to the truck … there was a man standing there." Sebastian glanced at the roof and balled his fists. "I had that bad feeling. You know? When your gut is telling you that something's not right."

I reached out and touched his forearm.

Sebastian flinched and then laid his hand over mine. "He was wearing this black mask but by the time I saw it… He shot Edward in the leg." Sebastian let go of me and stood up. "I'd never heard a gun before that. I know we lived on a farm, but my father grew vegetables and he hated guns. That sound, for years it made me freak out."

I stood up.

He paced to the edge of the roof and stared out. "I yelled for help. Edward was screaming. I tried to get him to his feet, but he couldn't stand so I fucking carried him. I dragged him, even though he was screaming at me to stop. Then this motherfucker shot me, too. I fell down a ditch and rolled right into the stream. The pain. Man, that pain was unlike anything I'd ever felt." Sebastian wiped at his face.

He was crying? Fuck me. This badass was actually crying. He must have truly loved Edward. I walked to him and hugged his back, squeezing tight.

"I was dragged by the current downstream and I think I passed out. When I woke up I was being pulled onto the shore by some fishermen." Sebastian turned in my arms and hugged me. "I told them what happened. The police came. Detectives. Friends. Family. It didn't matter. They found Edward later that day. He was raped and … and the fucker strangled him." Sebastian took a shaky breath. "The motherfucker strangled my Edward."

"I'm so sorry." There was nothing I could say to help ease that pain.

"It took two years and four other murdered boys to find him, but I did. The guy was our neighbor, Mr. Barker. He was a farmer with a wife and two girls. I found him. I shot him in his leg and I fucking strangled him. I took his life the way he took Edward's." Sebastian laid his hands on my cheeks and lifted my face to stare up at him. "There's a lot of blood on these hands, Mickey, but it's not innocent blood."

"I know that."

"I had to kill him. I had to try to kill your father. They're monsters, and the only thing that can kill a monster is another monster."

"You're not that, Sebastian." It took me a while to see that fact, but I did. I understood. If Sebastian hadn't done what he did, then there would have been more innocent victims taken by the man that sired me. "I'm so sorry about Edward."

"He was avenged." Sebastian brushed hair from my forehead. "I've been alone since then. I never needed anyone until I met you. You've got a way about you that made me slip up and make a mistake."

He made me sound special. Irresistible. "I don't normally date guys that tried to kill my father, either." Thinking about him made me cringe. I can't believe I called that man 'dad' for so long. "I'm afraid he's going to want to see me, to talk to me. I can't do that. I can't look at that man and see anything but evil." I laid my head on his shoulder. "The media's going to go crazy for months. They'll probably drag me through this shit. How could I have not known? How could I not be involved? We weren't close. I'm telling you, once my mother died, I moved out and I spoke to him once a month on the phone. I had no idea…"

"Shhh. It'll be okay," he whispered.

"How? I just wanted to open my own bar, get a house with a fucking white picket fence and raise a bunch of kids." That'd been my dream for so long, too long. It was bound to be yanked out from under me eventually, I guess. "I just … I just want to leave this life and start over."

Sebastian took a breath and then, it almost sounded like he was hesitating.

I glanced up into his handsome face.

"We can do that."

"Leave? No, we can't. Can we?"

"We can. I have enough money. Once the police say you can leave the state then we can go. Change our names. Start over, both of us."

This sounded like one of those dreams where everything works out and you hate when the morning alarm breaks the bubble. "That sounds fantastic." I hugged him tighter, thinking out loud. "We could open a bar in another city, a smaller one. The Cox Club."

"Excuse me?"

"My bar. I always wanted to the name it The Cox Club."

"Why?" He grinned as he asked.

"Because I think that'd be an awesome name for a gay bar. Start off with dancing and drinks. Maybe add a dungeon for those who like kink. A hotel. Spa." I snorted. "I have some pretty wild ideas for my future." Ones that were so far out of reach they might as well be stars.

"Our future."

Yeah, our future...

Chapter Seven

The insanity plea didn't work. My father was tried by a jury of his peers, or that's how the saying goes. I didn't go to a single day of it. The news followed me around for weeks so I stayed indoors. I took a break from work, but only because I had some money saved up. It was supposed to be for my bar, but I used it to stay afloat and hide from the world. My uncle's wills named me as their next of kin. I donated every fucking penny to charities. There was no way I would touch that blood money. A suspect in the bombing was never found, but there was an ongoing investigation into the victims' families. In four weeks, the jury was sent to make a verdict and it came back guilty. I was actually relieved when Sebastian told me. We celebrated that night with wine and woke up with Sebastian tied to the bed.

The next day I was up early, avoiding reporters asking the stupidest questions. "How do you feel now that your father's been convicted?" How the fuck did the world think I felt? Horrified at being related to a serial killer. Terrified that he'd get out. Relieved that I'd never have to see him again. Sad, because I couldn't stop him sooner.

It took about a month for the news to change to some other tragedy they could exploit and make ratings from. Finally, my life was getting a bit calmer and the time I'd spent with Sebastian was so much more special. He was my rock and I had no idea if he knew just how important he was becoming to me. It was in the afternoon when I came home after getting two interviews for some bars just outside the city. I was thinking a move further from the heart of New York City would be a good change. The stares from the neighbors and strangers that recognized me was becoming too much.

"Hey, handsome," Sebastian said from the kitchen.

I let out a squeal and threw my keys in his general direction. "Fuck, man!" I had to place a hand over my heart to make sure it hadn't leapt out. "Front door! Front door!"

Sebastian smiled. "You didn't say that when you found me naked in your bed last night."

I opened my mouth and then shut it. There was no good way to answer that.

"Besides, I'm not staying."

"You're not?" *Oh*. I was getting used to eating dinner with him and then watching some bad movies on TV. We always ended up in a tangle of limbs. It didn't always lead to sex; sometimes it was just about being close to him.

"Correction. We're not." Sebastian took my hand. "I have a surprise."

"Okay…" I was thinking of him naked, but he led me out the front door and to a waiting taxi. "Where are we going?"

"Somewhere." He held my hand.

"Somewhere close? Should I be wearing something else?" I had on a sweater and jeans because the end of winter was still cold, but if we were going to be outside for a long time I'd need my thicker jacket.

"Just shut up and enjoy the ride."

"Where have I heard that before?" I snorted.

Sebastian leaned closer. "Yeah, well, I can't exactly climb over you and start undressing in the back of a taxi."

"Sadly." My cock loved the idea; it thickened inside my pants despite the chill in the air. "Is it close?"

Sebastian just stared at me.

"Okay. Okay." I threw my hands up and stared out the window. An hour later, we had driven from the city and past towns that I didn't know existed. We came across a cozy town that was more on the verge of a city called Celestial Springs. I shit you not. It had a few large buildings, but a lot more farmland with a commercial area that looked pretty decent. We passed an Italian restaurant where savory smells filled the air. "Seriously, where the hell are we going?" I was getting cranky and I had to piss.

"It's right up here." His usual stoic manner was gone, replaced by … was that excitement?

We pulled into an empty parking lot. The small square building was surrounded by trees and brush, but I could see businesses on the other side. The sign said this had once been a dance hall, but from the look of the overgrown grass, it had been abandoned a while. Why would we… "Sebastian?" He didn't. He couldn't have.

Sebastian paid the taxi driver and then dragged me out of the car. The wheels kicked up loose dirt as the vehicle pulled away. "Well?"

My mouth just hung open.

"Okay, it's crap right now, but it's a great location. Good town. The wood back there is all part of the property so there's room to expand…"

"You're fucking serious? The Cox Club?"

He smiled, wide and genuine. I'd never seen such a look. "We can work on it together. Build a life here. I think we can rent a place until this is finished and maybe find a house nearby or add on and live here."

"You've really been thinking about this." My dream had become his dream. "Fuck. I…" Oh, God, this was going to break his heart. "I can't afford this." I had about two months of rent left in my bank account if I rationed my food.

"I'm not asking that, Mickey. Do you like it?"

"Sure. Yes. Of course." And it broke my will that I couldn't do this with Sebastian. I couldn't start a new life with him.

"Good. Because I bought it."

I swear I choked on my spit. There was a good thirty seconds of coughing before I could talk. "You what?"

"I bought the building and the land. It's under my name, but I want you to co-sign it."

"You're serious? You're totally fucking serious?" I think I was having a heart attack.

Sebastian's smile fell. "Yes." He grabbed my hand. "You were serious, right? About The Cox Club? About living together? Starting a new life?"

"Actually … yeah, but I never dreamed…" Wow. I was fucking speechless. New life. New town. New me. New us. "You do know fixing it up is going to be an issue. I can't use a power tool to save my life."

"You hammer pretty good." Sebastian wiggled his eyebrows.

I snorted and wrapped my arms around him. "Holy fucking shit. This is really happening. Wait." I held his face in my hands. "What about your … job?"

He sighed. "I'm tired, Mickey. I'm tired of all the death and the violence. I'm thirty years old and I just want … I just want to be happy. You make me happy. I love you, Mickey."

"Damn good answer. I love you, too." I hugged him again tighter and then we both stood there looking at the dusty, broken-down building. "You sure you know how to use power tools?"

Sebastian laughed; it was a rare sound that made me shiver and smile. He kissed me right on the lips. "You sure I can't get you to rethink the name?"

"Not a chance." I licked his lower lip. "But I know a few ways you can try…"

The End

You can read more about The Cox Club in *The Devil's Cum in His Eye.* Coming soon from Evernight Publishing.

www.evernightpublishing.com/james-cox

SUNSHINE AND SNAKES

L.J. Longo

Copyright © 2017

Chapter One

Today

What I know for sure about Bruiser Accorsi couldn't fill a Chihuahua's nut-sack.

I know his real name is Burgess. Second-born son. Took his mother's maiden name. He goes by Burr if you go back.

I know the Accorsis are the biggest family in the illicit "adult entertainment" industry. High-end escorts. He likes to brag about the movie stars and politicians his girls fuck. No direct human trafficking. A financial decision, not a moral one.

I know he's an amateur bodybuilder. I know his thick black hair is soft, not greasy. I know his eyes are the color of a sun-shot grapevine.

But I also I know he's worth sixty thousand dollars dead.

And I'm gonna be the one to kill him.

Chapter Two

August 2010

Bruiser Accorsi left no room in the six-by-eight cell for me.

Pictures of his family, his iPod charger, his portable DVD player, the DVD folder, a pink origami swan made for him by his eight-year-old cousin littered the shelf over my bunk. Necessities—his clothes, yard shoes, a tiny bottle of shampoo—he stored on his own shelf, but I lived among the cloud of his possessions.

And still, when a box from my uncles made it through security, I let him take it. He discarded the book like it was diseased. Unfolded the letter, saw it was in Spanish, dropped it. Then he cocked his head.

"That's a hella lot of candy."

I glanced at the letter. Only a few sentences long. Followed by an itemized list of the contents. When Bruiser opened a bag of candy, it had to be either chamoy, fresa, or sandia. The carton of orange Tic-Tacs wouldn't make that noise.

He ate a candy, and I waited. White boys make the best faces when they eat Mexican sweets.

Accorsi didn't disappoint. He had chamoy. The sweet and sour, the chill and tang surprised and revolted him. He spat the candy into the toilet where it pinged against the porcelain. "That's fuckin' weird. Are the rest that shitty?"

I nodded.

He tore out a pack of Tic-Tacs and swished the sweets around his mouth to cleanse his palate. "Christ, that's weird. What the fuck was that?"

I glanced over at the hard candy dissolving in the toilet. "Chamoy."

"Which is?"

"Chilis and sadness."

Bruiser snorted at my poetics. "Tell 'em to send cigarettes."

"I don't smoke. I eat chamoy and Tic-Tacs."

"Well, Tic-Tac, I'm tellin' ya, as a professional courtesy, get your people to send a better quality of fuckin' candy."

He dropped the box at my feet, then flopped onto his bunk. I uncurled long enough to gather the book and letter then returned to sitting with my knees crossed and my muscles tight.

Bruiser sprawled with one leg out to the cell's center. I could not leave the bed without walking over him. In August, Bruiser never wore the top of his prison scrubs or even an undershirt, unless a guard made him. Just leaned against the wall, wavy black hair cradled in his palms. His blue earbuds scraped his stubbled jaw as he bobbed his head. A teenager lying in wait.

I held my new book, feeling rattled and uncertain once the confrontation was done. The business with my package was the closest Bruiser had come to posturing.

I'd been in the cell with him for a week. He never noticed me—though he routinely talked to the cell block. He'd chat with someone across the way about baseball, or shout to someone else that he made too much noise. Bruiser Accorsi ran people with the brute naturalness of someone born to take control. Even the guards deferred to him when they weren't careful.

I was invisible, which was perfect. But when there's another man in your bedroom, you notice him. Get aggravated by his silent presence. Assert dominance over his dark skin. Though the casual way Bruiser managed his business like I never existed conveyed authority just fine.

Men who feared their cell mates didn't sprawl on their bunks, bare chested, tight belly exposed. A lion never worries about a rabbit.

And I knew how to act like a rabbit.

I wouldn't disturb Bruiser unless he made me. I was still too broken and sore from the last cell block king I'd crossed, and Bruiser put Jorge Matisse's power to shame.

No, I'd be a rabbit. A magician's rabbit disappearing into a book.

My uncles sent me an anthology of pulp crime fiction. Mostly about hitmen. Abuelito's sense of humor.

****

"You read fast." Bruiser's post-lockdown observation resonated in his big chest, and his casual delivery turned his thick Brooklyn accent into a drawl. "You're gonna read through the whole library."

I said nothing.

His voice slowed when he was annoyed. "You know, Tic-Tac, you're only in here because the warden came to me with a deal."

I glanced at him. Bruiser leaned back against the wall, head cradled in his bicep, staring at me. Movie star lounging. How long had he been staring? I avoided meeting his gaze directly.

He did not return the courtesy.

"Yeah. Warden came to me. Gave me an extra hour and two more visitors to keep your ass out of the infirmary." Something new strained his voice. I couldn't place it. "What'd you think of that, Tic-Tac?"

I had a lot of thoughts. I thought the warden was angry because the lawyer was nervous. I thought the lawyer was nervous because the doctor was upset. I thought the doctor was upset because I would not talk about what happened. And I thought she was a goddamned bleeding heart who spoke Spanish like she'd learned it in prep school and hadn't been paying much attention. I thought that those extra two hours and visitors meant Accorsi could still run the mob from prison. I thought that was kinda funny.

I said nothing.

"What'd they do to you anyway? Broke your arm."

And dislocated my shoulder. And stabbed me at least three times in the ribs. And given me the kind of rectal tearing that would put a warden out of work if I was middle-class and white.

"Everyone knows it was Matisse." Bruiser waited for me to speak. When I did not, he interrupted my silence. "Well, fuck it, no reason for you to tell me everything about it. Everyone knows."

He sat forward. "Doc has a thing for you. She don't come to the cell block to check on just anyone."

She also didn't ask anyone else "how are you seventy?" because she didn't have the right word for "feeling."

Bruiser chuckled. "Yeah, go on and smile. You think she's cute."

"I think she's stupid. She has a weakness for wounded beasts. It will get her hurt if she's not careful."

Bruiser's voice grew rigid and ominous. "Well, that's not creepy or nothing."

"Oh, no, I didn't mean—" to let my anxiety show, to threaten him through a proxy. "She annoys me a little, that's all. And I'm not…"

I shrugged, but the innocence of my drifting apology did not put him at ease.

He looked grim, threatening to put me in my place. "Finish your sentence."

"In this book, there's a man who says…" I

flipped back to where I'd read it. "He says here, 'I distrust a close-mouthed man. He picks the wrong time to talk and says the wrong things. Talking's something you can't do judiciously unless you keep in practice.'"

I closed the book. "I don't keep in practice."

"Not very judicious, eh?" Bruiser laughed. "Loved that movie. *The Maltese Falcon*. Bogart, Lorre, and Greenstreet. The femme fatale …"

He shut his eyes as the opening credits rolled in his mind. "Mary Astor. Yeah, they don't make films like that no more."

Sexist, racist, with as much homophobia as they could sneak past the censors if the book was any indication. But I didn't know the film, so I shrugged.

Bruiser answered my silence. "You're a quiet son of a bitch."

People said that about me in Guerrero, too. About the whole family. The uncles and Abuelito and I would sit for hours outside the house on crates and play cards without speaking. We drank coffee or mezcal when we had it. For hours, the only thing anyone would say was "good game" or "smart play" or "one more?" You never knew when someone would shake his head and the game would be over. Sometimes there would be an excuse, "time for work" or "the boy should practice.' but otherwise, golden silence.

I spoke because Bruiser stared, waiting. "It's not meant as disrespect."

"That how Matisse took it?"

I shrugged, pressed my back on the wall, and opened the book.

"Yeah, Matisse is an asshole." Bruiser agreed with words I had not said. "If he starts with me I guess I'll murder him."

Bruiser didn't mean it. They rarely do in this

country.

****

The lights went out while Bruiser listened to his music.

I'd already put the book under my bunk next to my box of candy. I lay facing the wall. It was not wise for me to look at Burgess Accorsi for too long, especially when he wasn't wearing all his clothes.

In the darkness, I listened to the cell block. The others did not know how to be quiet. Chatting, coughing, snoring, sniffling.

Bruiser was silent, though. It worried me.

But adrenaline and common sense can only power a man for so long. I was asleep when he grabbed me by the neck.

Before I caught up with my fear, Bruiser straddled my legs, pinned me, wrapped his fingers around my throat. I didn't scream or buck. Fighting was pointless. "Shit."

Bruiser's grip tightened. "Make another noise. I dare you."

I didn't take his challenge.

His other hand scared me more when it grazed gently over my spine, fluttering the prison scrubs. Nothing threatening in that touch, but the softness filled me with more dread than his violence.

His fingers clamped hard on my ass. "This doesn't belong to you anymore, Tic-Tac, does it?"

My cheeks clenched automatically to defy his statement. "I guess not."

Bruiser slapped my head. Even his half-assed punch left my brain swimming. "Don't get all chatty now, Tic-Tac. Did you need a noise to agree with me?"

I shook my head.

He stroked my hair. "Good boy."

My pants rustled under his hands. He rocked his cock between my cheeks.

Bruiser wouldn't come close to doing the damage Matisse and his boys did in the yard. I'd fought them, I'd lost, and for my own protection I ended up sharing Bruiser's cell. But Bruiser wasn't going to send me to the infirmary. He'd lose his extra hours, visitors, the plus marks on his parole, and his new toy.

No, Burgess Accorsi was smarter. He'd go easy.

"You know the deal, Tic-Tac." His breath smelled fresh and faint as stolen mints. His lips brushed my ear, and I jolted. What the hell? He needed to go easy, not be… Fucking seductive.

He had no right to remind me of the trucker in Des Moines, how he'd smelled like pot and beer when he slipped inside. Or the college boy outside of Austin who'd been nervous about kissing, but nibbled my ear when I sank between his thighs.

"I'm gonna fuck you, and you're gonna take it with your customary silence." Bruiser's accent made him more aggressive than either of those other lovers, but his hands were kinder. "You won't tell because if the warden fucks with my privileges or my parole, you're dead."

His grip on my throat crushed harder. His threat was hollow, but I nodded.

"Do the job right, and it will be easy."

Hot hate rose and burned my throat, but I swallowed it in silence. I liked the weight of the man. I liked his heat and the solidness of his well-muscled body. Everything about the bastard turned me on, but still, I'd kill him as soon as I could get away with it if he forced me.

Just like Matisse.

"Start by sucking my cock."

His heat and weight went away, but his hand

stayed firm on my neck. He tugged me upright, and I would've slipped off the bed if his grip had slackened. Instead, he trapped my face kissing distance from his ripped abs.

The emergency lighting painted his pale skin a devil red. He peeled down the hem of his loose orange and white striped pants slowly as if the fabric wouldn't let go of the ridges of his body without a fight.

His dick sprang out rock-hard, thick, and veiny. Even in the prison's hell-light, I appreciated its definition and power. Wished I got to play with it on the outside. Maybe in the backroom at some San Francisco club. Or a marina in the Southwest. Now, it was just business. Violent, sick business. It'd be over soon.

I slid my gaze from Bruiser's erection to his face. A listless glare to show my only resistance. This fucker needed to know I wasn't scared.

Bruiser grabbed the back of my head and pulled me toward his cock. Without ceremony or hesitation, I sucked. No need to finesse. I knew my way around another man's dick, but Bruiser didn't need to know that. Just in and out, lips tight, teeth out of the way.

That's how this transaction worked. Do the job right.

Something went wrong. Bruiser didn't pump his cock forward or hold my head. He didn't tease or threaten. His clenched hand softened, draped in my hair, an undemanding pressure more like a lover than an abuser.

I tilted my eyes up the man's solid body and accidentally met his gaze. Since I'd stepped into the prison, there were precious few times I'd looked someone directly in his face, and the intimacy startled me. Bruiser wasn't supposed to be watching his new bitch suck him. He was meant to close his eyes, tip his head back, and fuck my face. He certainly wasn't supposed to look so fucking... I don't know how to describe that moment. It stuck with me, changed everything. He wanted me, not to dominate or control, not to prove anything, not because he desperately needed to get off, but because he wanted me.

Sex was supposed to be about power. There was no place for his relaxed pleasure.

I didn't look away, and neither did Bruiser. The Italian's eyes were gorgeous. He seemed surprised by his own behavior, but doubled down on the strange affection. His fingers traced over my cheek, painfully tender. His cock throbbed against my tongue.

It was a needless risk, a potential trap, and fucking stupid. But before my brain could talk me down, my tongue reacted to the gentle caress, swirled around the cock to savor and not just service.

Bruiser choked on air. "Yeah, do that..."

Committed to my folly, I surrendered to the pleasure of sucking another man's cock. I watched Bruiser's face as I slipped the shaft out of my mouth, lapped at the head, swallowed it all again.

"Fuck..." Bruiser finally tipped his head back and sank his hips forward.

My cock stiffened and the rest of my body clenched with fear. Should not be enjoying this. Should not have consensual sex in prison. Should not treat a mob capo like a lover.

I gripped my knees to keep from touching him. Control the desire to hold the Italian god attached to the cock buried in my throat.

The only violence from the man came when he pushed me away. Forceful enough that I ended up on my back looking at Bruiser from between my own half-raised legs. My consent disgusted him, and he'd beat me to death now. Accident of rage.

He glared, furious, confused, ashamed.

"You a cocksucker on the outside, too, Tic-Tac?" He said my new nickname without confidence. He wanted to say my real name, but he didn't dare.

Against every survival instinct, I nodded.

"How bad did they fuck you in the yard?" The apathetic crudeness was right, but his tone belonged somewhere else. Belonged to a man who could be kind, even trusted.

I wasn't that stupid. "Does it matter? You're gonna take what you want."

He stared at the body he owned now, assessed my wide-spread legs, my hard cock, my steady glare.

Then Bruiser stepped away. "Guess I want somethin' different."

He collapsed on his own bunk. His bare chest barreled as he sprawled out and stroked his cock, beating furiously. His eyes were closed, jaw clenched, face tight as he focused on release, but the shadows of the prison bars fell in soft lines across his skin.

That image would haunt me for years.

I watched him masturbate, mouth dry with want. My cock throbbed, anticipating the hard fuck that should be coming.

That was the deal, wasn't it? That's the way it was supposed to be.

Except that nothing was the way it was supposed to be. Not since we'd accidentally seen each other.

Bruiser didn't notice when I knelt by his bed. He jolted when I took the tip of his cock back into my mouth.

And he knocked me back hard. "The fuck are you doing?"

I looked at him and showed more desire than I

had ever let any other man see. But it didn't reach my voice. "My job."

Bruiser slowly nodded. Maybe he could read the fear and the desire. Maybe he understood my longing, the impossible depths of lonely lust. Maybe he just knew he had a Mexican cocksucker in his cell.

When he held out his cock, I took it.

****

When the uncles sent me a Tic-Tac container with white pills, I knew it wasn't candy.

But Bruiser didn't. I opened my own packages now, but he always watched for things he might want. "Those peppermint?"

"No, they're Mexican Tic-Tacs. Papaya. You'd hate them."

"Fuck you, they're not. Says 'Tic-Tac' right on the front."

"It's spelled the same in Spanish."

"'Freshmints' is not Spanish. Give me the fuckin' Tic-Tacs."

"They're not meant for you." A slow dread filled me. I didn't like white Tic-Tacs. My uncles didn't intend them for me, which meant—

"Don't sass me," Bruiser growled. "Don't you dare. I have been very good to you."

Very good. It upset me how much I enjoyed how good he was to me. And he was only getting better with practice.

"You can have all the orange ones, but not the white."

Bruiser got up, towered over me, fists clenched. I didn't flinch.

"Christ, you got ice in your veins." He admired me. But it didn't matter. "Think it will last when I beat you to a pulp? Give me what I want."

It was the middle of the day. Free time. The cell doors were open and other prisoners milled around. There was a poker game in the cell next to ours. It was risky.

But these were not meant for him.

"No."

His nostrils flared, and he held out his hand. "Last chance, Tic-Tac."

I grabbed his wrist as I kicked out his knee. When he stumbled, I rose and hit his throat with my open hand. The big man crumbled backward, falling on his bunk and missing the edge. He plopped on his ass and looked up at me from the concrete, wheezing.

I didn't back down, dared him to rise and attack. When he was too stunned to move, I put the Tic-Tac container into the pocket of my shirt.

Bruiser jumped to his feet and looked out to see if anyone else saw how quickly I'd taken him down. No one reacted, so no one had. "The fuck was that?"

Luck. Training. Surprise. So I said nothing.

He sat on his bunk, straightened his shirt, touched his throat. "That's not candy, is it?"

I sat on my bunk and opened the newest book. Gabriel García Márquez. I knew it as "La Hojarasca" but its English title was "Leaf Storm." It had other stories including the one about the old man with angel wings.

Bruiser snatched the book and came dangerously close to shouting. "Don't you give me the silent treatment."

"Don't yell. Or you'll have to hit me, and you don't want that on your record." I held out my hand.

Bruiser licked his mouth, handed me the book, then paced. Eventually, he sat next to me on my bunk. "What are you in here for?"

"Stealing a car."

"Fuck stealing a car. Everyone says stealing a car. What'd you really do?"

I wasn't going to answer, but the truth worked so well. "Intent to sell marijuana. I got two years and six months."

He leaned back and looked out of the corner of his eyes, then down at my pocket. He assumed my uncles sent product for me to sell. Bruiser wanted no part of the drug market. It wasn't his family business, it dirtied his name, didn't interest him.

So, he returned to his side of the cell, comforted in the knowledge that he had something on me and that he understood my no. He wasn't pushing the matter. Not with the dull pain radiating from his windpipe.

Instead, he went on like we were having a conversation. "I'm in for aggravated assault. Lawyer says I'll get paroled in eight months."

"Isn't that a bitch?" I snorted.

"All these places legalizing. If New Jersey decriminalizes while you're in jail, you ought to fuckin' sue the state."

"I'll be out before that shit gets past this governor," I answered.

Bruiser said, almost shy, "Maybe I'll send people to get you when you come out."

That was dangerous territory. It made my heart beat faster, so I acted like it didn't matter and turned to my book again. "Maybe you will."

"You know I've talked to brick walls that have a better back and forth than you. Do you want me to or not? We friends or what?"

I looked up from the book, only long enough to meet his eyes. We were not friends. We were not lovers. We were cell mates, and he fucked me because I let him, and I let him because…

This is why I don't talk. My thoughts are fragmented as starlight, but my gaze is unflinching.

Bruiser frowned and wandered out of the cell to join the poker game next door.

When it was safe, when he was deep into the game, laughing and making stupid bets, I closed the book. I listened to his cheer and his conversation. Outside. Outside with him. He wouldn't be Bruiser out there. Outside, he was Burr. He'd take me to Italian restaurants and baseball games. We'd roll around in a real bed, and I could let him know how much I enjoyed his body.

The buzzer rang. Free time over. Fantasy done.

****

The fantasy returned that night as frightening and swift as a scorpion when Burr climbed into my bed.

I pressed tight against the wall to pretend I didn't want him to touch me, but also to give him enough room to stretch his tall body beside me. My muscles tightened with delicious lust when he reached under my shirt and stroked my chest. I practically vibrated when he kissed my neck and ran his hand through my buzzed hair. He smelled like my wintergreen gum that night, and my desire for him quickly moved past the point of toleration.

He didn't notice. His caressing was for his pleasure, not mine. As he took his careful inventory of my skin, his cock swelled against my ass. Each slow thrust forward rubbed my dick against the cell wall, more torment than relief. But he never noticed my accidental lust before.

So, when his hand slid down my abdomen, I thought nothing of it. Until his fingers wandered past the hem and brushed the curls at the base of my cock.

I grabbed his arm. "You're not supposed to."

"I do what I want."

Since he was stronger than me…since I wanted it, I didn't fight.

More hesitant, his fingers crept along my length. He petted my shaft, afraid of the contact since I'd broken my silence. He'd never jerked another guy off before. I knew it by the shy pressure of his fingers when he finally circled my cock.

He wasn't expecting what he found. "Jesus Christ, you always get this hard?"

I did. But I'd go through hell before I admitted it.

He focused on stroking me for a while. But I said nothing, regulated my breath so he would hear no change. So if he intended on finishing me before fucking me, he lost interest.

He nudged my pants only far enough to caress my ass and loosen my hole. He almost had me then, his fingers in my ass and his other hand around my cock, still kissing my neck. If he'd kept up…

Instead, he pushed his cock inside. Pain sobered me. I clenched my jaw and made not a sound. Still with his hard shaft pulsing deep, his fingers firmly gripping my cock, his lips on the back of my neck plucking in neat pecks, I was right where I wanted to be.

Burr had no idea.

He groaned, rocking in and out slowly. Not thrusting yet. He focused on my cock, trying to make me come. I didn't fight it. Not just because I wanted to come. I wanted him to have that.

But soon, Burr's kisses were not so neat and small. Bites and licks mixed in and he forgot to stroke. Just gripped the base of my cock as he fucked me. Soon he forgot even to do that and pushed me onto my belly and pummeled me hard.

I couldn't take it. I wanted to scream, to punch him, to demand he make me come. Instead, I squirmed so

I could get my hand on my own dick and squeeze.

Bruiser grasped my neck and pinned me. "Don't you start fighting now, Rick."

"Finish what you start then."

Burr backed off, rose to his knees, grabbed my hips to steady my body while he fucked harder. But he let me lift my ass and stroke my cock.

I'd never dared come before. Afterward sometimes, when he snored safely on his bunk, and I could sink into my own imagination. Sometimes when he left the cell, and I could hide under the covers. But never during, never as he fucked me. I bit the pillow to stifle my moan when it happened, fantastic flood, the glorious death of the fire in my veins and the temporary lulling of lust.

I don't know if Burr noticed when I came or if the shuddering and clenching of my ass brought him. He collapsed on top of me, and my strength gave out. He crushed me in his embrace, caressed my chest, kissed my neck. Right back to where he started, until the kisses grew further apart and even softer.

Stupefied by satisfaction, I confessed. "It's Rico, by the way."

"Wha?" Burr slurred with sleep. "Oh, Rico. Sure."

A deep anxiety flooded me. This had gone too far. The whole thing had gone too far ages ago, but this was the next country over from gone too far. Falling asleep with his cock buried in my ass... Fucking cuddling. It scared the shit out of me.

Still, I didn't have the courage to shake him off.

Burr eventually sobered. "Fuck."

I didn't move when he hurried away from me. I held onto his warmth, even as his cum grew cold on my thighs. I didn't tell him I wanted him to stay.

In the silence, he sighed from his bunk, a heartsick sound. Longing for me when I wasn't even six feet away.

****

As a personal favor to Burr, so he couldn't be implicated if everything went totally sideways, I waited until he was paroled to kill Matisse.

The uncles were quite smart with that one. The white Tic-Tacs were pure caffeine, and I could tell the paramedics the truth as soon as he went into seizures. One pill wouldn't hurt a person, just give him a little kick like an energy drink. I told them I put them in my coffee and I didn't think it was contraband. But Matisse stole them in the yard the day after Burr was released, ate the whole pack, had a heart attack when he tried to pin me down and get my pants off…

The police filed his death as accidental. Hardly even questioned me, though I suspect our kindly doctor wanted to shelter me from the trauma.

Chapter Three

Today

It's cold enough in the Rainy City to justify winter wear. My mark left his conference in a lovely scarf and a stupid wool cap. He's too old for the hipster look, and he forgot his accessories when he stumbled out of the jazz lounge. Nice place to spend the last four hours of your life.

His hotel stands five blocks to the East, so he's waddling in the wrong direction. Good news for business.

I follow with long slow strides and his scarf and cap stuffed under my windbreaker.

"Ninety-eight bottles of beer on the wall." In his hometown of Greensburg, North Carolina, someone would put in a noise complaint. But he's in Seattle, and no one gives a shit.

His wife was so specific. She'd packed his clothes. She knew his habits. She'd sent dozens of photos—the kind a P.I. would take. Explained her motives like seeking absolution. I doubt she got it from my abuelo. The P.I. photos worry me, but getting caught is the wife's problem. We are anonymous.

"Ninety-seven bottles … no, ninety-eight bottles of beer." He steadies himself on a brick wall, checks his math by counting his fingers. "Ninety-nine. Ninety-eight. Ninety-seven. Ninety-six."

The man resolves to continue walking and sings, "Ninety-five bottles of beer on the wall."

And this was an accountant? I hope he did his job sober. We near the alley I'd prepared to the west, so I quicken my pace to catch up to the man. "Excuse me, sir. You're drunk."

"I'm not drunk. I'm on vacation." He starts with a smooth and friendly drawl, judging me by my voice. When he sees my skin, his demeanor changes. "And it's none of your business, you … you!"

He cuts off his Southern hospitality before I find out if his slur of choice is the charming "spic," the more trendy "illegal," or the classic disgust for a whole country wrapped up in one venomous "Mexican."

"Listen, let me get you an Uber, sir. Give me a ten, and I'll use my app and get you home." I spread my gloved hands to show I'm safe. "You're not in a good neighborhood to be white and drunk."

His already flushed face gets redder. "I'm not drunk. I'm on a business vacation."

I glance around a final time. It's a lonely street and dim, a scary place to be if you're middle-aged, white, and from the South. Particularly with a creepy Spanish man talking to you.

"Give me a ten, and I'll call you an Uber. Last chance, mister."

"Fuck you." He pulls out a long hunting knife. Nice twenty-inch blade. He probably uses it to gut fish and show off at weddings.

The wife mentioned his prize. I took it as an opportunity.

"You couldn't cut yourself with that thing, old man."

"Fuck you, spic!" There it is. "Go back to Mexico!"

He staggers, brandishing the knife. Someone passing in a car, or watching from the window would be scared. He's loud enough to call attention.

I'm not scared. "Listen, you racist old fuck, I'm just trying to help you. You're so drunk you're about to shit yourself."

"Fuck you. Fuck… Go back to Mexico. Before we finish the wall." He stabs at the air. Miles away from cutting my shadow.

Until I close the distance between us and take his wrist in my hands. The startled man tries to pull the knife away, to control his own arm. But he's weak, drunk, and it happens too fast.

The knife cuts his own throat.

Too late, his other hand flails at my arm. Blood spurts over his sleek black coat. The blade creeps deeper. His eyes roll in frantic loops. He gurgles without understanding.

I help him along by paraphrasing a certain Southern woman. "A good wife can't abide infidelity, but she doesn't want the shame of divorce."

It's amazing to watch the fluttering of understanding, guilt, justification, anger, fear. Then the man dies, shits himself, and collapses.

I release the dead man's wrist as soon as he falls. Stagger back with a mockery of shock, flee down the alley toward the dumpster I'd picked.

I shuck off the dollar-store cotton gloves, the oversized jeans, the windbreaker. I use the sanitizer to wipe what little blood is left on me. The jeans absorbed most of it, and my slick running slacks are waterproof, so the blood beads rub away. I check the thick gray sweater I wore all night under the jacket. No trace of blood.

The clothes go in the dumpster. The split garbage bag goes on top of the bloody clothes. I put on the dead man's wool cap and scarf and stroll out the alley's other side.

A few blocks later, on a more populated street, I hear the sirens and lift my head in mild interest with the crowd. Sometime later, when I pass a homeless man sleeping, I put the hat and scarf next to his hands.

I hail a taxi, return to the cheap motel where I left my bike. I checked out hours ago, but like the nice manager said, no one bothered my bike.

****

I notice Abuelito's missed call because I stop to look at the sun rise.

Due to a thick cloud cover, the Oregon sky drips with molten orange light into a burning sea. The ocean is softer on the west coast. The bay sits like a lake, with waves moved by wind ripples and not the distant moon.

I take off my helmet and return the call. "How's the news?"

Abuelo—there's nothing little or kind in his voice—says, "No details. Missing person."

"Good." I open my jacket and pull out a chocolate lollipop.

"When will you be in New York?"

To kill Burgess Accorsi. "I said I don't like that one."

"It's a lot of money."

I say nothing, just suck on the candy.

Abuelito reads the silence and shrugs with his voice. "I'll send one of your uncles. Maybe a cousin."

I sigh. The uncles are too old and the cousins are too green for a man like Burr.

Abuelito agrees with my silence. "He's hard. Two people have already tried him."

"Two?"

"That we know. Someone will get him soon."

Might as well be us. You don't sneer at sixty thousand. Professionals and amateurs are already scratching. Bruiser might end up jailed for homicide before they kill him, though. He won't die without a fight.

"So," Abuelo's sternness returns. "When can you

get to New York?"

I ruffle my hair, stiff from the helmet. "Day or so."

"I'll wire funds." He hangs up.

I look at the phone, annoyed because I hadn't actually agreed. But we're a closed-mouth family. We talked more about Bruiser just now than when Abuelito gave me "the talk."

My fifteenth summer, I was practicing behind the house when he waved me over to the gun table. "Rico, you don't dance with the girls."

"No."

"Are you shy or don't you want to dance with girls?"

"I won't dance with anyone, Abuelito."

"Dance with whoever you like. Boys. Girls." The old man waved his hand with a dismissive warmth. Then the warmth died. "Just don't let it interfere with the job."

"Never." I had promised.

The wind blew from the south, bringing a little California heat to the chilly morning and the empty rocky beach.

My e-mail is short. "Hi Burr. Coming to NYC. Want to meet?"

I lean on the guard rail and look at the ocean until I finish my lollipop. I'm nowhere near the gooey center when I get Burr's answer. He gives me a New Jersey address, and a goddamned missive. Asking for details and times, excited as a schoolgirl, gushing about the neighborhood and the restaurants. Like we ever make it to restaurants. We always try. He's even made reservations, but … sex takes priority.

His e-mail makes me smile. His accent carries in the words as if the lift and lull of his voice live in the spaces between the letters.

I don't answer him right away, but watch the tide slip along the shore and finish my candy. When I mount the bike again, I switch destinations to a motel somewhere in Hoboken.

Chapter Four

February 2013

I'd been out of prison for half an hour, and I'd spent most of it planning the murders of the other people at the bus stop. This mother would walk into oncoming traffic if I threatened her screaming baby. That hipster would smile politely as I walked up to him and snapped his neck because he was afraid to be racist. The bodybuilder, tough as a needle, would be the biggest challenge. She might have been coming from the prison herself. Off-duty police. But for the first time in two years and six months, I had shoe laces. I could strangle her if I wanted.

I did not want to strangle a stranger. My morbid fantasies distracted me from the problem of what to do next. I needed a bike, a laptop, and new clothes. I ought to call Guerrero, but I needed to get a phone.

I leaned over my knees and stared at the iPod. I'd never been entirely sure if Burr left it on purpose for me or on accident because he didn't want it. He hadn't written or sent someone to get me.

The bright sun floated through the sky, cold and dry as frozen tinder. The flat expanse of dead greenery overwhelmed me. No dreams lived there.

Someone touched my shoulder. Before I remembered prison was over, and New Jersey was not Guerrero, I was on my feet and my hand stung from punching a block of muscle.

But the muscle caved, and the big man folded over. For a moment, I was certain I'd just gut-punched a member of the Secret Service. His shoes shone on the cracked gravel, the tailored suit glowed with darkness, and the wavy hair reflected the sunlight.

Then he burst, "Jesus Fuckin' Christ, Rico! You tryin' to kill someone?"

Shame and an unsettled pleasure reddened my cheeks. "Burr?"

"Who the hell else would be here for your sorry ass?" Burgess Accorsi straightened. Swept his hands over his chest to firm the lines of his crisp white shirt and black jacket.

His handsomeness was unfair. I'd never imagined him in a suit, but of course the world saw him as a businessman. The uniform of wealth was his camouflage.

Maybe the cage had broken me. Maybe the isolation and the fantasies had destroyed my understanding of reality and I imagined him. But no, the bodybuilder stood between the mother and me, protecting them from the crazy man who punched some CEO motherfucker. The hipster's phone was poised either to record or call for help.

"Relax, I didn't tell him I was coming," Burr spoke to the crowd of three and gave them a broad, kind smile. He clapped his hands on my shoulders, and I crumbled under their weight. "Should know better than to surprise you, right, Rico?"

"Yeah." If I had a knife, he'd be dead. "You should have written."

Burr laughed—a big, booming noise trained to compete with New York traffic. "Come on, the Cadi's around the corner."

Instinctively I didn't move when Burr took my arm. My resistance surprised him. His big hazel eyes carried the kind of innocence that only exists on men with long lashes and a five-o-clock-shadow. "What's wrong?"

Where did Burr want to take me? What did he mean to do there? How far had he traveled in 'the Cadi' to be rejected? Was I rejecting him? Why? Was this a trap?

There were too many ways to answer Burr's confusion. So, I stared in silence.

Burr released my arm. "Well, shit, man. If you feel that way, take the bus."

I shook my head to cancel my glare. "Where are we going?"

"Preferably toward NYC. But you know, whatever." Burr tilted toward the bus. "Where were you plannin'? Atlantic City? You got a hotel or somethin' out there?"

"No plans."

"That's not like you."

He was right. I'd hoped for him.

****

As the man poured himself into a new Cadillac, he looked like a commercial. Maybe selling sleek, study, American-made luxury. Maybe selling the next Bond movie.

I crawled into the passenger side. "You always this fancy, Burr?"

"She's my reward to myself for getting through prison without killing anyone." He grinned and buckled in.

"All I got was a lousy iPod." I took the blue strings out of my ears and wrapped them around the little blue shell of music. My only company after he left.

Burr smiled wider, glad I'd kept it, not acknowledging that he'd left it for me. He turned on the car. "You bulked up, Tic-Tac. You run out of books to read?"

"Naw, after my shitty roommate left, I had no one to talk to."

Burr had a good laugh.

He drove away from the bus stop without hesitation. He had a destination, and he didn't hide it. The road quickly turned rural as we headed away from the highway.

"Where are you taking me, Burr? Out to the pine barrens where you bury people?"

He scoffed. "I ain't gonna bury you."

"I know it." I'd bury him first, and he'd never see it coming. "But what's the plan? You gonna make me an offer I can't refuse?"

"You being funny or what?" His hand clenched and unclenched on the wheel. "It ain't like that."

I couldn't make myself ask what it was like.

My silence made him a little desperate. "You could've gotten on that bus, Rico. I didn't force you into any car. I didn't."

Relentless quiet.

"I got no plan. I just … I don't want you to get the wrong impression, but I … I just had to…" Burr floundered as I watched. "Man, you are hard as shit to talk to, you know that?"

"Worse than a brick wall." I didn't make it easier. "You had to…?"

"Look. I just wanted to see you." Burr's gaze flickered over me, then snapped forward. "I wanted to get you a job, but you can say no."

"Don't need a job."

"Come on. You'd be a great fence. That steely glare. I bet you scared the shit out of junkies when you were selling."

"I never sold."

"You were arrested for intent to sell. I've seen the court records."

Outside, the dead buildings and empty trees rolled by. "A client sent me after an addict. I posed as a dealer. Turns out the mark was posing, too. He arrested me before I could hit him."

"Hit him? Like—" Burr jolted. "You're a cleaner?"

"Nothing clean about it. I usually leave the body for the police to worry about."

Burr leaned back in his seat and took a long look at me before turning his attention entirely on the road. "Leave the body, eh? What happened to Matisse?"

"Just what the coroner said. He overdosed on powdered caffeine." I smiled. "Never had myself as a client before. I can tell you, the pay for that job? Not so great."

Burr ran a hand through his hair. He looked nervous about this new perspective. "Jesus. What? Do you work for the cartels?"

"We're not unaffiliated. It's more of a partnership. The bosses don't know us. They think we don't know them."

I pulled out a packet of orange Tic-Tacs and offered them with a friendly rattle. "That enough reason for you to stay the fuck away?"

He didn't take the candy, which delighted me. I popped a handful in my mouth.

Burr sat in silence, his eyes narrowed. Eventually, he asked, "Why get in the car if you didn't want to see me?"

My heart leaped to my throat, and I couldn't stomp it down before I answered, "Never said I didn't want to see you."

Immediately, I knew I could expect nothing but scorn for a sentiment like that. I tried to make up for it, curling deeper into the seat. "I just wanted you to know who you were seeing."

Burr didn't mock me. He smiled, kept his eyes on

the road, then he held out his hand. I poured some Tic-Tacs into it, relieved.

"Guess it's good to know. What are your plans, Rico?"

I leaned back far in the extravagant comfort of the passenger seat. "Love to take this car to some backwoods place. Get you to fuck me in the backseat. Does cum stain leather?"

It was the most direct thing I'd ever said to Burr. Maybe to any man. It electrified him, and the car purred as it shot forward on the empty highway.

****

He'd already checked into a Ramada about twenty minutes from the jail. He faltered as he opened the door with the key card, "Like I said, I don't want you to get the wrong impression."

I walked into the room; fresh, cheap luxury. Big bed. Deep tub.

Burr shut the door behind him and dropped the bolt as a matter of habit. "I know when I got out all I wanted was a hot bath, so if you—"

I was only able to slam him against the wall because Burgess wasn't expecting it. My hands were on his shoulders and his muscles coiled, ready to punch me away. The power in his body drained in shock when I kissed him.

In the cage, he'd fucked me every chance he got, but this was the first time we'd kissed. His full lips remained warm, dry, and inactive. His big hands hung at his sides. Maybe this was the first time he'd ever kissed anyone. He leaned against the wall like he was afraid I'd disappear if he touched me.

"Come on, Burr." I stepped back, teased him with my absence. "I didn't get in that car with you to take a fucking bath."

When I close my eyes, I can still see the wicked grin he gave me, still feel the chill of desire that trembled up my spine.

His arms crushed behind my back and his teeth knocked against mine as he kissed me. I held his face and his neck, teaching him the basics, the open mouth, the searching tongue. It drove him wild, like offering a man dying of thirst tiny sips of cold, clear water.

He groped at my back, my ass, my shoulders, my neck. Tore the already-too-small hoodie. Yanked at my jeans without loosening my belt. He wanted me naked, but he wasn't coordinated, too maddened with passion to get what he wanted.

I controlled him. Teased his lips by licking. Drew back enough to threaten his hold on my ass. Ran my hands over his crisp white shirt. Dove back into the kiss.

He groaned and buckled against the wall already breathless. "Fuck, man…"

His cock bulged in his tailored trousers, and pre-cum saturated the spot at his tip. He ripped the hoodie over my head and dragged me back into his big body. He kissed my neck and growled, "You miss me or what?"

His fingers played over my naked back, the first time anyone had touched me without violence since he'd gotten paroled. It made my muscles sing with longing. "Naw. I just like the suit."

"Should have said." Burr tugged at my jeans, determined to either break my hip bones or the belt. "I coulda worked something out with the warden."

I slipped away to undo my belt, and he pushed me toward the enormous bed. Had to be king-sized. Big brown and white comforter. I hardly saw it because Burr tore off my jeans. Nearly broke my foot to get my sneaker off. I tried to help, but I'd introduced him to kissing. Now he was determined to drown me in his lips, to crush me with his mouth, break me with his tongue.

He manhandled my clothes, rushing to get to my naked skin. I expected him to unzip just enough to free his cock and fuck me right there. Instead, when I was naked, he stepped back.

And looked at me.

He'd never seen me naked. Glimpses in the communal showers, but he couldn't risk it. He might have ended up staring like he was now.

It made me uncomfortable. I'm a person who hides, who is never seen. Gazes slip off me like oil and return to phones, or friends, or beautiful things. But he drank in the sight of me.

His hands trembled when he touched my knees.

I parted my legs, reclined, and closed my eyes. I waited for his cock, thrilled for the invasion.

Molten desire radiated through my core when instead of a cock in my ass, I got a mouth on my cock. I jolted, made a sound that was partly "fuck" and partly 'yeah' and utterly incomprehensible. Burr smiled around the head of my cock, the brown shaft sinking past his rosy lips. He slurped more in and held my gaze, transfixing me with his big green eyes. I couldn't make myself look away, but I also couldn't bear the pleasure of his full lips, his tentative tongue.

"That's it, Burr, suck it like a man."

Encouraged, he attacked my cock, bobbing his head and taking it deep, keeping his lips tight around my shaft. He didn't know what the fuck he was doing, but that was fine. I rubbed my hands through his hair, slowing him, gripping the soft strands and savoring his strong jaw and his beautiful mouth.

The man on his knees—so powerfully built, so put together in his tailored suit, so undone with lust for me—didn't know what to do with his hands. As he sucked my cock, his fingers gripped his knees, my ankles, then fisted lamely in his lap.

"Unzip your pants, Burr. Let me see your cock."

He groaned and obeyed. When his cock burst out, the tip was red and creamy. He gripped his shaft in one hand and his balls in the other and bobbed on my cock.

"Stroke it," I instructed.

He shook his head no which made my shaft shudder.

"Aw, are you about to come, Burr? Did you miss me?"

He slipped back on my cock. "I missed fucking you."

I pushed my dick back into his mouth. "Make me come, and you can fuck me all you want."

Burr returned to his task with renewed energy and this time I could not stifle my groan. I leaned on the bed to support myself as he worked my shaft and groped my balls.

"Yeah," I promised him, startled and aroused by my own speech. "You can fuck me all you want, as loud as you want, with the lights on. Just keep…"

I moaned, and he hummed around my cock. He stroked his now. Hard and slow, squeezing until a drop of pre-cum drizzled down his fat head.

"Careful, Burr." I pumped my hips into his face, positively verbose. "If you don't get that cock of yours under control, you won't be able to shove me face-down on this bed. You won't be hard enough to ram that fat dick up my ass."

He gripped my ass with both hands, pulling me to my feet, pressing my hips to his face. His big tool swayed in the cold air. One finger snuck between my cheeks and sought my hole. I wiggled so he could find his way inside.

"I really want it, Burr. I've missed that cock, been thinking about it ever since you left. Then you show up looking goddamned hot as fuck. You're lucky I didn't jump on your dick at the bus stop."

His cock spasmed and he came in a shower of thick cream. It ran down his hand, shining like starlight on his fingers.

I smirked with a kind of victory.

He drew off my dick with a hard suck and looked up at me with the rich sensuality of thick eyelashes and pale skin. "You ever think about this ass of mine, Rico? About what you could do to it with this fucking beautiful thing?"

His words struck me so hard I could not be silent. "What?"

Burr kissed the head of my cock, and it nearly knocked me over. Then he slipped out of his jacket. Left his pants on the ground and stood. His white shirt fell open enough to show the dark curls on his broad chest.

"You ever think of fucking me?"

I hadn't. I hadn't dared. I was now, though. The desire consumed me, filled my head with so much want that I couldn't move.

Burr kissed me, tossed me back onto the bed, then straddled me. He'd planned this, too. His hole was clean and lubed. My cock slipped inside easily.

I gripped at his chest finding my voice only long enough to express my shock and delight. "Jesus Christ, Burr!"

He hissed and flinched. He hadn't done this before. But he rolled his hips and dealt with the pain. Fucking amazing. Every twitch of my cock made his tight ass shudder. His body was so dense with muscle, I could barely move him when I started bucking.

I grabbed at his shoulders and pulled him down to

my face. He groaned with pain as I kissed him and thrust. But he ground his ass back into my dick.

My breath came faster as I fucked him. Everything tightened in my stomach and balls. Orgasm. I held back because he'd hardly started.

He nibbled my ear. "Don't give me the silent treatment now, Rico. You got your dick under control?"

He rose on his knees and rolled over my cock, showing off his broad chest, the clean white lines of his shirt, the huge muscles underneath. The beautiful bastard stroked his body with one hand and his cock with the other. "You miss this?"

I had. Jesus Christ, I'd missed looking at him. I wasn't about to confess it, but I suppose he figured it out when I tossed my head back, groaned, and thrust. A few white-hot seconds later, I unloaded in his ass.

Grinning with pride and drunk on sex, Burr rode until my cock slipped from the vise grip of his muscular ass. Then he bowed over me to kiss my mouth and stroke my body.

I never let a stranger touch me like that. I only let him because I was so used to giving Burr his way. Or maybe it was that only Burr bulldozed through my scorn and silence and insisted on touch. His hands were magic, judging and only finding perfection, easing my muscles and stirring my skin.

It lulled me. I was practically asleep, comatose with a satisfaction like he'd killed my survival instincts. I only noticed he was hard again when he stopped feasting on my body and rubbed his cock along my inside thigh.

"Rico, can I…" He whispered, but didn't finish.

I opened my eyes to sneer at him, but lost myself immediately in the soft hazel of his gaze. Still, I'm not the sentimental sort. "Come on, Bruiser, you know I fuckin' want it. Since when did you need written permission?"

He grinned, "You're such a bastard."

I stretched my arms behind my head, flexing a little for his sake. "Serves you right for getting cuddly."

A second later, with his cock deep in my ass, he wasn't getting cuddly. He was getting rough. Rough as he could, and the man was built to fuck hard. He had my knees by my ears before long and was doing his best to break the bed. I held my breath and enjoyed the ride.

I stifled my groans, biting my mouth to keep from gasping. But… there was no reason to. I was free to shout and scream and beg him for more.

So, I did.

He rewarded me with answering grunts and growls. And soon another explosion of cum.

He slipped out of my ass, but not out of my arms. Rolled on his side and sprawled out next to me in the massive bed. We both had room to spare, but he jerked me under his arm like his favorite stuffed doll.

"That's how it's supposed to be, Rico."

I said nothing. But maybe, I didn't disagree.

****

After I took that shower—he was fucking right, I forgot the pleasures of a private, hot shower—I found him sitting on the bed with my hoodie in his hands. He looked like someone kicked his kitten to death.

He glanced at me, and it only got worse. I ignored his brooding and dried my hair. He reached for me. "Christ, I want to keep you naked forever."

"Yeah, yeah. I know. Keep your hands off. Did we pass a diner on the way here?"

"I'll order delivery. You want pizza or Chinese?"

I lowered the towel. "Afraid to go out in public?"

He grimaced because I hit the problem exactly. "No. It's not that. There's no one around here who knows me… I just…"

Burr tried to get all suave again and grazed his hand over my ribs. "Don't think I can keep my hands off for long."

I stepped out of his reach and put the towel around my waist. "Does your family know?"

Burr deflected. "Does yours?"

"Mine is in another country." I leaned on the dresser. "And we kill people for money. They don't give a shit who I fuck."

Then I crossed my arms and gave him a real answer. "Yeah. They know."

He rubbed his neck, such a strangely helpless gesture from such a powerful man. "Yeah, well. It would be … I don't know, a weakness. Something enemies could exploit or whatever. No one knows."

Burr stood and tugged at the towel, so I was naked again. He tickled his hands over my sides and kissed my shoulder. "But they don't have to. That's not a problem, right?"

"No. It's no problem."

I'd be getting on that bus after all.

Chapter Five

How the hell did I end up in the suburbs?

I check the address, recheck it, and then take off my helmet to gawk at the house.

It's a fucking rancher. Not like a rowhouse, but like a one-story, private residence, surrounded by a moat of manicured lawn. And it's not alone. The whole neighborhood is populated by single family houses with two cars in the driveway.

In the house behind me, a kid throws a baseball at the garage and catches it.

The address Burr sent me is particularly private. There's a tree in the front shadowing the little white mansion. Potted plant on a concrete porch. New luxury Cadillac in the driveway.

Yeah, that's his house. Jesus fucking Christ. What am I doing at his house?

That last time we hooked up slams into my mind. At least five months back in the late spring, out in Vegas at the Stratosphere Casino. I made fun of him for being fancy. He said next time he called it'd be more homey. He hadn't called. And five months was a long stretch for us. I'd considered the significance before now. Wondered if he had moved on. Tried to get a more normal life, more open.

Maybe that's what he meant when he talked about exploitable weakness. Maybe that's why I was going to collect $60k for killing him.

"Hey, mister, are you a private eye?" The baseball kid clumps across his lawn. He's white, still tanned from the summer but with a new school-year haircut. Brassy little shit. But maybe not. The suburbs are a brave new world for me.

I look over my shoulder and down. "Wouldn't be a good one if a kid noticed me."

"You could be," the boy says. "Meddling kids always see stuff."

Cute. "Aren't private detectives the good guys?"

He considers, then changes topics. "Are you visiting Coach?"

I point at the monster in the drive. "Does Coach drive a Cadillac?"

"Yup. Mama said he must be having a lady friend visiting because he spent all week cleaning and doing yard work. My sister thinks it's the princess of Italy because Coach talks about her sometimes."

I smile. "Well, I'm not allowed to name names, but if Coach talks about the princess to you sometimes … I'm here to make sure the place is safe for her visit. Think this is a safe neighborhood?"

He admits, sheepishly. "Someone stole my bike when I left it in the front yard. I was five, but that was ages ago."

"How old are you now?"

"Six and a half. I like your bike."

"You gonna steal it?" He looks so shocked it makes me laugh. "Shit, kid. I was joking."

"That's a bad word."

"Sorry. Do you see the police around here a lot?"

"Well, sure. Like when there's a fender bender and they stand in the middle of the road after school and at parades. I got a picture with one at a parade."

That *is* a good neighborhood. I never lived any place where a kid was proud to take a picture with the police. I think about giving the little guy a piece of candy—bet he'd love chamoy—but there's something unspeakably creepy about sharing sweets with a strange kid.

"Last question—and the princess thanks you very much for your due diligence—are you one of the coach's star pitchers?"

The kid beams. "Yeah! He says I have a good arm."

"You better get back to practicing then."

He darts off with a renewed vigor.

Good kid, in a good neighborhood, where a gay mobster coaches little league. What's the newspaper headline the kid's nosy mother will wake up to? "Local Coach Murdered," and later "Murdered Coach had Mob Ties." Wonder if his mama will pay attention when little star pitcher talks about a man in a black leather jacket. If he'll get to talk to a real live police officer about a real live murder. He couldn't identify me.

I feel the weight of the Glock 26 in my jacket. Loaded, safety on, suppressed. That's the first mistake most thugs make. Guns that are too big. If it doesn't fit in your pocket, it's useless. I put it all together back in Ohio when the highway was empty, and I've crossed two states without anyone noticing because it's a baby gun.

"Hey, mister., the kid shouts from his own empty driveway. "Why's an Italian princess coming to see Coach Burr?"

I wink at the kid. "If I told you, I'd have to kill you."

****

Here's how I plan it. I go in bringing the Smirnoff and my duffel, so I don't arouse suspicion. If he's survived two attempts now, the mark will be on edge, wary about even his old cellmate and occasional fuckbuddy. Nosy neighbors see nothing stranger than a friend dropping by for drinks.

The Baby is well-concealed, well-maintained, ready for action. When the mark gets handsy, I'll push him away, which will give me a chance to see if he's wearing Kevlar. If he isn't, I'll ask him to give me a minute to rest from the road. Finish the Smirnoff, pull out the Glock and finish him.

I should be able to leave his body in that recliner I see through the living room windows. Just walk out of the house and disappear. He won't be missed until he misses Little League with any luck.

And if he is wearing Kevlar? Well, I could shoot his head. My stomach knots at the idea of destroying that face, until I harden up again. I'll wait until he isn't wearing the armor. He's not gonna fuck me with a bulletproof vest on. He's not gonna fuck me at all.

Large, flat stones lead to his door like the grass is poison I need to skip across. The potted plant looks well-tended, but might be new. The porch is swept and clean.

Sixty thousand. That's retirement money. Not just for me, for the whole family. That's open-a-coffee-farm money. That's move-everyone-to-America money.

Burr opens the door before I get a chance to knock. "Rico!"

I can't help but smile when I see him. He's wearing long brown shorts, no shoes, and a dark, unbuttoned Hawaiian shirt that's just the wrong side of tasteful. What his ensemble lacks in dignity, it makes up for in sex appeal. His broad chest, densely hairy, striated with muscle, peeks in between the bright yellow and purple flowers that decorate the silky black of his shirt. His belly is trim, but not ripped. He'd need a week or so of strict dieting for sharp definition. His whole body is tanned so he's nearly as dark as me, but with a polished pinkness that marks his skin as white with a summer glow. Not born brown.

He grabs me and hugs me, the unhesitating warmth of an Italian-American. The quick, choking squeeze and the hard back-thump rattles my bones. I suspect it's half out of affection and half to remind me how fucking strong he is. "Welcome to the sixth borough of New York. What'd you bring?"

I tip the bag to show the six-pack of Smirnoff.

"That's right." Burr waves me inside. "I forgot you were a pussy."

"Oh, yeah? What have you got that's harder? Yuengling? A couple of wine coolers from big brother's baby shower?"

"Blow me." Burr closes the door, latches the bolt.

"Sure, but we both know you're gonna come after two seconds. Then I'll have to fuck you. But if that's how you want it, whatever." Jesus Christ, I've got to get in the right headspace. You don't proposition the fucking mark. He's not Burr. He's the mark. I'm going to shoot him.

"Well, we know where your mind is at." The mark laughs. He moves through the den—I guess, it's a den. There a little fireplace built into the wall and two couches—and into the kitchen. He gets two glass tumblers and fills one with ice from the fridge door. "Want ice?"

I twist off the top of a Smirnoff and drink.

He puts the tumblers on the counter. Nice big granite counters, though judging by the recycling bin, he doesn't cook much. He fetches a Yuengling from the fridge.

"Oh, yeah, real hard-ass you are." I tease him. I fiddle with the bottle cap, about to pocket it. Leave no trace. Instead, I toss it into the ash tray on the coffee table and sink onto the couch. "So, you're coaching Little League?"

"Yeah…" He sits in the recliner across from me. Next to me on the couch would be too intimate right now. Maybe later. No, not later, because I'm gonna shoot him in that recliner. "I always liked baseball. What, were you talking to my neighbors?"

"Kid with a baseball thought you were getting the house cleaned up for an Italian princess."

Burr grins and gets a little red. "Yeah, that's Jackie Davis. You never met a more uncoordinated kid."

"Friendly though. Ran up to me when I pulled up."

"He likes bikes," Burr says. "Don't take it personally."

I sip the Smirnoff. Once I finish, out with the gun. Sixty thousand dollars for a dead man.

Burr leans back in the chair, legs spread wide and relaxed. He rubs his neck which opens his shirt enough to give me a clear shot at his heart. I think of running my fingers through that dense patch of hair until I find his nipples, think of how he hisses when I pinch just right, how he squirms when I'm straddling him and sucking on his pecs.

"So..." Burr says. "How have you been since... Fuck, was it Austin or L.A. last time?"

It was Las Vegas, and he fucking knows it. That damned fancy Stratosphere hotel, with the shower attached to the Jacuzzi bath. We'd showered together, and he'd traced the water falling down the ridges of my back, watched the way soap bubbles gathered at the base of my cock.

"I can't complain. The job's been quiet."

"Around here, too." Burr lies. I suspect he's thinking about the two attempts on his life. But then, he might be thinking of Vegas, too. His gaze rests firmly on my jeans. Which are too tight. Especially for my stiff dick.

When I squeeze my cock, he jolts like an altar

boy caught dreaming dirty. His eyes jump to my face, and I smirk, delighted to catch him in the act.

"You get any action since Austin-maybe-L.A., Burr?"

"Couple of twinks." He averts his eyes. He's lying because he doesn't want to seem lonely or pathetic. "You know how it is."

I do. No one else is quite enough. No one else knows me like him. No one else triggers this automatic lust. I swig the Smirnoff, forgetting to drink in sips, to make it last, because once it's gone, I'm going to shoot him.

"You still out in Arizona?"

I nod. I *am* going to shoot him.

He prompts. "How's that?"

"Full of sunshine and snakes."

Burr smiles at my poetics, runs his hand through his hair, and gazes out the window. Fucking beautiful.

God, I'm not gonna shoot him.

"You are still hard as hell to talk to, Rico. I mean, how am I supposed to answer that? Full of sunshine and snakes? What's the even fuckin' mean?"

Can't shoot him. Gonna save him instead. From his family. From mine. Shit.

But first, I finish the Smirnoff and spread out on the couch. "You really want me to talk, Burr? After I rode across the country to get here?"

Burr licks his lips and shakes his head.

I open my jeans just enough to get my cock out. "Then you come here and blow me."

If 'a couple of twinks' do exist, and Burr deigned to give them head, they were lucky. Then again, Burr knows me. That's the problem with having the same bang-piece for seven years—he gets better at you. He's mastered the best tricks for my dick, from the way I like him to squeeze my balls, to the pressure on my head to make me hiss with pleasure, to the private allusion to our first time when he looks up and holds my gaze.

Today, in particular, it makes his face look at once terribly innocent and incredibly masculine, and my reaction, like always, is to moan, grip his hair at his ears, and fuck his face.

Burr takes it well, sucking hard as I pump my cock. I'd been thinking about sex too much, thinking about our past, about him, but I'm not ashamed that I come quickly.

It's more than Burr can swallow and the excess dribbles down his chin when he gasps for breath. I rub my cock over his face to collect it and rub into his neck and cheek. Which I happen to know is something that gets him off.

He kisses the tip of my cock. "You haven't gotten much action since Vegas, either."

I knew he fucking remembered. Asshole wants to make me think it wasn't important. I stuff my cock deep in his throat again, and Burr hums and sucks it hard. "I get plenty. Only from my hand. But you know how that is."

Burr suckles until my cock is too sensitive and I shift away. He pulls my jeans the rest of the way off my legs and crawls up on the couch, pinning me under his big body.

I push that fucking stupid shirt off his chest as he kisses me. Yuengling, cum, and the fresh mint of toothpaste. He saw me on my bike and ran to brush his teeth.

I rub my hands over his chest. I'll never ever get enough of him. The way the muscles flex against my palm, both soft and unyielding, the way the hair parts around my fingers, the heat of his skin, the distant thud of his heart.

He kisses a path from my mouth to my neck, slowly maneuvering me so that he can fondle my ass. I move where he wants me. Up on my knees, bent over the arm of the couch, ass raised to be fucked.

Burr, because he can never take a goddamned hint, rubs against my ass and keeps kissing, running his lips up and down my spine over the leather jacket, groping under my sweater. He tugs me up against his chest and lifts me upright so he can force my head back and kiss me again. His hand grips my neck. The hold, almost violent, ought to frighten me. But I can smell his cologne, and the heat and scent of him stir my cock again.

I relax my arms when he pulls off my jacket. The Baby Glock clunks heavily on the floor, and I stiffen. I glance over my shoulder. Burr's hand slackens on my throat as he studies the puddle of black leather. His expression goes dark.

If he asks, I'll tell.

But he doesn't, so I say nothing.

He gets rough. He tears the sweater off and pushes me hard over the arm of the couch. Holds my head down, grinds my face into the fabric. He stabs me with his fingers, not hard enough to really hurt, but close enough to make me flinch. He spits to stretch and widen my hole.

When he starts fucking me, he doesn't let up on the aggression. He rams his cock. Ragdolls me around. Squeezes my legs until they are pressed tight together. He gets the squirming and gasping he wants, but if he's expecting me to tell him to stop, he's underestimated how much pain I'm willing to take.

He fucks me so hard the slapping sound of his body colliding with me is a continuous applause. I slip off the couch, not strong enough to hold his weight and mine while he's tugging at my hips and pushing at my neck. He lets me fall to the floor. Before I can turn to face him, he follows me down. He stands and drills my ass, then crouches as he plows me; eventually he falls to his knees and at last starts kneading my dick.

I'm rock-hard for him, a glutton for his punishment. He knows that about me, too, and he makes me come again while he tears into my ass.

Like my release is permission, he growls in my ear and unleashes inside me. He keeps fucking until the cum has rubbed away and the friction hurts him. Then he tosses me aside and backs off.

Burr, far from being sated by the sex, glares at me like a raging animal. But his attack is casual. He throws an arm over the coffee table and catches his breath as he stares. For the first time in years, I recognize the hardness that made me so cautious when I was locked in a cage with him.

That's a man I might have to kill to save my own life.

"How about it, Rico?" His voice is cold. "You get your fix?"

It stings to sit, but it's a good pain. "Yeah. Worth the ride. Even without the contract."

"You in New York on business then?" He glances at my jacket.

I nod.

"Anyone I know?"

I smile faintly and answer honestly. "Sure. The younger Accorsi boy."

"I don't think that's a very good joke."

"Well, I'm too professional to tell." I lean on the couch, to appear relaxed, glance up at my empty Smirnoff. Not touching my coat. "Wanna shower together? Like in Austin-maybe-L.A.?"

"It was Vegas, May twelfth through fourteenth. Corner room on the fifth floor."

"Room 534," I agree. "The Stratosphere Casino."

"Let's not pretend it didn't matter."

"You started it."

We both sit in silence, sweating and distrustful.

Eventually, I kick my coat over to him. "It's a Baby Glock. Fully loaded, suppressed, safety on."

Burr reaches into the jacket's inside pocket and takes out the gun. He turns it in his big hands, weighing its presence, its significance. Then he lays it on the coffee table.

"So, tell me, Mr. Professional. How would you hit a guy like me?"

"Me personally?" I drape an arm over my knee. "I'd arrange for a booty call. Ride to your house. Shoot you in the recliner while we reminisced. Certainly, I wouldn't get distracted and get my brains fucked out instead."

There's no change in his stoic face. He didn't let me see those bruises on his ribs before. Big dents. He'd been wearing a good bulletproof vest, but he'd taken multiple shots. If the shooter had been more persistent, he might have punched through.

"If I didn't know you, I'd probably try to get in a bar fight with you. Kill you in public, like it was an accident. Which would be tough, because you're not a drinker."

Burr smirks and snatches his Yuengling off the coffee table.

"So maybe I'd try to jump you in a parking lot. Make it look like a mugging, but then you're a big guy. Who the fuck would try to mug you? So, I might try to shoot you from a distance instead. If I can't get my hands on military grade firearms, I'd probably use a regular hunting rifle and hope you weren't wearing armor."

I stand, stretch, lean against his couch. "Of course, I can get my hands on military grade tech, and I know not to stop at three."

Burr raises his eyebrow. "He stopped shooting because I killed him."

"He wasn't me." I wander into his kitchen. "Want some water?"

"Yeah." Burr stays near the gun.

I pick up the two tumblers, notice the bottle of wine on the table and the two place settings. I'd bet money if I went into his bedroom I'd see a hastily discarded suit on the ground. He'd dressed up for me, saw me in my road clothes and changed into something casual. Delivery might be on the way. He might not have intended to jump right to fucking either.

I fill the tumblers with ice water from the fridge. "My contact thinks it's internal."

"Your contact? The fuck is that supposed to mean? Someone hired you to kill me? Someone knew about you to hire you?"

I hand him the water and wait for him to ask.

"You were going to kill me?"

"If I were I would have done it already, wouldn't I?"

He drains the water in one go and sets the tumbler on his bookshelf. "Yeah. But you seriously considered it?"

"I seriously considered sixty thousand dollars."

"Sixty…" Burr's eyes widen. "Jesus Christ!"

"Yeah." I sip my water. "Have you been fighting with Daddy, your brother, or some rich lieutenant?"

"You don't ask shit like that." It's not a generalized "you." It's a personal one. His Mexican fuckbuddy doesn't ask shit like that.

Burr paces around his living room. "It's not supposed to go like that. Family is supposed to be…"

He pauses and looks out the big picture windows at the neighborhood. It's the face of a man who's realizing he doesn't belong where he's made his home. And that leaving the place he did belong is going to get him killed.

Or maybe he's just pissed.

"Family is family. I trust them more than—" Burr looks at me quickly, then finishes. "More than anything. Your contact is wrong."

I raise my brows and make no comment.

"Do not give me the silent treatment!" he roars.

I cross my arms and say nothing.

Burr drains the rest of his beer. A lesser man would start another. Instead, he sinks into the recliner again. "What are they saying in Arizona?"

"In Guerrero, they're saying, sixty thousand for your death. They want to see the body. Cash on delivery. They want it quick and painless. Something about removing a weakness before someone exploits it."

Burr rubs his left hand over his right fist. "That's Joey."

"Forgive me for not knowing who—"

"My brother. Fucking prick. I'll fucking kill him. Little shit. I did everything he ever fucking asked, and this is how he repays me? I'll fucking kill him myself. Beat his goddamned face in."

"That's not very wise." I sip my water.

"Fuck you and—" Burr remembers my particular expertise and calms, which is wise. "How would you do it?"

"If I was his little brother? I'd meet him alone in some out-of-the-way place. Probably tell him, he's the only one I trust and I think someone wants me dead."

"Out to the diner." Burr nods along. "Or the pine barrens. I'd have to deal with Tony and Pete."

"Before you start planning, you'll want to prove it's him. And since this is personal, you can't just hang around. The police and your family will suspect you. So, you'll want to consider how quickly you can get to money."

"How much?"

"All of it." I rub my lip, considering the angles. Should I call Abuelito?

"That's a damned dangerous look," Burr says. "What are you thinking?"

"I'm thinking we need to talk." I hate even saying the words. "You know, about us and your family and where you see yourself in ten or so years."

Burr chuckles, suddenly more shy than angry. He glances out into the kitchen. "Not the way I hoped this conversation would come up, but I'm game. You wanna order takeout?"

"Well, we've got no business talking like this in a restaurant."

****

Even though it's past midnight and I've never seen him, I recognize Joseph Accorsi when his guards let him out of the Jaguar. He's shorter than Burr, more chunky, though I wouldn't call him out of shape. He has a keenness that's distracted and nervous today.

Getting a call saying your brother's corpse and his assassin are both waiting in the suburbs is likely to do that.

I greet the three men at the door.

Joe Jr. asks without subtlety, "Where's the body?"

"In his bed." I point over my shoulder toward

Burr's room. "Where's the money?"

"In the bag." Joe Jr. waves his hand at one of his guards. "How'd you do it?"

"Poison," I say. "It looks like he had a heart attack."

"Shit." That's more than Joe Jr. expected. "Really?"

I nod.

"How did you get—"

"I brought a case of Yuengling. The beer was laced. I had one. He had five."

This line should give us away, but Joe Jr. either doesn't know his brother very well or is too distraught to pay attention.

I tease him about it, "Hey, you look awful upset about this all, Junior. Don't worry, Daddy's not gonna find out unless you act funny."

He whips out a gun. "Don't you sass me!"

I raise my hands innocently and shrug. "Dude, you've got zero chill."

"Boss," one of the goons says gently. "This guy is with the cartels. You don't wanna shoot him."

Joe Jr. touches his own chest with the gun. "You wanna know what my father is gonna say when he I tell him this? My father is gonna say thanks. He didn't want a faggot running things any more than I did."

"That's a comfort. I never like these mob jobs. Never know what kind of reprisal you're gonna get." I scratch the new growth of beard I've developed over the past few days. "Can I have the money now or are you gonna actually look at the stiff?"

Joe Jr. glares at me, then tucks the gun back into his arm holster and passes me into the hallway. The two goons follow, one with my bag of cash tucked under his arm.

I cross my arms sliding a hand into my pocket around the Baby Glock.

Joe Jr. opens little brother's bedroom door and peeks into the darkness. A gun shouts. His brains splatter against the soft sunshine yellow of the hall wall. Hell of a warning.

I free the Baby and shoot the thug with free hands first, though he's nowhere near his gun. The second guy drops the cash and has his piece out, but he's dead before he can decide where to aim. Head shots all around.

"Shit, you're fast," Burr steps into the hallway.

"I practice a lot." I survey the bodies. Dead. I open the chamber and unload the Baby. "I thought you might want to talk to him."

"Heard all I needed." Burr picks up the bag. He peeks in. "Good. I was worried they were gonna rip you off."

"Not paying a man who kills for money is not healthy." I put the bullets in my pocket next to the candy. Return the decommissioned Glock to my pocket.

Burr goes over to the bodies and gets the keys off one without even digging. He knows exactly where the driver kept the keys. Sad. He tosses the keys and the cash to me and I carry Burr's two suitcases out and load them into his brother's trunk. I put the money in my bike and bring out the gasoline.

I meet Burr and his brother's corpse in his basement. We douse Joe Jr. in gasoline, spread the stuff around the floor, and onto the support beams of the house.

Then we go back outside. We crouch together by the open basement window and Burr sighs. "It's a damned shame. I liked this house."

I put a hand on his shoulder to comfort him then pass him the lighter. He sets a wad of paper on fire and tosses it into the basement.

The gasoline catches and heat flares at the window. Burr closes it.

"You got that letter?"

I nod.

Burr stands. "Let's get out of here."

He gets into his brother's car, and I get on the motorcycle as soon as I drop Burr's suicide note into Jackie Davis's mailbox.

****

We watch the local Hoboken news online from a diner outside Baton Rouge. It's hot and humid as hell, and I'm not sold on beignets.

The newscaster talks about the house fire that took the lives of at least three men last Thursday and about how each revelation makes the case stranger.

"Burgess Accorsi's suicide note/confession, delivered to a neighbor's mailbox before he set fire to his home last Thursday, has broken the criminal operations of his family wide open."

"Serves them the fuck right," Burr mutters.

"Already police have made twelve arrests and shut down a ring of high-end escorts in the New York City area. Police remain searching for Joseph Accorsi Junior who fled the scene of the double murder suicide in a 2017 Black Jaguar."

The newscaster goes on to the next news item. Burr says. "That's it? No one has even mentioned the money I left to the Little League."

He'd gotten most of his money out of his bank accounts, but there was a healthy chunk left behind. I shrug. "Like the H.A.s say, 'When we do right, nobody remembers. When we do wrong, nobody forgets.'"

"You a Hell's Angel?"

"Am I white?"

He snorts, takes my laptop, and Googles his name again.

I push the beignets away. He gives me a funny look, so I explain, "Too sweet."

Burr's confusion only grows. "You love sweets."

I smirk. "I like sucking on things. Used to do seeds, but you can't leave a trail of shells at a crime scene."

"Like I don't even know you." Burr eats the rest of the powdered donuts. "Think they found his car?"

I shrug.

"Think they'd tell us?"

"Burr, you're lucky they're still talking about it. If we'd done things my way, this shit would be old news."

Burr reaches across the table and pats my hand. "Healthy relationships are built on compromise, darling."

I give him such a glare that he laughs.

Then I say, "I think it's trust, actually. Trust and good communication skills."

"Well, we're fucked," Burr says.

He turns the laptop to show me pictures of tropical beaches. Rental properties. "What do you think of the Cayman Islands?"

"I prefer the States. How about California, if you like beaches?"

"How about Hawaii?"

"Never been."

"Well, let's go and if we like it, we can buy a candy store." Burr chuckles. "Put your abwa…how did you say Grandpa again?"

"Abuelo." It'd take a couple years for Abuelito to say anything to Burr.

"Yeah, that. We'll park his bar right next door. What do you think of that, Tic-Tac? Wanna live over a candy store?"

"If you're living with me, it doesn't matter."

Burr blushes and drinks his coffee. He doesn't understand affection yet. I squeeze his leg under the table. He'll learn.

We both will.

The End

www.evernightpublishing.com/l-j-longo

LIVE OR DIE

Kai Tyler

Copyright © 2017

Chapter One

Zakhar

Sitting on an ivory leather chair, fingers steepled against his lips, dark, hooded eyes watching me, Alexei Smirnov brimmed with controlled aggression.

Barring an open black laptop, nothing else marred the surface of the polished walnut desk that separated us. The floor-to-ceiling glass to my right showed a panorama of the city—gray skyscrapers, cerulean sky, and the silver, winding river shimmering in the distant horizon.

In here, pearly white walls and slate floor tiles, stylish teal sofas, and a charcoal rug completed the sleek effect of this executive space.

The minimalist haven of serenity imprisoned Alexei's natural, savage energy, just like his expensive, stylish suit projected the image of prosperous businessman.

None of these things fooled me.

Caging a wild Siberian tiger wasn't the same thing as taming it.

Get locked up in the same space with it and prepare to be mauled. The warning sent a chill down my spine like an omen and doubt prickled my mind. Had I signed my death warrant by coming here?

Outside and on the floors below, the busy offices buzzed with activity like any lawful corporate premises. Nothing would indicate that this was the hub of a criminal organization, the MIRNO Cartel, whose offenses included digital espionage, cyberterrorism, and money laundering among others.

MIRNO left no paper trail, no digital footprint of their transactions. They had optimal technology and first-rate hackers.

As head of the consortium, Alexei Smirnov was number one on The Agency's most wanted list.

Jones Bellamy, head of The Agency's intel group, had assigned me to infiltrate MIRNO and secure the evidence needed to take Alexei down.

That's the reason I sat here, feigning nonchalance while surrounded by Alexei's trigger-happy bodyguards who looked ready to spray bullets and splatter my blood all over their boss's pristine ivory walls like contemporary artists dabbling in abstract paintings.

"Mr. Stone." Alexei said my name with enough contempt to cap an iceberg. "Why are you here?"

Not the welcome I'd been expecting from an old friend. To him, I should've been Zakhar, not Mr. Stone. There had been a time when we'd been inseparable. Best pals willing to do anything for one another—*kill or die*.

My lungs constricted, making it hard to breathe. Black spots flashed in my vision.

Stress, according to the shrink I'd been forced to see after my last assignment—a side effect from ten years of working undercover, dealing with criminals, thinking like them, and living with them. Years of disguising my true self, of assuming fake identities, of living from one lie to the next.

Everything threatened to unravel if I didn't get my act together.

I forced air into my nostrils, easing the squeeze in my chest and clearing my sight. "I need to talk to you privately."

"You disappear for ten years. No contact. Now you turn up out of the blue." He placed both palms on the desk, fingers fanned out. "The only reason you even made it up here is because I wanted to look you in the eyeballs and confirm for myself that it was really you."

He had a point. I expected him to be shocked at seeing me again after so long. Perhaps I could take advantage.

"Now that you have me eyeball to eyeball, don't you want to know why I'm here after all this time?"

His broad shoulders rose and fell with an indifference that didn't quite match the dark flare of his eyes. "Go ahead. Tell me why you've crawled out of your cave."

The corner of my left eye twitched, a sure sign that his biting tone got to me.

"Not in front of them." I tilted my head to indicate the three heavies standing in the office—two behind Alexei and one behind me.

"Then you can get out." He returned his attention to the laptop screen, instantly dismissing me.

My grip on the padded arms on the chair tightened as I got pissed off by his attitude. The twitch in my temporal vein transformed into full-blown constant ticking, a time bomb waiting to explode.

So what if I'd been away for so long? Did I deserve this level of disrespect? What the hell was he so goddamned angry about, anyway?

"Perhaps you're afraid." I was capable of goading him in return.

"Watch your tongue!" His head whipped up as he sat up, back ramrod straight. His glare had enough voltage to fry a moose.

I should've heeded the warning, should've kept my mouth shut. But I remembered the laws of the streets we'd grown up in. Whoever said "the meek shall inherit the earth" had never lived in an orphanage or on the streets. The meek inherited jack shit.

Not about to play lamb to Alexei's lion, I mocked him. "That why you need all these men to protect you?"

In a flash, Alexei shot out of his chair, gun in his right hand pointed to my forehead. "I don't need anyone to protect me from you."

Adrenaline spiked, and my heart nearly exploded in my chest.

Damn. Where did the weapon come from?

He must have had it on the desk, in front of the open laptop where it would've been obscured from my view. The unconcealed guns worn by his security team had distracted me into thinking they were the only physical threats.

What a foolish rookie mistake to make. Not something expected from a seasoned pro like me.

The image of Alexei as a respectable businessman had duped me after all. Or perhaps, at a granular level in my subconscious mind, I'd allowed myself to think that he would never let any harm come to me—something he'd always done in the past.

With tightness around his eyes, his unwavering dark pupils glowering at me, it looked like he would pull the trigger any second and forever erase the notion of him as my protector.

Holding my breath, I sat perfectly still and held his gaze. Undercover work involved being in volatile situations, and I'd mastered being cool under pressure.

Yet, as my heart raced and cold sweat ran down my back, instinct reminded me that this was Alexei who had always been unpredictable and had no qualms about spilling blood. On previous occasions, I'd been by his side, not the person staring at the nasty end of a stainless steel Beretta 9mm semi.

This wasn't the way I'd envisioned our meeting going down, and I hadn't planned on dying today.

Exploring my options of getting out of here alive, my muscles tightened as I calculated the distance between Alexei and me—about five feet. I could take down the man behind me and recover his weapon. But that gambled on Alexei being slow on the trigger.

His cold, hard, flinty eyes dared me to move, fingers primed to follow through on his threat.

Perhaps backing down would earn me a reprieve. At least I hoped it would.

"Alexei," I breathed out his name, not quite a plea, but with enough gentleness to convey deference. "You've never needed anyone to protect you from me. You've always been able to kick my butt all by yourself."

Something flickered in his gaze and was gone just as quickly. Did he remember the past? Our shared history? One of the training sessions where he'd taught me to defend myself, perhaps?

Whatever it had been, my words seemed to have an effect. After a few more tense heartbeats, he flicked his left hand.

With a quiet click, the door behind me opened. The bodyguards walked out without a word and the low buzz from the rest of the building muted once the massive slab clicked shut again.

Alexei settled back into his chair, hand still on the gun which now lay on the desk, his expression unreadable. "Start talking."

Now that his undivided attention focused on me, my throat dried out, and my hands shook as the adrenaline ebbed in my veins. I needed a drink or two, perhaps something stronger to take the edge off.

When I'd agreed to this assignment, I hadn't realized it would be so difficult to sit before him and do what I've done so often for the past ten years—tell a series of made-up stories to maintain my cover. Tell lies to Alexei.

My gaze bounced around the room while I worked saliva into a parched mouth and rubbed my hand over a perspiring neck.

Like a hawk, he watched every move I made, his eyes the color of an obsidian night. As if he could see through to my anxiety, see through to the man I hid from the world.

Then again, a little nervousness wasn't a bad thing considering what I was about to tell him.

"Someone is trying to kill me," I blurted out, wanting to get this done no matter the outcome.

"Ha." He barked a short, ugly laugh. "Whoever it is will have to wait their turn. If anyone is going to kill you, it will be me."

My mouth dropped open and I gaped at him. "You

want to kill me?"

"I'm thinking about it." He didn't even blink.

This was no joke. I stared at him as if he'd grown two heads. He might as well have been an alien for all I knew about him. Ten years had changed him into a bitter man.

I had loved him once.

And he wanted to kill me.

Talk about bad romance.

"What did you think would happen when you came back here?" he gritted out. "You're a government agent, for fuck's sake."

Shit. Blood drained from my head. I blinked rapidly as all my muscles tightened.

No wonder he was so bloody pissed off. I would've reacted the same way if I'd been in his shoes. Government agents and cartel bosses didn't make great bedfellows.

How the fuck did he find out about my job?

Due to the nature of my work, my file remained highly classified. No more than a handful of people with high-level clearance in The Agency knew about my work. We couldn't take the chance of covers being blown.

It seemed my luck had run out this time. I'd been screwed over. Someone I worked with had leaked the information. If I couldn't trust my colleagues, whom could I trust?

My mind raced at a thousand thoughts per second as I scrabbled for a solution. If I couldn't recover the situation, I would be dead, food for the fishes or birds or whatever other creatures Alexei wanted to feed with my putrefying flesh.

Fatigue made my body sag. I sighed in resignation, as my mind spun a tale. "You're right. I'm an agent. But I've been burned. Someone in the agency framed me, and there's a hit on my head. I have a disk that contains an encrypted file. You have the people who can decode it. That's why I came here. I need your help."

His intense gaze bore through me as if he could see through my lies. Seconds felt like minutes, and I struggled not to tug at my collar or shift in the chair under his scrutiny.

When he spoke, his voice had lost the harshness, although the words announced his continuing suspicion. "Why do you think I'll help you?"

The question caught me off-balance. My cheeks burned, and I diverted my gaze to the expansive city skyline.

"We're friends," I whispered the obvious, the most fundamental thing about us.

"We're not friends." Trust Alexei to yank me back to reality. "Friends don't leave. They don't walk away without saying goodbye. Friends don't betray friends."

Unable to confine myself any longer, I shot out of the chair.

He didn't even flinch, back to being cool, calm, and collected. Damn him.

My agitation spiked, I walked to and from the windows at a frantic pace. Not a good idea to turn my back on Alexei, considering he had a gun and wanted to kill me.

Wound so tight and full of adrenaline, I couldn't sit still if I wanted. Not to mention that I was close to not caring. Close to not giving a fuck.

Taking this assignment had been a bad idea. I'd had misgivings right from the start.

My investigative remit covered organized crime and usually revolved around drugs, as well as human and weapons trafficking. Bellamy had called me into a one-on-one meeting to discuss an ongoing investigation. When he'd mentioned he wanted me to infiltrate MIRNO, a chill had run down my spine at the thought of seeing Alexei again after so long.

There were too many memories, too many unresolved issues. I didn't want to rake up old feelings.

"Isn't this more suited to the cyber crime unit?" I'd raised my concern.

"MIRNO falls under organized crime, and I have overall jurisdiction," Bellamy had replied. "In any case, you know the target well."

"I don't," I'd been quick to respond.

My boss leaned forward on his desk. "It says in your file that you were in the same orphanage with Smirnov?"

"That was a long time ago. I haven't seen or spoken to him in years."

"Well, it's time to rekindle your old friendship. You need to get into his organization and bring us the information to shut him down."

Then, I'd hoped the time apart had made me immune to Alexei.

Now, I stood in Alexei's office, realizing I'd never gotten over him. Seeing him again was all it took to have him under my skin as if the past ten years hadn't happened.

I balled my hands into fists and turned to face him. "I get it. You don't want to help me. I was wrong to come here. I'm going to get out and leave you to whatever you were doing."

The agency would have to find another way to take Alexei and MIRNO down. I was done with this life. I wanted out.

The sound of the slamming laptop made me flinch. The raw nerves heightened my senses.

He stood up, fury evident in his clenched fists. "You're not leaving, Zakhar. You don't just show up after ten years and then walk away without telling me why you left in the first place. You came to me for help. You're going to get it."

My brain must have short-circuited because I swear I heard him say he would help me. Although, I was more caught up in the fact that he'd said my name—the rough, savage way he'd spoken "Zakhar" sent a tingle down my spine. Heat radiated through my chest, and I quelled the urge to grin like a fool.

"You are … going to help me?"

"Of course. Let it never be said that I didn't help a person in need, especially someone I once called my brother," his voice dropped.

For the first time since I arrive at Smirnov Tower, Alexei sounded disappointed.

Thickness in my throat made me unable to speak. He'd considered me his brother, treated me like one. I'd let him down by walking away.

But ten years ago, I'd wanted more than brotherhood from him. I'd wanted him. Period. Walking away had been the best thing to do. For me. For both of us.

He inserted his gun into the shoulder holster, grabbed the laptop off the desk, strode to the far end of the office, and pressed a button on the wall. The panel slid sideways, revealing an elevator. It had to be a private one since it hadn't been the one we used to come up here when I arrived.

A palm print and retina scan from him made the doors pull apart.

"Come on," he said and stepped inside the shiny metal box.

I had no option but to follow. Perhaps all wasn't lost. Yet.

My hands clenched and I had to force them to unclench. I hated elevators, the enclosed space, ever since I'd been trapped in one as a kid for a few hours. Alexei had been with me, standing shoulder to shoulder just like today.

I rubbed the back of my neck with a clammy palm and sucked in a deep breath. Alexei's scent filled my nostrils—a mesmerizing mix of sandalwood and citrus, personality, and class—precisely like the man, reminding me of orange groves and turquoise oceans. And like many years before, being in his presence took the edge off my panic. And the side panels of the enclosure had reflective surfaces that made the lift appear larger.

The elevator ride was short and ended in a lofty, semi-open penthouse where I had a view of the city in every direction.

Alexei had come a long way from the orphan boy who had run away from the foster system, and had ended up living on the grimy streets only to survive by his wits. He'd been a young teen when I'd met him for the first time. Even then, he had all the alpha qualities that he exuded now.

I remembered what he'd said to me the day we'd run away from the children's home.

"Zak, our future is bright, but they are going to snuff it

out in here. We have the choice to live or die, which one do you choose?"

Of course, I'd chosen to live, and we'd left the place together. He'd been like a big brother, looking out for me, making sure I had whatever little food we could find. He'd done whatever it had taken for us to survive.

Now, look at him. His spacious apartment was more expensive than we could've dreamed about as kids. He'd done well without me. As head of MIRNO, he had influence among the upper echelon of society and enough money to buy whatever he desired.

He'd always said he would make it big one day. I hadn't doubted him. He was still the smart one.

And the sexy one.

This was proven as he took his jacket off and flung it over a coat rack.

Pulling his tie off with one hand, he unbuttoned his shirt with the other. Broad shoulders stretched the fitted pinstripe shirt. He had never been big, but he'd filled out from what I could see.

I'd been the big one—Fat Zak, as the other kids had named me. Children were vicious sometimes. Once Alexei had become my protector, no one dared utter that name in my presence or his.

Sighing, I followed him through a circular, gallery-style hallway with impressionist paintings hanging on see-through walls. Our footsteps echoed, my heavy boots thudding on the hard flooring as we walked past a sitting room, dining area, kitchen, and study. Although they were partitioned, the design made it flow from one section to the other, retaining the open plan look.

Alexei strode into what seemed to be his bedroom, an ample space with minimal furniture and clean lines. The whole place was breathtaking, but it was as if something was missing. Alexei's soul.

Clinking sounds drew my attention to Alexei as he removed his cufflinks and placed them on a dark wood dresser before tugging his shirt off.

Entranced, my breath hitched as I stood and watched him undress.

He had aged. The sprinkling of grey on his dark hairline and trimmed beard attested to that. He hadn't worn those the last time I was this close to him. Strong jaw, black-rimmed eyes, and straight nose made up a remarkable face.

Tight muscles rippled on his torso, reminding me of the lean, mean killing machine trained in various forms of martial arts.

He unbuckled his belt, leaned over, and pushed down his trousers, kicking them off along with his shoes until he stood naked.

Healthy-looking golden skin covered well-toned sinews. Everywhere. No tan lines.

Fuck me. Blood rushed south, and I hardened instantly. My mouth watered and my fingers itched.

Alexei glanced at me with a smirk. "Is that an invitation?"

My cheeks flamed. I hadn't realized I'd spoken out loud. "Of course not."

I looked away, angry at myself for the slip. I had been in the closet for so many years. Nobody knew I was gay. Not my colleagues and not the perpetrators I interacted with during an operation. And yet within an hour in Alexei's company, I gawked at him with no shame. It certainly didn't help that he paraded around in his apartment in the nude.

He had no body shame. I had plenty, a remnant from my days of being Fat Zak.

"Why the fuck are you undressing?" I bit out, still keeping my gaze averted, although his naked image burned behind my retinas.

"I need a workout to release all the excess adrenaline."

Was he talking about sex again? I glanced at him and caught a view of a bubble butt on firm thighs as he walked through an opening into another room.

Bad idea to look at him because now I didn't know which was sexier—the well-hung penis or the tight ass.

Stifling a groan, I shook my head to disperse all the images of things I'd like to do with naked Alexei and followed him into a private gymnasium.

Rower, treadmill, stepper, elliptical machines, as well as free weight benches, were all positioned so the user could keep the city in sight while working out. But it was the boxing ring in the corner that drew my attention.

Alexei earned his reputation for being savage in the ring as an MMA fighter. It was good to see that some things about him hadn't changed.

"What do I get for helping you?" His question seemed to come out of the blue.

Me, I nearly said. I would've offered myself to him if I'd thought for one minute he had an interest in me.

Oh, I knew Alexei liked men. The little information we had on him showed he'd had sexual encounters with men. Always casual. Nothing serious.

He'd been married to a woman, though. I couldn't forget that.

At least he would be bisexual, but as he'd said himself, I'd been a brother to him. Brothers didn't fuck brothers.

Hence my reason for leaving. I'd wanted him to fuck me so bad. And if the tightness in my denim was anything to go by, I still wanted him to fuck me.

He pulled a folded pair of white shorts with blue stripes from a shelf displaying other gym outfits. Everything was handily available. No wonder he could wander naked.

He glanced at me, eyebrow cocked, waiting for a response.

The boxing ring at the far corner of the gymnasium gave me an idea. I cleared my throat. "How about a chance to kick my ass?"

"You mean you and me in the ring?" He glanced in the same direction I was looking. "Are you sure about that?"

He had the right to smirk. He was a beast in the ring, and I was crazy to even suggest it.

Still, a part of me yearned for the punishing pain he

would deliver. "I'm sure."

His lips curled into a wicked grin as he pulled on the shorts. "Come on, then. You can change into this."

He grabbed another pair of shorts, these ones with red stripes, and tossed them to me.

Holding the shorts, I glanced around, trying to find a private spot to get changed.

"You're not getting changed. Have you changed your mind?" He threw me another glance over his shoulder.

"No," I said a little too quickly.

I'd never been comfortable in my skin, unlike Alexei. Never walked around in the nude.

I preferred to pretend to be someone else which was why I was excellent at infiltrating crime organizations.

Spotting what looked like an alcove at the far end beyond the ring, I walked over. It was the entrance to a shower room. Luckily it also had more locker-style shelving.

Shrugging my leather jacket off, I hung it on a hook before tugging my t-shirt over my head. I placed the top on a shelf and sat on the bench running along the side to pull my boots and socks off.

Whip. Whip. Whip. I leaned over to look and found Alexei using a skip rope to warm up.

He was disciplined, had always been. I'd never had that level of self-control. He'd been my motivation, my reason to work hard. When I'd been doing my training for The Agency, I'd found a new focus. My family history—my father specifically, who had also worked for The Agency before his death. I'd wanted to make my father proud.

After so many missions and so many years, I'd lost some of that focus and self-restraint. Working undercover wasn't a suitable environment for routine or stability. Things were always changing, and I had to adapt to every situation.

There was no point bemoaning the past. I was here on the job, and I had to remember that. While there was a personal tinge to being here, I had to stay focused on the ultimate goal.

When I got dressed again in the shorts, I realized I had

no training shoes. There were a few pairs of sneakers on the shelves. I'd worn his boots previously, so we were roughly the same size. Another glance at him showed him barefoot, so I ignored the gym shoes and joined him by the ring.

"I can't see any gloves," I commented as I shook out my arms to loosen my limbs.

"We don't need them." He tossed me a roll of clean fabric hand wrap. "You can use these or go without."

In the streets, we'd brawled bare-knuckled. While he had no qualms about it, I wasn't about to give him any more advantages over me.

"I'll go with these." I settled on a bench and wrapped the fabric over my hands. The lightweight material stretched and conformed to my fingers and palms and didn't loosen with movement.

I grabbed the skip rope and hopped for a couple of minutes, alternating from one leg to the other in sets while Alexei got on the treadmill.

Testosterone hummed in the air. My entire body vibrated from the excitement of the upcoming fight. I got transported back to the old days and the buzz of fighting.

This place didn't have the musty smell of the public gymnasium we used to train in. I remembered the fear and excitement, the rush of adrenaline, smelled the sweat, and heard the force of the blows and the snap of bones. The controlled street brawl. The injuries and people limping home with bruised egos. Terrifying and exhilarating all at once.

Holding onto the rope, Alexei climbed into the ring. With undeniable presence, he looked ready to kick my ass.

My heart sped up again. Being in close proximity to him always had my ticker going wild as adrenaline rushed through me. I wasn't about to roll over for him, though.

Chapter Two

Alexei

Zakhar stepped into the ring, all big and buff. He'd always been the chunky one even when we were kids. Then, the other kids in the orphanage had taunted him about it.

In those days being big didn't equate to strength, as gentle Zakhar had demonstrated.

On the other hand, I'd been the scrawny one with a mean streak a mile long, and the ability to fight dirty. I could dish out as much pain as I got and more.

The first time I'd met him had been in the dining hall of the Special Residential School, a place for minors aged three to eighteen. He'd been shuffling from the queue at the counter, his brown plastic tray clutched so tight his knuckles had been white, a cute, chubby boy with sandy blond hair and freckles.

He must have been about eight then. None of the other kids his age would let him sit at their table. He'd looked lost, and I couldn't resist getting his attention.

"Hey, kid!" I'd waved, indicating for him to come over. "Sit with us."

Thirteen at the time, I'd been at the table with fourteen- and fifteen-year olds.

"He can't sit with us," one of them had protested.

Inviting a preteen to one of the teenage tables was one of those unspoken rules—even siblings didn't sit together at dinner.

Never one for rules, I made my own. Even then I'd had influence and had been able to get people, including the adults, to do what I wanted.

So when I'd said, "I'm inviting him. Got a problem?" None of the other boys responded. I'd ordered them to shift along to make space.

The kid had settled beside me and placed his tray on the table, head bowed and hands clasped together.

"What's your name?" I'd asked.

It had taken a few seconds before he'd lifted his head and looked at me as he'd spoken, "Zakhar."

The other teens at the table snickered because Zakhar had been praying.

I'd ignored all that as my attention had become riveted on his eyes. He'd had the most captivating pair of eyes I'd seen—electric blue that shimmered like an ocean when he was sad and blazed like a hot flame when he was excited.

Like now. Those electric blue babies shone with what seemed like anticipation as he climbed into the ring.

After that evening in the dining hall, the boy that he'd been had attached himself to me. Not that I'd complained.

I'd adopted him as a kid brother, warned the other children from harassing him, and taught him how to defend himself. With the years of training, his baby fat had eventually turned to the solid muscle of youth.

Staring at the chunk of a man he'd become, it hit me.

I'd saved him.

I'd made him.

And how did he reward me?

By abandoning and betraying me.

A flash of anger went through me, and before he could straighten in the ring, I struck with a left jab. His reaction was fast as he countered with a forearm block. I jumped back and followed immediately with a roundhouse kick which caught him by surprise and sent him staggering back.

He came at me with punches; *whoosh, wham* his fists went. I blocked and dodged, but one connected with my solar plexus, knocking the wind out of me.

Like fuel, the pain reenergized me. My fist went flying, and as soon as I saw an opening, I grappled him, kicked his leg out, and sent him tumbling forward with me on top of him.

As soon as he hit the deck he yielded, his muscles going limp.

I sat on his rump and jerked his arms back. "I want to know the truth about why you left, Zakhar."

This one question had bugged me for ten years.

"Alexei." He sounded out of breath as he tensed up beneath me, back muscles rippling. "The past is best left in the past."

"Bullshit." My cock hardened from his movement. I suddenly had the urge to be buried inside him. Instead, I yanked his arm, causing him to wince. "We did everything together. We were *bratan,* and you left without a fucking explanation. I want to know why."

"Things changed. It was time to move on."

"That's crap, and you know it."

I twisted his arm again, inflicting pain.

"Fuck! Take it easy," he yelled, panting heavily.

"Tell me the truth!"

"Fine!" His chest heaved. "I had to go and build my own life. I couldn't live in your shadow forever."

As if he wielded a sword, his words sliced into me. I released him, scrabbled to the corner. My mouth opened, but no words formed.

He moved slowly, finally sitting with his back to the ropes. He didn't look at me.

I'd found his docility attractive when we'd been boys. It had drawn me to him. Now it only got me more pissed off as I knew he hid things from me.

"So that's how you saw me," I said as I pushed off the mat. "I was blocking your light? I didn't let you shine?"

He shook his head slowly. "That's not what I meant."

"What then?" I gripped the ropes tight, my back to him. Otherwise, I would lay into him and unleash the beast inside me I struggled to restrain, the part of me that had loved dishing out pain just for the sake of it.

I slid out of the ring and headed to the treadmill. I couldn't hurt him. Not yet. Each time I looked at him I saw that boy who needed my help. Not to mention that he'd turned into a man I wouldn't mind fucking.

Brothers don't fuck brothers—

"You got married, remember?"

His words cut off my train of thought and had me halting my steps. "You left because of Eva? You wanted her for yourself?"

Eva had been my wife of eight years until she'd died from cancer. Marrying her had been a mutual agreement between us. She'd benefited from my protection against her abusive, controlling father and having her as my wife had opened doors for me among certain circles that had aided my rise in the cartel world. Although she'd been a mafia princess, she'd also been a lost soul who'd needed the security I'd provided just like Zak had done.

"No!" he shook his head vehemently. "It's not what you think. I didn't want Eva."

"What else can it be? You left while we were on honeymoon."

"Alexei, listen. I left because I thought that since you had her, you didn't need me."

"Why would you think that?"

"Because … because it had always been the two of us against the world until she showed up. I saw less and less of you, and you got involved with *Gospodin* Krasinski, mixing with the high flyers. I felt left out."

"It *was* you and me against the world. I'd been trying to build a future for us. For you. I told you we were going to make it big. I was trying to make it happen."

He scrubbed a hand over his face and shook his head. "I know what you said. But the reality of it all, I couldn't live with it. I just had to leave."

"And you couldn't tell me all of this. You couldn't talk to me? You left with just a brief note to say you'd gone traveling and that I shouldn't bother searching for you."

"I didn't think you'd mind that I wasn't there anymore. I thought you were happy."

I'd thought I'd been happy until I'd returned from a brief honeymoon ready to tell him the exciting news about my new position in the Krasinski network, only to find him gone. I hadn't felt that shitty since my parents died. It had felt as if I'd lost another member of my family. He had been my family until he'd gone.

"Of course I had to look for you. I went nuts for

weeks searching and wondering why you'd gone. Eva had been a means to an end. I thought you knew that."

We glared at each other for a few seconds before he puffed out a breath.

"I'm sorry, Alexei."

His apology didn't make me feel any better. It didn't change the fact that he hadn't trusted me in the past. Nor did it change his reason for being here this time.

Ignoring him, I walked into the shower room, stripping off the shorts and tossing them in the laundry bag for the housekeeper.

How could Zakhar not have trusted me? After everything, we'd been through? Everything I'd done for him. Even after we'd run away and lived out on the streets, I had his back every single day.

How could he think that I would've tossed him out because of Eva?

I should put a bullet through his thick skull.

Slamming my fist into the locker, I put a dent in the wood as pain shot though my arm.

Damn Zakhar.

Damn me for being a fool and for even caring.

In the wet room, I lathered my body with the shower gel in the bottle on the metal rack. With my forehead tipped against the limestone tiles, water beat my skin as suds swirled and washed into the plughole at my feet. The padding of footsteps made me glance back.

"Alexei, are we cool?" Zakhar stood at the entrance to the wet room.

Swiveling, I faced him. I wasn't going to pretend even if he was. "Cool? No, we're not fucking cool."

I switched the faucet off and walked out, liquid dripping down my body. "You can use the shower."

He turned away as if not wanting to look at me, but I caught the way he stared at my groin.

With the thrill of the fight still in my veins and the sight of him covered in sweat, I was hard. But unlike him, I wasn't ashamed of it and wasn't about to hide it.

From the first time I'd known what fucking was, I'd had a hard-on for him. He'd been my *bratan* and off-limits as far as I was concerned.

Now, he wasn't my brother anymore. He had betrayed me. This meant he was fair game.

With the bulge stretching his shorts, I'd say he wanted me, too.

I was going to drag him out of the closet one way or the other.

"You need to clean up," I said. "We're going to the club."

With that, I grabbed a towel and headed to my room.

Chapter Three

Zakhar

An hour later and after a brief helicopter ride, we were in Exilado. A den of iniquity as some people described it, a place where all things were permissible.

And Alexei had brought me here. Why?

As an agent, I wasn't supposed to be in here without arresting everyone. Still, working undercover meant I had to go wherever Alexei went.

We sat in low, dark leather chairs in a muted private lounge with a glass wall overlooking the vibrant, noisy club below. The server left a bottle of whisky with glasses as well as a small silver tray with lines of white powder and a thin ceramic cylinder that looked like a straw.

Temptation on my already frazzled nerves. I'd developed a nose for coke after living in environments where it had been readily available. As a stimulant, it had provided the boost I'd needed to do certain things.

Alexei poured the drinks and slid one across the table in my direction. To my utter shock, he pushed the small silver plate towards me, too. "This is for you. I know you enjoy it."

Shit. Did he know everything about me? "You know nothing."

He shook his head. "I've had my eyes on you for years, Zakhar. So cut the pretense."

He'd been watching me all the while I'd thought he didn't know where I'd been. My hands shook as I snatched the platter, lifted it, and snorted down two lines. I dumped the tray, tipped my head back, and closed my eyes briefly as I pinched my nostrils.

My mind buzzed with alertness as adrenaline surged through me.

Alexei just watched me, dark eyes probing, eyebrows raised and chin jutting.

God damn! He was handsome, even when his sensual lips curled into a smirk. The harsh angles of his face gave him a brutal attractiveness that hooked me, and his firm, athletic body reeled me in.

My mind flashed with the image of him in the shower earlier today—man, muscles, and moisture on erotic display. I'd wanted to lick and tickle, caress and cajole his solid, slick skin.

Now, blood rushed south. My dick swelled, pressing uncomfortably against the tight silk trousers Alexei had given me after he'd informed me jeans wasn't suitable attire for this venue.

As he sat across from me with his perfect posture and smug expression, I knew he'd never want me that way. Even if we weren't *bratan*, he now saw me as an enemy because of my job.

"What the hell is going on?" Sipping the whisky, I pushed thoughts of naked bodies aside in a bid to keep things businesslike between us.

"What's the problem? You want to arrest me?" He clasped his wrists together, taunting me to handcuff him.

Even if I had the tool to restrain him, he wasn't breaking any laws. Well, except for procuring a controlled substance. But he'd never been in possession, and he wasn't the supplier so it would be hard to make it stick in court. In any case, I was the user. If this place was raided, I'd be the one testing positive for a drug.

"You never used to want to be involved in this shit." The narcotic had taken effect, making me more talkative, more energized.

In the years I'd know him, he'd always been disciplined about what he put into his body. He'd sworn never to get implicated in the narcotics business as a manufacturer, dealer, or user.

Ironically, I'd ended up dealing and using as part of my cover for the covert operations.

"That was then. Things change," he repeated my earlier words. Damn him.

Just then a dark-haired, muscled man walked in, dressed in nothing but a jockstrap. He wiggled across the room, hips snapping in an exaggerated motion. He didn't give me more than a perfunctory glance before he straddled Alexei's lap and placed a kiss to his mouth.

"*Gospodin*, it's good to see you."

"It's been a while, *mal'chik*. Have you been good?"

Sensation burned across my chest and spots flashed in my vision.

Alexei used to have a nickname for me years ago— *malyshka*. Kiddo. It wasn't exactly the same thing or loaded with as much sexual connotation. But hearing him address the man in such intimate terms made me dislike the stranger instantly.

"Yes, Sir," the newcomer replied as he stroked his hands down Alexei's chest. "I'm going to take good care of you this evening."

"You know what I like."

"Of course." The man grinned and wiggled down, rubbing himself all over Alexei and going on his knees between his spread legs. He reached for the buckle and pulled the leather out of the hoop.

My nostrils flared, and my hand around the glass tightened. I gulped down more whisky, the burn acute as my senses heightened, making the colors bright and sounds sharp.

"He's not going to do what I think he's going to do?" I snapped. I should've been feeling euphoric from the drug. Instead, thoughts of violence entered my head, visions of hacking off the interloper's hands for touching Alexei. I wanted to kick the man until he was a bloody mass.

"If you mean suck my cock, then yes, he's going to do it like a good boy before I fuck him." His eyes darkened and his lips lifted in a smug tilt. "Or do you want to take his place, Zak?"

The spot belonged to me. Alexei belonged to me. The words screamed in my mind. I should be the one kneeling before him, deep-throating his cock.

The derision in the way he said my name made me slam the glass on the table and jerk upright. He wasn't going to drag me into whatever game he was playing, not in front of witnesses.

"I don't know why I came here. But you're of no use to me. You're not man enough for me." I don't know why I said the reckless words except that the drug had loosened my tongue. I pushed off the sofa and walked towards the exit, turning my back to Alexei.

Bad move. I should know never to turn my back on a predator.

He slammed into me, gripped my neck in a chokehold and swept my feet from under me. I careened forward, using my hands to break the fall as he landed on top of me on the sofa.

"It's obvious you don't know me, Zak." The depth and the danger in his voice sent a sizzle down my spine to my balls.

My heart raced, my body heated, and my breaths shortened.

His body bore down on mine, and I hardened. His scent filled my nostrils, his aura in every pore. My belly quivered the way it usually did anytime I was near him. And I was a goner.

"Alexei." I'd wanted to warn him to move away. Instead, his name came out like a plea, a sob of pleasure.

"I know who you are, Zak." His warm breath whispered on the skin of my nape. "You've been hiding in the closet for so long, you don't know who you are any more. You can't even admit to yourself that you want me to fuck you."

His taunt hurt because it was the truth. I twisted and bucked, trying to shake him off. "Get off."

His grip didn't loosen. And if I was honest I didn't want him to let me go. He reached across and rubbed my already swollen dick through the fabric of the pants as he nudged my legs apart with his thigh.

"Mhmm. This proves me right," he growled in my ear.

There was something in his voice, something almost animalistic. Combined with the way he held me down, his weight pressing into me, I craved him, all of him.

My skin itched and my mind buzzed with the urge to be naked under him, covered in sweat, filled with him. I strained, pushing back against him, needing more contact.

He abandoned my cock.

I groaned, driven to the edge of desperation.

His hand massaged my balls, perineum and then fingers pressed against my hole. Even through the fabric, I felt them and clenched with the yearning to be plugged with the thick dick I'd glimpsed twice already today.

"Sir?" a whiny voice called out, and it took me a few seconds to realize it was the jockstrap man. Alexei's boy.

My anger flared up again. "Tell him to go."

"Why should I? Are you offering to take his place?" He caressed my balls.

I swallowed and mumbled. "Yes."

"I didn't hear you."

"Send him away, and you can fuck me any way you want," I said, loud enough for the guy to hear.

Alexei stopped touching me, and I wondered if he was going to pull away.

Instead, he ordered, "Leave the kit and get out."

"Sir?"

"Get out," he growled.

The man gasped, mumbled something like "sorry Sir," dropped something I couldn't see on the low, dark table and hurried to the door.

I heard it open with the whoosh of sound from the club, and then it quieted again as it shut.

His hands were on my fly, and before I could do anything, he had my trousers pulled down my legs, exposing my butt to the cold air. I thought he would want me to suck him like his boy was going to do.

By the way he grabbed my ass cheeks and pulled them apart he had different plans.

"How long have you wanted me to fuck you, Zakhar? How long have you been dying for my cock?"

"Unh," was all I managed. I wouldn't have even known what to say if my brain functioned, as all the blood rushed to my groin and I felt a wet tongue rimming me.

"I've got to say, I like the way you smell and taste." A

hand covered my dick and squeezed.

"Unh," I groaned again.

"You like that?" He leaned over me again, his voice close to my ear, fingers finally penetrating me.

I rocked between his palm on my cock and fingers in my ass. I was so close, but it wasn't enough. "Mhmm."

"I want words, *mal'chik*." He withdrew from me.

Desperate, I didn't know when the words left me. "Fuck me. Please, Alexei."

Something broad and hefty nudged my hole. "Do you want my cock?"

"Yes … please." I tried to rock backward, but his hand gripped my neck, holding me down.

He pushed in, the pressure and pain split me open as he filled me an inch at a time. I wasn't lubed up, but I didn't care. His shaft must have been oiled, because when he pulled back and slammed forward, he was in me, hips to butt, balls to balls.

Gasping for breath, sweat soaking my shirt, I sprawled face down on the leather couch, fingers digging into the cushion as the man I'd once loved fucked me raw in a night club, while revelers danced the night away beyond the doors.

I could tell myself I was doing this for the job. But the truth remained. I'd wanted him like this for over ten years, and I did this because I craved Alexei with every fiber of my being. Nothing more. If this was going to be the only time he fucked me I wanted to savor every aspect.

The pain merged with pleasure, the sensations out of this world when he pegged my gland again and again.

"Oh … oh … oh … oh," I gasped each time, my mind reeling as I hurtled towards the edge of bliss.

"Who is the man now?" he gritted out.

"You … you are."

"That's right, *mal'chik*." He smacked my ass before reaching around and wrapping a lube-covered hand around my dick.

Just one stroke and I begged for more. "Please…"

Breathless, adrenaline pulsed through my veins and

my body trembled.

"And who is my bitch?"

Even through the fog of pleasure, the insult registered. I stiffened and then bucked against him, trying to push him off me. I knew I'd hurt him by leaving. Couldn't he let it go even for this intimate moment as he rode my ass?

He pressed his weight against me, holding me down. I could've fought him and escaped from his grip. But I didn't have him rip me open for nothing. I wanted the conclusion, the fulfillment that he would give me.

His grip on my neck tightened, almost cutting off my breathing. "I asked you, who is my bitch?"

My skin tingled all over. I relaxed my body, submitting to him with a sigh. "I'm your bitch, Alexei. But you know that makes you my dog."

His grip on my neck grew painfully tight, and for a moment, I thought he would strangle me. In my recklessness, I didn't care. I'd happily die with him buried inside me.

Instead, the sound of deep laughter filled the room. The natural kind and the first I'd heard from him since my arrival today.

"Yes, I'm your dog. The top dog," he growled close to my ear, making me smile.

After that, he seemed to give himself in to the pleasure as he rocked into me. His warm mouth pressed against my shoulder and he caressed my skin with his free hand. A sizzle went down my spine.

Old emotions returned, the heat radiating through my chest. This gentle side of him unraveled me. I didn't want to fall in love with him all over again.

His hand on my cock and dick in my ass focused me on the present and sent me rushing to release. Bright lights exploded behind my closed eyelids. I jerked and groaned while ropes of cum splattered on the sofa.

Alexei pressed another kiss to my shoulder, and then pumped into me a few times. Warmth filled my insides before he collapsed on top of me.

We stayed that way, him on top of me, panting to

catch our breath and get our heart rates back to normal.

He pushed off, tore a small heated towel from the pack, wiped himself, and put his clothes right. He picked up another hot napkin from the table and tossed it at me. "Clean up."

Alexei stood over me while I lay prone on the sofa, trousers shoved down around my knees, and sticky cum ran down my thigh. Where was my dignity? I was a highly-rated member of an elite investigative unit. Yet I'd just played bitch to a man I was monitoring.

Slowly, I levered myself to the side and wiped his dripping cum from my sore ass. While it was a shame to clean his seed off, the ache would remind me of this encounter for some time.

I fumbled with my trousers and pulled them up. When I'd dressed again, I asked, "What now?"

He met my gaze. "Now, we go home."

Chapter Four

Alexei

I jerked upright, awoken by a disturbance. Something wasn't quite right. The sky was cobalt through the sun-sensitive screen covering the floor-to-ceiling windows.

Tilting my head, the sound came again—loud mumblings I couldn't quite make out.

Zakhar. He was in the room next door. He hadn't earned a space in my bed. Not while he was still pretending and telling lies.

Without thinking, I swung my feet over the edge of the bed, concern for him taking over. The hall lights came on automatically as I yanked my door open and dashed across to his.

The light spilled in, dappling his prone body on the mattress. He tossed around, whipped his head from side to side and raised his arms as if fighting someone off, the sheet tangled around his legs.

He had always had nightmares from what I could remember from the days we lived together. There had been only one way to calm him then.

Before I knew what I was doing, I walked over the rug at the foot of the bed and climbed in. I scooted close and whispered, "Shhh, *malyshka*. I won't let anyone hurt you."

What was I saying? A band tightened around my chest.

I hadn't said those words to him, to anyone, in over ten years. Yet they came as naturally as if I still meant them. As if I remained his protector and his "brother."

Well, I wasn't his "bro" anymore. Not after what I did to him tonight in the club. There had been several private suites in the building with comfortable beds for guests to use if the need for sex overtook them.

Instead, I had claimed him, raw and savagely, in the lounge within full view of security cameras. To send a message to his employers who I knew would get to watch the video as part of their surveillance. They needed to see that they couldn't mess with me.

Everyone else would know that Zakhar was mine. Had always been mine. Would remain mine.

Of course, his being mine hadn't stopped him from betraying me before. It probably wouldn't prevent him from selling me out again. A knot tightened in my belly.

"Xei?" His eyelids fluttered but didn't open. He seemed to be sleeping, but now in a calm dreamscape.

That had been his nickname for me so long again. The sound of it now chased my suspicion away, and I stroked his arms and brushed my lips to his nape. "Yes, it's me. I'm here now. Go back to sleep."

He shivered and snuggled into my arms as I pulled the sheet back up to cover both of us.

We hadn't slept this intimately since we were teens and had to share the same cot in the dingy bedsit I'd barely been able to afford with the odd jobs I'd done. He'd been eleven, and I'd been sixteen when we'd left the children's home. We'd slept rough on the streets until I'd been able to save enough money to rent a place that had been barely large enough to swing a cat.

So much had changed since then. Including Zakhar. He'd been Zak or Kiddo to me in those days depending on my mood.

He wasn't that kid anymore. He was all man, emphasized by the muscular back I felt under my hand and the sturdy legs draped over mine.

A smile curled my lips. He'd always been eager to drape himself over me while he slept. In those days I'd considered his actions innocent, just his own way of trying to keep warm under the thin blanket. I remembered having to pry him off me when he was finally asleep and turning my back to him so he wouldn't have my morning wood prodding him when he woke.

I hadn't wanted our interactions to turn sexual then. He had trusted me like a kid brother would, and I hadn't wanted to betray that trust. And of course, he'd been younger by five years. By the time I'd been twenty years old, he'd still been a minor of fifteen. Any such interaction between us would've been forbidden, not just because being gay had been prohibited in the environment we'd grown up in, but he'd been a child, and that would've made me a ... pedophile.

My grip on his shoulder tightened.

As a teenager, I'd sprung him from the orphanage just so he wouldn't be preyed on by the monsters in that place. As an adult, I would've killed anyone who had so much as looked at him in the wrong way.

So I certainly wasn't going to become the monster I'd been protecting him against at the time.

Instead, I'd focused my pent-up energy at building a future for us while I'd waited for him to grow up. We were going to be a proper family. I was going to give him the world.

Until he'd left me.

And now he was back, and in my arms again.

But for the wrong reasons.

I drew in a deep breath, shifted so that I gazed out of the window. The screen allowed a view of the outside but blocked prying eyes from seeing inside. Not that there would be anyone close by. But there were other high-rise buildings within long-distance camera lens range. Zakhar's employers would have someone scoping my building throughout his assignment. They'd been spying on me long before he arrived.

He'd been sent here to spy on me. The Agency sent him on this wild goose chase.

But the mastermind behind his assignment was an old enemy. Not The Agency, although they weren't my friends over there for obvious reasons.

The real foe was someone who had a personal axe to grind and who wanted control of MIRNO—Boris Medev, Eva's brother. Jones Bellamy, Zak's boss, was his stooge.

Perhaps Zakhar didn't know that he'd stepped into an old-fashioned cartel turf war.

I hoped he didn't know because it would be easier to forgive him being a government agent than it would be to overlook him working for a crime boss who wasn't me.

In the meantime, I would give him the benefit of the doubt. Well, I wasn't about to kick him out. Not yet. I wanted more of him. I was going to have him, damn it.

Sighing, I turned on my side and scooped him in, so his back was to my chest and my groin to his bubble butt.

Hell. He made me so damn hard I could easily fuck him again right now.

But he was mine, and I didn't want to hurt him any more than I'd done already. I'd proven my point in the club. They wouldn't see any weakness in me. Even if they'd sent the man, who might prove to be my Achilles heel, to bring me down.

They wouldn't know that having him in my arms like this was all I'd ever wanted. What they didn't know couldn't hurt me.

I pressed a kiss to his nape and breathed in his musky scent. With him in my arms, I drifted off to sleep.

****

The sky outside was gray as I took a last look at the sleeping Zakhar with mussed hair and morning wood. I could stay with him and wake him up with my mouth wrapped around his cock.

But routine and self-discipline won. I padded over to the gym for a workout as I'd done every other day—this time, a circuit involving the treadmill, boxing bag, spinning, free weights, and treadmill to cool down.

Sun rays made the sweat glisten on my body as I stripped off the clothes and headed to the shower. I stood under the cascading warm water, soaping my body when I heard a sound and turned around.

Zakhar stood at the entrance to the shower room in his briefs.

My cock filled out. Damn. He looked hot standing there with a tentative smile, his blond hair sticking up in all directions, and his body calling for me to explore.

"You're awake," I said, unable to hide the smile curling my lips. There were some things about the boy I'd known that were still there. Still warmed my heart to see.

"Yeah. I'm…" he raised his right hand as if unsure of what to say. "Did you come to my room last night?" He jerked his thumb backward over his shoulder as if pointing to the room.

"Yes, I did. You had a nightmare, and I thought getting into bed with you would help to soothe you."

"You did?" His mouth dropped open and his brows rose to almost his hairline.

"Yeah. And it worked, too." I grinned as I remembered how he'd said my name and burrowed close.

"It did." He took a step into the shower room. "I dreamed that you held me. But why would you do that? I thought you were angry. You didn't say much after we left the club."

"I'm not angry with you, Zak. At least not at the moment. And not when I saw you tossing and turning last night. It reminded me of when we used to live together, and I would hold you when you had nightmares."

"Oh." He glanced away before looking at me again. His eyes were the same brilliant blue I loved so much. "Thank you."

"If you want to thank me, join me in here," I said with an inviting smile. I wasn't much for pussy-footing, and I wanted to feel him skin to skin.

At the club, he'd been clothed aside from his pants at his ankles. And in the bed, he'd been asleep, and I hadn't wanted to wake him.

Now that he was fully conscious, there was no reason I should hold back.

Without a word, he pushed down his briefs and stepped out of them, his full lips in a lopsided smile. Steam rose around us as he came close.

Fully clothed, he was hot. Naked, he was edible, his power evident in every delineation of muscles. I don't think I'd wanted him more before now.

He breached the gap between us and pressed his lips against mine.

On reflex, I jerked back. Men didn't usually initiate

kisses with me. At least, none of my previous lovers had done anything remotely close.

Zakhar stared at me, his eyes bright and challenging.

With a smile, I leaned my head forward, and he resealed our lips. His mouth was surprisingly softer than I'd imagined it would be, but exactly what I needed at this moment.

Lifting my hand to his nape, I gripped him, tilted my head and devoured his mouth. Passion took over, teeth clashing against teeth, tongues tangling.

And just like that, I was hard as a rock. I slammed his back against the tiles. The two of us groaned as we gulped in air while water cascaded down our bodies in rivulets.

He maneuvered me around, so my back was now to the tiles and went down on his knees.

He was a sight to behold, glistening with water, as he took my crown into his mouth.

A deep groan reverberated in the room. That must have been me, although I had no recollection of making the sound, so lost in the pleasure of his warm mouth and his wet hand.

He did something incredible to my balls, and I jerked my hips, ramming my cock down his throat in reflex.

"Damn!" I shouted and gripped his head, ready to fuck his mouth.

He looked up at me, blinking to get the water off his eyes.

The adoration I saw in there made my breath catch. This was the boy who'd trusted me with his life, my *malyshka*.

I tugged him, making my dick slide out of his mouth with a pop, and pulled him to his feet. Then I slammed my mouth against his.

I turned him around to take my position and kissed him with the crazy longing that I had always felt for him, my free hand wrapped around his dick.

"Oh," he groaned as I lined up our shafts in my hand.

Grinning, I leaned back. "Get the shower gel."

He cottoned on to my meaning and pulled the bottle

off the shelf, popped the cap, and tipped it over my hand. It wasn't the best lube but I didn't care because it was divine having his dick next to mine as I worked both of us to completion.

Holding each other as close as possible as we kissed and jerked our hips in tune to my movements. He came first, white jizz pumping onto my stomach while his face was twisted in bliss.

The sight of it sent me over, and with two jacks of my wrist, my balls tightened, and creamy cum erupted from me and splattered onto him.

Forehead to forehead, we stood there panting, watching the water sluice the semen away down the drain.

"That's a good way to start the day," he said, a little out of breath.

"The best way." I kissed him briefly. Then I pumped more gel into my hands, worked some foam and started massaging his chest.

"I've always wanted to do this," I confessed.

He gasped and stared at me, mouth open. "You have?"

"Don't look so surprised. This thing between us didn't just happen overnight."

I turned him around, so he didn't have to see my face and know the depth of my feelings for him. I'd shown him a crack in my armor.

He braced the wall with his hands, and I rubbed down his back in a rare moment of tenderness. I'd never done this with anyone else. Not even Eva.

I trailed a finger down his crack and over his pucker. He winced.

"Shhh," I whispered in a soothing tone and placed a kiss on his ass cheeks before rubbing his legs.

"So why didn't you ever say anything or do anything?" he asked, as his breathing sped up.

"Because fucking you wasn't important before. We had places to go and things to do. I thought we had all the time in the world. I never thought that you would leave." Heaving a sigh, I stepped away as my chest tightened and my disappointment returned.

He turned around, head cocked to the side and eyes narrowed in a wary expression. "I'm sorry for leaving."

Nodding, I turned the shower head in his direction so he could rinse off the lather. "It doesn't matter now. You're back, aren't you?"

I hoped he would stay this time. But only time would tell.

Something flickered in his gaze. "Yes, I'm back."

I didn't believe him, and his lie soured my stomach. I forced a smile to remain on my face. "Come on. Let's get something to eat. Then we can get started on finding out who is trying to kill you."

Chapter Five

Zakhar

Something was wrong.

Actually, everything seemed to be right.

Alexei was a different man. A different man from the one I'd seen yesterday. The one who had put a gun to my head and threatened to blow my brains out. The one who had fucked me on the floor in the middle of a busy nightclub.

This one, the one who came to my bed when he'd heard my cries. The one who worked my body into frenzy in the shower. The man who had made breakfast for us this morning. This was a different man.

It seemed he'd turned into the man of my dreams. The man I'd pined for years ago.

I was enjoying his company so much as I sat at the table chatting with him.

Shit. What was I doing? Could I forget what he'd done in the past, not to mention what he did for a living? Honestly, I didn't care how he earned a living. I'd only joined The Agency to spite him.

On the surface, I'd done well professionally with several successfully completed operations.

But I'd missed him. He'd been my family. In the past, I hadn't been able to make any connections with other people. My job didn't allow me the time to build relationships, and I couldn't trust anyone.

Being here with Alexei made me feel as if we were in a relationship. As if we were a family again.

Something had to be wrong with me for craving something I couldn't have.

"So, what is this trouble you're in?" he asked and pushed his empty plate aside. "You're usually the one taking down others."

"True," I agreed, scrambling in my mind to remember everything about my cover I seemed to have forgotten. "But I've made enemies it seems, and one of them wants me dead."

"It shouldn't be the first time that's happened."

"It's not. This time is different. This time it seems the people I work for are the ones targeting me. I need your help to find out who it is."

"Does it matter who?"

"It matters. I did a job recently in Buenos Aires where I had to retrieve a digital device only to get back to my hotel room and find a hit squad waiting for me."

"Buenos Aires. That was you? Six people killed."

Shrugging, I took another sip of coffee before speaking. "That was a setup, and I think they wanted this."

From my back pocket, I pulled out the mini-disk.

"I think this is the reason someone is trying to kill me. The contents are encrypted, and I need your help to decode it. I know you have people who can do the work."

He shrugged. "There's no guarantee my people can do it."

"You employ the best hackers in the world. If it can be done, then someone in your organization can do it."

"If that is government property, hacking into it will bring trouble to my door."

"Well, it's not like you've never had trouble before."

"True. I'm well overdue for trouble." He gave me a sexy grin.

Alexei pressed the button on a small remote control, and a monitor screen on the wall flickered before a bespectacled blond guy appeared.

"Good morning, Mr. Smirnov," the man said.

"Morning, Denis," Alexei replied. "This is Mr. Stone. He has a file I need you to work on immediately."

"Of course, sir."

"Pass it over." Alexei beckoned with his hand as he opened his laptop.

"Sure." My stomach rolled as I slipped the device across the table. This was really happening. One minute we'd been eating breakfast like a couple, the next minute I was about to set something in motion from which there would be no return.

I had to glance away when he inserted it into the

laptop drive. I should tell him to stop, but I couldn't bring myself to do it. This was my job. I had always completed every mission. No matter what we had shared, it didn't change our pasts or make right the wrongs. I couldn't give up now.

"I've made a copy of the file, and you can now access it," he said to Denis.

"Great. I've got it. I'll get working immediately and let you know as soon as it is decrypted."

"Do you know how long that will take?" he asked.

"This looks complex, so it could be hours or days."

"Okay. Let me know as soon as it's done."

"Will do." The monitor went blank as the call ended and Denis disappeared.

Alexei pulled the disk out and handed it to me. "You heard him."

"Yeah. So … what happens in the meantime?"

"We can't do anything until he's decoded the file." He closed the laptop. "I want to show you something. We're going out."

More guilt prickled through me. I didn't know how much longer I could continue the deceit. He would definitely kill me when he found out the truth.

****

Thirty minutes later, we were in our old neighborhood—rundown buildings, graffiti on the walls, debris on the streets, and weedy car parks. Memories assaulted me. We even drove past some of the dingy alleys we'd slept in when we'd first become homeless.

My gut tightened in knots, and I struggled to take in deep breaths. "What are we doing here?"

"So I can show you this." He pointed ahead at a block in the middle of the ghetto that seemed to be going through regeneration with what looked like new and renovated buildings. There were other lots with scaffolding or cranes to indicate ongoing work.

"Is that the children's home?" I asked as the car slowed down.

My mouth dropped open. The old orphanage building

wasn't there anymore. Nothing remained except mowed grass, a flower garden, and trees.

The chauffeur opened the door for Alexei, who stepped out into the sunshine.

"What's going on?" I asked as I followed, glancing around the place. Could my memory be so wrong? "I swear the orphanage should be here."

"You're right. This was the site. When I first made lots of money, I bought the building, closed the place down, and had it demolished. Eva suggested we should turn it into a park. There you are."

The green space in the middle of an urban jungle was beautiful with a children's playground as well as a section of grass that seemed like a soccer field.

"What happened to the orphans?" I couldn't help asking. There were still kids who needed social welfare.

"Come on." He walked along the pavement before climbing the steps of a new large brick building.

I looked up at the name on the plaque above the doors. *The Eva Smirnov Children's Home.*

"I dedicated the place to her. She loved children, but couldn't have any," Alexei said and pulled the antique doorbell.

There was a squeeze in my chest, but I didn't say anything.

The door swung inwards, and a middle-aged woman with salt and pepper hair held up in a loose bun stood there in a blue sundress and black flat sandals.

"Hello, Helen," Alexei greeted with a warm voice.

Her lips curled up, and her brown eyes twinkled. "Ah, Alexei. It's good to see you. Come in."

She stepped aside to let us in to the bright, open hallway.

"It's good to see you, too, Helen. This is my friend, Zakhar."

"Zakhar." She tilted her head to study me. "The Zakhar you told me about?"

"The same one." Alexei clasped my shoulder. "Helen

runs the place."

"It's nice to meet you, Helen," I mumbled, caught off-guard as I wondered why Alexei would discuss me with the woman. That he discussed me at all over the years of my absence. "You told her about me?"

He gave me a sheepish smile and shrugged. Was that a blush on his cheeks?

"He told me all about you," Helen said, leading the way into an office. "And you're just as handsome as he described you."

Now it was my turn to blush. What exactly had Alexei said?

"Helen," Alexei spoke before I could. "I brought Zakhar here to show him around. I know it's impromptu, but I hoped you wouldn't mind."

"Of course I don't mind. You're welcome to come over any time." She bustled around and grabbed a bunch of keys. "It's Saturday. Some of the children have activities like the music and sports clubs. Otherwise most should just be in their rooms or common areas."

She led us back into the hallway. We found one group of children in a small hall practicing in the choir. Another team played on instruments in a different room. We entered what looked like a lounge and found a few children watching TV. They recognized Alexei and greeted him.

As we walked upstairs, Alexei's phone rang.

"Go on," he said and headed to the exit. "I have to take this."

I followed Helen upstairs as she showed me the dormitories, divided into age groups and gender. Unlike the old orphanage, there were no more than four bunk beds to sleep eight in the rooms. Each bed space seemed personalized with different colored bed sheets and stickers on lockers. We didn't have such luxuries.

"The classrooms are in the adjoining building. Would you like to see?" Helen asked.

This wasn't like the old children's home at all. It could've been a private boarding school, except these kids didn't have wealthy parents. Or any parents at all.

"No. I think this place is wonderful. You're doing a great job."

"Thank you. It's because of Alexei's generosity that we're able to take care of the children." She paused at the top of the landing and looked at me. "It's a good thing you came back. You inspired him to build this place."

"Me?" I swallowed hard. "The place is dedicated to his late wife."

She shook her head. "Eva was a sweet soul, and yes, he put her name on the building. When he first came to me with the idea of running this place, it was you he talked about. He never talked about Eva, but he talked about you. A lot."

"That was probably because we were in an orphanage together."

"Probably. Or it could be because he loves you."

"Men like Alexei don't love," I blurted out before I could stop myself. "He's a…" I was going to say criminal, but I kept my mouth shut before I did.

But it didn't change the fact that Alexei controlled an organization that cost global businesses millions of dollars due to their activities. I had an illogical distrust of everything and everyone, including Alexei.

"What do you think this place is?" She waved her hand around. "This is a monument of love. This dedication he has to the welfare of children can only come from love."

She gave me a pointed look before descending the stairs.

Did that make Alexei a modern-day Robin Hood who robbed the businesses to take care of children? Did that make his actions right? He had benefitted from his crimes, hadn't he?

I scrubbed a hand over my face and walked down with heavy footsteps. The line between right and wrong had been blurring in my mind for a long time. Too much time spent with criminals and I was beginning to sympathize with them.

Chapter Six

Zakhar

"Why did you demolish the old orphanage?" I asked in the car on the way back to Smirnov Tower. "I mean, the new one is great, but I don't get why you felt the need to build it."

He pressed the button to raise the privacy screen between the driver and us. Then he closed his eyes briefly and then opened them. "Do you remember why we ran away from the children's home?"

"The place was crap."

"Crap doesn't begin to describe it." He scrubbed his face. "There were so many things wrong with it. But one of the main problems was that the staff were pimping the children out to pedophiles."

"Fuck. What? How?"

"It had been going on for years. Many children were abused."

Suddenly the penny dropped.

"You were one of them?" Nausea rolled my stomach as I asked the question and dread filled me.

He gave one nod. "When you arrived and followed me around like a puppy, I had to protect you from them. You were pretty with your blond hair and blue eyes and I knew it was only a matter of time before they targeted you, so I made a deal with one of the pimps."

My stomach heaved again at the horror of what he'd said. "You did what?"

"I wasn't important. But you were, and I had to do whatever it took to make sure they didn't touch you. It worked for a while. But when the staff that I'd made a deal with left and a new one took over, he refused to keep the deal. He said I was getting too old and they needed a fresh body. You. That's why we ran away. I couldn't let you suffer the same things they'd done to me."

The car came to a stop, and I didn't wait to check where we were before yanking the door open. I stepped onto the sidewalk, bent over with my hands on my thighs and gulped in air as dizziness swept over me.

What the fuck had I done? Why didn't Alexei tell me all this years ago?

I would never have left him if I'd known.

"Zak?"

I looked up to find Alexei standing over me.

Worry lines furrowed his brows. "Are you okay?"

I gulped in air. "Yeah. Just give me a minute."

"Come inside when you're ready. I'll instruct security to send you up to the penthouse." He turned around and strode into the building.

I straightened, turned my face up to the warm sun, and closed my eyes.

Fuck. What was I going to do now? Alexei had already made a copy of the file, and once it was downloaded onto their system it would start doing its work. Agents would show up soon afterward to arrest Alexei.

Once that happened Alexei would have the perfect reason to kill me for my betrayal.

The only option I had was to go up to his apartment and tell him the truth. Perhaps he could stop Denis before he actually decoded the file.

Mind made up, I hurried inside. The security at the desk indicated the elevator I should use. When I got in, the doors closed and the cab traveled upward without me doing anything.

"Alexei," I called out when I got out of the elevator and followed the circular hallway.

He stood by the window in the office, talking on his phone. A pensive expression on his face, he looked up, saw me, and ended the call. "We have a problem."

He walked over to his desk and typed on the laptop.

"What's going on?" I asked, walking across the room toward him.

He looked up but seemed to stare straight through me. "Our network is under attack."

Damn. It was happening already. I hadn't had time to

stop it.

This was the part where I should get out as quickly as possible. My job was done. The rest was for The Agency.

But the thought of disappearing into the sunset, of leaving Alexei, had my stomach in knots. I couldn't abandon him. The decision to stay might cost me my life.

"You need to call your lawyer."

"Why?" He glanced at me between typing furiously.

"Because you're going to be arrested."

He froze. "What have you done?"

The fact that he accused me implied that he knew something was up. Had he figured it out already?

"The network invasion is a Trojan virus. It's a cloak for the real attack which clones every data on your systems and gives The Agency access to everything, including decoding files."

"They get all the intel, I get arrested, and you ride off into the sunset? Was that the plan?"

Swallowing, I couldn't meet his gaze. "I'm sorry."

"You're sorry? Fuck you, Zakhar!" He opened a drawer, withdrew a gun, and pointed it at me. "How do you think I was able to find all those sickos who kept targeting children? It is from work that MIRNO does with tracking pedophile networks on the Dark Web. Yes, some of what we do here is illegal. Yes, I've ordered those people to be killed off. But I have no regrets, damn it. In this world, you can't effect change as a poor man hustling in the street. You need money, connections, power. That's how I was able to build the children's home."

He scrubbed his face with his free hand. "You know you're a dead man."

"I know," I said with solemn acceptance, suddenly realizing I'd sooner go by his hands than live a life without him again. I'd wronged him and probably deserved death after what he'd done for me. I wasn't afraid, just remorseful. He had sacrificed himself to keep me safe, and my reward to him was to deceive him and get him arrested. I deserved to die.

"Do you want to live or die?" he asked in a calm

voice.

Jerking back, I stared at him, surprised he extended the same choice he'd offered me when we'd been kids. Then he'd provided me with the chance to escape molesters. Now, I wasn't sure what he was giving me.

"Live," I said, hoping I'd made the right choice.

"Good." He waved at the chair in front of the desk. "Tell me the real reason you came back. The truth this time."

Doing as he asked I told him the full story about the assignment to upload the file into the MIRNO systems so they could access hidden data and acquire proof of his crimes.

"You should know that I would never have joined The Agency if I'd known what you did for me. I would never have betrayed you like this," I said at the end.

"I believe you, and I want to give you the chance to make up for it. Are you willing to do what it takes?"

"Of course, tell me what I have to do."

He opened the drawer again and took out a storage disk similar to the one I'd given him previously. "I want you to upload the file on it into The Agency servers. It will wipe out any information they have on me and you."

****

Three hours later, I was at The Agency's regional office. Alexei had been arrested and I'd just been debriefed by my boss, Bellamy. I sat at my desk typing up the report. The words were refusing to flow as I kept picturing Alexei's face as he was arrested. He'd been staring at me with the same intense expression that reached my soul and uncovered my secrets until he'd disappeared from view into the car.

I glanced around the place. Being a weekend, the floor was almost empty; only those involved in this investigation were present.

I should've been celebrating a successful outcome to the operation, but I felt no warmth or excitement. My stomach was still queasy, and I didn't feel like I belonged here.

Needing to wake my brain up, I strode over to the coffee machine. I walked past one of the conference rooms, and I could hear people laughing and talking loudly.

"That is just gross," one person said.

"I didn't know Stone liked taking it up the ass," another commented.

I pushed the door wide and got a better view of my colleagues watching a video on the screen in the corner we used for playing back surveillance tapes.

That knot in my gut curled. The image was familiar. The nightclub. Alexei on top of me, partly on the floor and on the sofa.

The men all shut up when they realized I'd walked into the room. For the first time in my life, I didn't feel ashamed for wanting other men. In truth I'd only ever wanted one man—Alexei—and he was the one fucking me on screen.

Defiant, I stared at each man one by one. A few of them looked away. I couldn't believe they would betray me like this. It was one thing to view videos of other people caught in the act. But to sit here watching one of their colleagues as if I was nobody to them infuriated me.

"So this is what passes for entertainment around here? Yes, getting fucked in the ass is the best. You should try it some time," I said in a scathing tone.

"Homo," someone shouted.

"Oh, please! Just remember when you're jacking off, it'll be me you'll be picturing. And what will that make you?"

I swiveled and walked back to my desk. Fuck them. Fuck them all. They were people I'd worked with for years, and this was how they behaved toward me. Not to mention that one of them had leaked information about my work. Well, I was done.

At my desk, I typed out a resignation letter, printed, and signed it. I walked over to my boss's office and dropped it on his desk. Then I returned to my computer, pulled the disk Alexei had given me from my leather jacket, and loaded it into the drive.

Once the file downloaded onto the network, I took the disk out, grabbed my jacket, and headed out.

I didn't want to go to a hotel and Alexei was not at his place. I found myself in front of the children's home an hour later. Helen let me in, offered me coffee and a bed in the staff quarters. It was a small room, but I didn't care. I didn't sleep for a long time. When I eventually did, I dreamed that Alexei held me and chased my nightmares away.

****

On Monday morning, I was in court for the arraignment. The judge dismissed all the charges against Alexei as the prosecution didn't have any evidence. Everything about Alexei had been wiped from The Agency servers, including the old digital information they had on him.

Satisfied that Alexei would be okay, I hurried out of the courtroom, hoping to get away. I had a train to catch to another city and perhaps another country altogether.

My old boss had a red face as he confronted me outside the courtroom. "I know you had something to do with this."

"I don't know what you're talking about. I've handed in my badge. I don't work for you anymore."

"I can have you arrested for obstruction of justice—"

"Back off, Bellamy. If you do that you'll be the one in jail." Alexei stepped to my side along with his lawyer. "I have information about you and your involvement with the Medev Mafia. Do you want me to continue?"

My boss blanched, looked from me to Alexei, and walked off with a huff.

"Medev?" Something clicked in my brain as I recognized the name. "Isn't that—"

"Yeah. Long story for another time," Alexei cut in, apparently not wanting me to mention the name of his late wife in public.

"Okay." I was happy to not mention Eva, but the curiosity of why his late wife's relatives would want him incarcerated didn't escape me. Nor did his mention of another time. Did he still want me around after everything?

"You resigned?" His sensual lips curled into a smile.

"Yes," I grinned at having him so close after the last two days. Getting through had been torture, and now I couldn't stem the weightlessness or breathlessness from happiness. "I needed a change of career."

"You can work for me."

"No need for that. I already have a job."

"You do?"

"Yes, Helen offered me a job at the home."

"Wonderful. Well, can I take you out to dinner tonight?"

Warmth bloomed in my chest as I stepped close to him. "Only if you let me sleep in your bed afterwards, Xei."

"It's a deal, *malyshka*."

And I knew I had Alexei back. He had suffered for me. I had hurt for not trusting him. This time we would be inseparable and would live or die together.

The End

www.evernightpublishing.com/kai-tyler

$250,000 LOVE

Jessie Pinkham

Copyright © 2017

"Another profitable month in the gambling industry."

I grin at the boss. "Very profitable."

He flips through his take, which I've just given him in hundred dollar bills. The boss deserves his share. If he hadn't taken a chance on me, mentored me, and funded my early efforts, I'd never have made it. Illegal gambling is lucrative, but you have to know what you're doing.

"You're one of my best students," he says.

"I had a good teacher."

I don't stay long because other people are waiting to give the boss his cut of their earnings. My phone rings as I'm walking back to my Corvette. It's my sister, which is unusual. Shelly doesn't approve of my business. It's easy for her to judge, because she'd already moved out when Dad's heroin problem got out of control and shit hit the fan. Her being high and mighty didn't feed the younger kids—my work for the boss did. The boss paid a hell of a lot better than McDonald's, which was the only other option for me when I was a seventeen-year-old high school dropout. Our younger half-siblings know it's me who's been making sure they had food, clothes, and a roof over their heads for the last nine years, so they're closer with me than Shelly and she hates that.

"Hello," I say, cool but not rude. No point in letting Shelly rile me up. Maybe if our mom had stuck around, or our stepmom had lived, everything would've been different and Shelly and I would like each other, but life is what it is and I stopped worrying about my sister's opinion of me a long time ago. She can keep her moral superiority and I'll console myself with financial security.

"Malachi."

She calls me by my full name just to piss me off, because I hate it. It's a shitty name given to me by the shitty mother who ran off when I wasn't even a year old. I used to think it'd have been better if I was never born, but then my younger brother and sister would've starved or been taken into foster care where who the hell knows what could've happened, so I guess it's a good thing Mom stuck around long enough to have me after all.

I don't give her the satisfaction of insisting she call me Mal. "Yes?"

"Evan is in trouble."

That gets my attention. Evan Kourakis is the little brother of her best friend, and also the first guy I ever loved. Hell, the only guy I've ever loved, though that hasn't stopped me from fucking my fair share. I haven't seen him in over a year, since Shelly's second wedding, but I still care about him. Even ruthless businessmen (I prefer "businessmen" to "mobsters," though I'm sure my sister would disagree) can have a soft spot. I'm cursed with a soft spot for Evan, a guy I've never been with and never will.

"What happened?"

"I don't know all the details," she replies, which is so unusual I suspect it's a lie. "I just know he's in trouble and Anna called me crying. Apparently, Evan called her to say he's probably going to be killed tonight. Judging by the way you eyed him at my wedding, I thought you might want to look into it."

I definitely do. "You've got to give me more to go on."

"I'll text you his number. I'm sure you need somewhere to channel your protective instincts now that the kids left home. Maybe you can break someone's kneecaps for him."

She only says that because our siblings love me and they can take her or leave her. I don't rise to the bait. Besides, I don't break kneecaps personally. I have people for that. "I'll see what I can do for Evan."

"Good." She hangs up without saying goodbye. A minute later, I get the text and I don't waste any time in calling Evan. I start the car so I can go meet him ASAP.

"Hello?"

"Evan, it's Mal. Just got a call from my sister that you're in a bad spot."

"That's one way of putting it."

"Thought I'd see if I could help."

"I'm not sure anyone can help me now."

"So you're just planning to give up without even trying?"

He sighs. "I don't want to get you in trouble."

"I can take care of myself."

"And I can't, obviously." He mutters this to himself, not to me. "If you want to stick your neck out for me, I'll take you up on the offer. From what Anna's mentioned, you might have some connections."

If by connections he means I'm part of the area's most powerful mafia, then yes, I have connections. "I know a few people," I say noncommittally.

He snorts. "I'm sure you do."

"Meet me at The Brick Oven?" The Brick Oven

is one of the boss's money laundering operations, so nobody will try to off Evan there. Besides, I get free pizza.

"I'll be there in fifteen minutes," he says.

I get there a few minutes early, so my pizza is already cooking when Evan walks in. He looks wary, but sits down across from me.

My heart beats faster at the sight of him. He's still got the same sexy, pretty-boy looks he did when I first started to crush on him, though he's added bright blue to his fancy blond haircut, and he has black plastic glasses that are way hotter than any glasses have a right to be. He's not short, but I'm tall enough to have a good five inches on him, and he's appealingly slight. I have a thing for smaller guys.

I fell for Evan when we were sixteen, and you'd think in the last decade I'd have gotten over him. Nope. I still smile just because he's here, as though I've lost my mind and started believing in happily ever after.

"I appreciate the offer," he says, "but I really don't know how much you can help."

"Try me."

He looks around with concern. "Shouldn't we talk somewhere more private?"

I almost laugh. "Trust me, unless you've pissed off my boss, this is one of the safest places you could be right now."

"Not your boss," says Evan. "Congressman Whitmore."

"Whitmore?" I'm not especially worried about facing off against a congressman, more curious how Evan got on the wrong side of one. "What'd you do to him?"

"Nothing!"

I raise one eyebrow.

"I swear. I didn't do anything wrong, I was in the wrong place at the wrong time, I overheard something I shouldn't have, and now Whitmore is going to be after me to make sure I don't talk."

I hadn't known Whitmore was so dirty. Doesn't surprise me, though, since his ambition knows no limits.

A couple of the other guys look over, curious. I glare at them until they go back to their checkers. Benefit of being six-four and solid muscle, which is why I make plenty of time to work out.

"Start from the beginning," I say.

"I met up with the congressman earlier this afternoon."

"Why?"

"If you must know, to fuck."

He's finally out of the closet. Good for him. I think he was the last person to acknowledge his sexuality, because the rest of us knew. That made loving him an exercise in frustration. "Was he good?"

"If you must know, I was mostly in it for the thrill. He was okay, but gave lousy blowjobs."

Well, shit, I'd be happy to give Evan an excellent blowjob. "Okay. Go on."

"He took a call in the other room. Some kind of emergency, he said. He's not as smart as he likes to think he is, though, because he accidentally put it on speakerphone."

"I'm guessing this is when you overheard something you weren't supposed to."

"Yes."

I have to prompt him. "Which was?"

"His senior aide, O'Donnell. I, uh, ran into the guy a few times when I was over." Evan says this like it's something he should be ashamed about, which it isn't. People get way too hung up about sex. "Anyway,

O'Donnell said, 'Taken care of, sir. Justin reports that Paulson is at the bottom of the Atlantic.'"

He looks around nervously, as though he expects to be killed any second. "Do you have any idea who Paulson is?" I ask.

"I looked online. I'm guessing this is the same Olivia Paulson who interned for Whitmore recently and was reported missing yesterday."

"How do you know she was reported missing?"

He shrugs. "I have my ways."

We can have that conversation later. Right now, I need to know the rest of the story. "What did you do?"

"What do you think I did? I ran out of there, went home, and made sure my will was updated. There's no way Whitmore is going to let me live after I overheard that."

Never likely to begin with, but he sure as fuck won't now since Evan ran. "Anything else?"

"I think that's plenty."

The pizza arrives. "Thanks, Lucie." I give her a winning smile even though she knows I'm gay. Makes her feel good to know she doesn't only get appreciated for her boobs.

I think about everything Evan has said over a couple bites of pizza. He nervously plays with a napkin. "Whitmore isn't going to have you killed," I say. "I'll take care of it."

"Seriously?"

"Yeah. Sit tight, don't leave this place, and I'm gonna go make some calls." I take the rest of my slice to go, since I hate working on an empty stomach. "Enjoy the pizza."

He gives me an incredulous look while I walk away.

****

Outside in my car, I call Junior. He's the boss's son and right hand man, so I use a respectful tone. Respect is important in business. "Good afternoon."

"How's business, Mal?"

"Great. Friend of mine's in a bit of trouble, though. How do I get in touch with Carlos?"

I've never put out a hit. Broken bones are nearly always sufficient for collecting on gambling debt, if not in cash then in favors—I prefer cash, of course, but I'll consider the right favor. Therefore, I need Junior's help to get in touch with the agent who arranges hits.

"You don't. I'll call him."

"Much appreciated."

We hang up, and I wait to hear back. This is going to be expensive. Good thing my latest venture, an exclusive and luxury high-stakes poker event, is earning nicely.

A few minutes later, I get a call from a private number. "Junior asked me to call, and he vouched for you. Can you be at the coffee shop on 21st and Elm in forty-five minutes?"

"Yes. The friend I'm doing this for is in danger, though, so he can't leave The Brick Oven." At least not until I've taken some precautions.

"If this friend has relevant information, I need to speak with him." Carlos sighs as though I've asked him for the world on a platter. "I'll be there in an hour. Bring a deposit," he says, and hangs up.

I'm not entirely sure how much I should bring, so I drive home and grab fifty grand. That ought to show I'm in good faith.

Evan has barely touched the pizza when I get back. Too bad, because it's damn good pizza. "We've got a meeting," I say. "He should be here soon."

"Am I ever going to be able to leave this

restaurant?"

"Of course, once we've made sure you're safe. In the meantime, we have a bunker beneath here. Nobody will be able to get to you." Well, we call it a bunker. It's really more of a safe house without the liability that is windows. It's rarely used and I've never needed it before, though I know the boss was holed up in it for a couple weeks last year.

"Is there any chance you can get some equipment from my place?" Evan asks.

"We've got toiletries and some spare clothes down there."

"I mean computer equipment."

He has odd priorities. "A congressman wants you dead and you want your computer?"

"What the hell, it's not like you're going to judge me for illegal activities," he says.

He's right about that. "Laws are put in place by people too weak of will or body to protect themselves any other way."

"That's one way to look at it," he says. "I'm more inclined to think that some laws are useful, but far too many are put in place by our corporate overlords for their benefit at our expense."

"We can agree to disagree. So, why is this computer equipment so important?"

"Have you heard of Anonymous?"

"The hacker group?"

Evan grins. "I'm one of the best."

That explains how he knew Olivia Paulson was reported missing. "Is that a hobby or a day job?"

"More of a passion. My day job is in digital security for the banking industry. At least it is for now. My boss is a hardass who might fire me for disappearing."

"He can't fire you if you're in the hospital."

"What are you going to do, forge a doctor's note?"

"Don't be ridiculous. It's far easier to buy a real one."

Evan looks at me for a few seconds, then laughs. He looks great when he laughs, and my stomach does this little flip. "I guess I'm playing with the big boys now. Hacking satisfies my moral outrage at the systemic exploitation of the common man, but it doesn't pay well."

"And digital security?"

"Pays respectably. Not much for connections with people open to bribes, though."

"Maybe you just don't know what to look for."

He's looking at me in a very assessing manner now. "And what about you, Mal? Are you exploiting the common man?"

I prefer to exploit rich men. It pays better. "I'm in gambling. Adrenaline junkies come to me looking to be exploited."

Evan laughs again. "Damn, I've missed you."

My chest tightens at that admission, because I missed him, too. "Yeah. You know how things were, though."

He nods. "Someone had to step up to take care of Ben and Angie."

Damn straight. My good-for-nothing father was too busy looking for his next score, and Shelly inherited Mom's selfishness, so that left me. "They're doing well," I say. "Angie's in college, wants to be a dentist. Ben works for the post office."

Ben's job was one of those payments made as favors. He's my kid brother and I love him, but he's not the sharpest crayon in the box, so I got him set up in a stable job with decent salary and benefits which is working out great. Angie, now that girl is smart and I'm making sure she'll graduate college without owing a dime.

"They're lucky to have you." Evan loads the sentence with some kind of emotion or further meaning I don't quite understand. Does he realize that it wasn't just the work, and I stopped seeing him as frequently because it hurt too much wanting a guy I couldn't have? It's a special kind of torture to hang out with a guy you love when he only sees you as a friend.

Whatever moment we were having is broken when someone walks into the restaurant. It's a mom with two kids, and not far behind is a serious man who might be Carlos. He's a very nondescript guy who could blend in anywhere. People notice me because I'm six-four and muscular, so I could never blend in the way Carlos, or whatever his real name is, is able to.

"Mal?" he asks, coming right over.

"We can talk in the back," I say, leading the way to a small private room.

"What can I help you with?" he asks, all business. I can respect that.

"My friend has a problem with Congressman Whitmore."

Carlos's lip twitches. "A congressman."

"He wants to kill me," says Evan. "I was in the wrong place at—"

Carlos holds up a hand. "Your reasons are your business, not mine." He passes a small spiral notebook and pen over to Evan. "Write down everything you know about him. Address, routine, favorite coffee shop. Don't worry about importance; it's not your job to decide what's important. Just write everything."

"Up to and including favorite sexual activities?

Because that's where most of my knowledge lies."

Something that wants to be a frown appears on Carlos's face. "Sex clubs are important. Positions are not. Start writing."

While Evan writes, I lead Carlos over to the corner. "A congressman doesn't come cheap," he says, as though I hadn't already realized.

"What are we talking?"

"You looking for sooner rather than later?"

"Yes."

"Bargain job is two hundred. I'd recommend the sneakier bastard for two-fifty."

I can't say many people are worth a quarter of a million dollars to me. Ben and Angie, absolutely. I'd do anything for my kid siblings. Shelly, maybe, but I'd hold it over her for the rest of her life. And then there's Evan. Damn, love is expensive.

"I want this done right."

"Two-fifty it is, then."

"I brought fifty," I say, giving him the envelope. He examines it with satisfaction. "I can have the rest to you in a couple hours."

"Five o'clock at the pawn shop on Eighth and Market."

"I'll be there."

"So, what's the plan?" asks Evan.

Carlos gives me an exasperated look. "Don't be late. Bring his list." With that, he tucks the fifty thousand in his sport coat and walks out.

Comprehension dawns on Evan. "You're putting a *hit* on a *congressman*?"

"The alternative is letting him get one on you."

"I thought we were going to expose his evil ways."

How charmingly naïve. "That would take too

long." Besides, this is neater.

"I should probably be horrified," he says. "Instead I'm just grateful that I might not die in the next day or two."

"Survival has a way of changing your perspective."

"Why are you doing this for me?" He looks at me through those sexy glasses and I wonder if he really doesn't know, or he just wants to hear me say it.

I'm not committing to anything. "You can't continue your crusade against systemic exploitation if you're dead."

"Somehow I doubt I have enough money to pay you back."

"Don't worry about it."

"Thank you, Mal."

"Sure thing." He might be starting to figure out my real motivation, so a change of subject is in order. "Finish that list. Time is of the essence here."

"Right." He goes back to writing, but he still keeps giving me these thoughtful looks. Maybe he's onto me. I hope not, or it's going to be a long week.

****

I get back to The Brick Oven just after one in the morning. Evan has set up the computer equipment I brought back from his apartment earlier and is busy looking at a screen full of symbols that mean nothing to me. Probably computer code.

"I thought you'd be asleep," I say.

"Hard to sleep when someone is trying to kill you. Do you always work this late?"

"More or less." I don't have to personally supervise every event, but I prefer to when possible.

"Good night?"

"Mediocre." I had to pay out more in blackjack

than I'd like. These nights happen, and I still made money. "The house always wins. Some nights it just wins more than others."

"This is why I don't gamble," he says. "I don't like losing. I think I know why Whitmore had Olivia Paulson killed."

"Why?"

"She had pictures on her cloud which must've been surreptitiously taken on her phone."

I'm not much for technology, in part because I don't trust anything I don't entirely understand and in part because it's too easy for people like Evan to access. "Are we talking about an internet cloud?"

"Of course. That's the only kind that matters. Look at this."

I walk over to one of his three computer screens. "What am I looking at?"

He presses a couple keys and a picture pops up. Looks like a document of some kind. "Can you zoom in?" I ask.

Evan presses another button and I see what he's talking about. This is a slightly fuzzy picture of a computer screen showing a wire receipt from China to an account in the Cayman Islands. I state the obvious conclusion. "Whitmore was taking bribes."

"Not just bribes. Chinese bribes."

Bribes make the world go round, but they're frowned upon in government circles, particularly bribes from foreigners. I have no problem with bribes. In fact, I find them very useful in eliminating difficulties, though I suppose people would prefer not to have foreigners interfering with the U.S. government. Most people are hopelessly idealistic about democracy.

"I'm sending these pictures to CNN," he says. "Partly because I want to make sure he suffers even if he does kill me, and partly in revenge for Olivia Paulson."

"He's not going to kill you." I'm going to make damned sure of that.

"Hope for the best, prepare for the worst. I wonder how long before this is breaking news."

"I thought anonymous sources sent their information to WikiLeaks."

"Only if they aren't good enough to cover their tracks on their own."

"Which you are."

"That's elementary." He closes down whatever he was doing and stands. "Done. I can't wait to check the news tomorrow."

"It'll give Whitmore something else to worry about." I wonder if a distracted target is easier for a hit man.

"I'll see what else I can dig up tomorrow. Are you sleeping here?"

"Yes." I don't want to leave Evan alone and unguarded. Sure, there are a couple guys upstairs, but I feel better being here, which really goes to show that I never got over this man. "I'll get that doctor's note first thing tomorrow. Pneumonia sound like a good excuse?"

"I'm not particular about my faux illness. I just need to do a little research so I sound authentic when my coworkers ask about it."

"I prefer coworkers who don't ask questions."

"I work with some decent people. It's not terrible that they care."

"As long as they don't get too nosy about your leisure activities."

"They think I hike on the weekends."

Evan makes that statement as he peels off his shirt, letting me see that for a guy who spends most of his time in front of computers, he's in impressive shape.

He's not as scrawny as I thought; rather he's lithe and toned. And he knows I'm looking, because he smirks and says, "I don't hike, but I keep up with my calisthenics."

I'm a weights man myself. Never thought much of calisthenics until now when I see the results in front of me, though of course that may be more good genetic fortune than calisthenics.

"Out of curiosity," he says on his way to the bathroom, "how often do you have to utilize a hit man in the illegal gambling business?"

"This is the first time, believe it or not. Dead customers are bad for business."

He gives me a wide, not at all innocent smile. "Your first hit is for me? I'm honored."

I'm starting to wonder if I might have a chance with Evan after all.

****

I wake up to Evan yelling, "Fuck!"

"What?" I check all around the room, but nothing looks alarming. It's also ten past eight in the morning, a solid hour before I want to be awake.

"My apartment building burned down around four this morning."

"Fuck."

He scowls at his phone. "I just wanted to see if the photos are in the news. They are, by the way. Whitmore's office is making noise about them being fake."

"Meanwhile, he's been busy having your building go up in flames."

"At least nobody died." Evan flops back on his bed, frowning. "But over thirty people are now homeless, and it's my fault."

"It's Whitmore's fault."

"Is it?" he asks. "I mean, yes, I think it's safe to

say this wasn't an accident and Whitmore was behind it. What if I hadn't leaked the photos? Would he still have had my building torched?"

"For all we know, he ordered that before he even found out about the pictures."

"The pictures made breaking news at two twenty-seven."

"That's not much time to order arson." I can't say I know a lot about arson, having no use for it myself.

"We can't rule it out."

"This is not your fault, Evan. If Whitmore wasn't such an idiot that he broadcast a private conversation, we wouldn't be here."

He stares at me. "Most people would say 'if Whitmore wasn't a corrupt and morally objectionable man.'"

"I'm not most people. I couldn't care less that Whitmore took bribes, and while I can't say I approve of murdering interns—did he try buying her silence first? I bet that would be attractive to an intern with a mountain of student loans—she should've realized what she was getting into when she took those pictures. A wiser intern would have shut up and walked away, and therefore still be alive."

"So it's her fault she was murdered?" Evan blinks slowly, as though he can't believe what he's hearing.

"No. It's Whitmore's fault, if you care about blame. I'm merely pointing out that you can't play with fire without taking precautions, or you'll get burned." That's just common sense.

"Where does that leave me? Aside from homeless."

"Still alive, which is what matters."

Evan gives me another knowing look. "You don't care that Whitmore murdered Olivia Paulson, but you do care that he wants to kill me."

"She's just another person. There are over seven-point-four billion of us. You're a friend, which makes you different."

"A friend, hmm?"

I head into the bathroom to avoid further conversation. Evan takes the hint, because when I come back out he's already hard at work on his computer, presumably fighting for the little guy. His mission is idealistic and his devotion to it is charming. If that thought doesn't show how gone I am for this man, I don't know what would.

My phone rings and caller ID tells me it's Dad. I mentally groan. I don't want to talk with him, now or ever. However, the conversation can't be put off indefinitely, and I might as well get it over with while Evan is around to make the world a brighter place.

"Hello."

"I got an eviction notice," says Dad.

"Good morning to you, too."

"It's not a good morning, because I'm getting evicted."

"That's what happens when you don't pay your rent."

"I haven't been able to afford my rent for a while." Translation: he spends all his money on drugs, when he manages to keep a job, that is.

"I told you a few months ago I wasn't paying it after Angie moved out." My sister practically lived with me for the last year before she left home, but I paid Dad's rent anyway in case Family Services came sniffing around.

"Sure, you'll help her with rent, but not your father."

"Angie is a full-time student with a part-time job.

There's nothing stopping you from paying your own rent except your heroin habit."

"Addiction is a disease, Mal," he says in his best wounded voice. "I'm sick."

That's just another excuse to avoid taking responsibility. "I told you I'd pay for rehab."

"Rehab didn't help."

"You stayed three days. That's not even trying."

"I do try!" He attempts to crank up the "poor me" act, though that stopped working on me the second time he pawned some of my stepmom's jewelry. I managed to buy back a couple pieces—her engagement ring for Ben to use when he proposes someday, earrings for Angie to remember her mom by—but I'll never forget how devastated my little sister was to find her heirlooms gone.

I think that's when I started to hate my father. Not when I had to drop out to put food on the table, or the first time I found my cash missing, but when my sister was crying over her empty jewelry box.

"You're going to let your own father be homeless."

If the accusation is supposed to sting, it fails miserably. "You were content to let your own children be hungry and homeless, not to mention you stole from them."

"Mal, I need your help."

"I'm not going to enable your drug habit. Call me if you decide you want to take rehab seriously."

"But Mal..."

I end the call by pressing the red disconnect button with more force than required.

Evan's looking at me with sympathy, something I wouldn't tolerate from almost anyone else. After an awkward couple of seconds, he says, "You really got the dregs of the dad barrel."

"Don't I know it." He was actually a decent father before heroin, but I'm not feeling generous enough to acknowledge that at the moment.

"You've done well for yourself despite him."

"It was sink or swim. I swam."

He nods and turns back to his computers. Damn, I never understood the phrase "fuck-me glasses" before and now it makes perfect sense. He's got this sexy-cool nerd vibe going with the plastic frames and the blue streaks in his hair, while his fingers fly over the keyboard.

I go back to the bathroom. Maybe jerking off in the shower will help me control myself around Evan.

****

Business must have been so much easier in the days before income tax and the IRS. Now we have to account for every damn nickel in order to fund the government's ever-increasing meddling in private lives. When your business isn't strictly legal (not that the government has any business determining who can and can't offer gambling activities in the first place), dealing with the IRS is that much trickier. I have to keep a close eye to make sure a reasonable percent of my earnings are being laundered, and the rest I keep in cash. It's a complicated balancing act and the most annoying part of my business.

I'm sitting down to a meeting on the subject of money laundering with Jones, an associate and a nephew of the boss who specializes in this service. "I hear you've got a friend hiding in the emergency bunker." He makes the comment with emphasis on the word 'friend.'

"Everyone should have access to an emergency bunker," I say in reply. "You never know when you'll need to lay low for a few days."

I refuse a cigar because that shit can kill you. One, I'm in no hurry to die, and two, when I do go I'd like it to be quick and painless, not a nasty ordeal like my grandfather's emphysema. The scotch I do accept, because Jones is a scotch snob and always serves good stuff.

He puffs on his cigar. "This friend trustworthy?"

"Yes."

"You sure you're thinking with the right head?"

I never let my dick endanger my business or well-being, and Jones knows it. "Positive. Besides, I've got dirt on him, too."

That meets with his approval. "Mutually assured destruction is a powerful deterrent. You owe this guy or something?"

If I want to do a friend a favor, it's my business, and I don't appreciate the interrogation. "What is this, the Inquisition?"

Jones chuckles. "Someone's getting defensive. I might not have been entirely off-base about you thinking with your dick."

It's actually my heart, which is far more dangerous, but I'll be damned if I let Jones on to that detail. The best defense is a strong offense, and I have an observation or two which will hit home. "This from the man who follows a certain hooker around with a perpetual semi."

"Stripper, not a hooker." He punctuates this with a stab of his cigar into the air. "There's a difference. Meanwhile, I've never brought her into the bunker."

"If Evan goes out, he might turn up in the morgue." Or possibly end up at the bottom of the ocean, since Whitmore's people have an affinity for that method of body disposal. "If your stripper was in that much trouble she'd be in the bunker, too."

"Maybe," he says.

"Your uncle have a problem with it?"

Jones shakes his head in a cloud of smoke. "Nah, he's fine with it. Didn't think you cared enough to go into crisis mode for anyone but your kid siblings, so he's amused that you've gotten yourself so involved with this pretty boy."

I glare at him. Jones gets the message, coughs, and changes the subject. "How's business? You said you're ready to increase the dollar amount with me."

We get down to business, and if I leave a little more abruptly than usual once we're finished, Jones is smart enough not to mention it.

****

I come back from the meeting with donuts from the shop down the street. Best donuts for miles around. "Frosted or glazed?" I ask, holding them out for Evan to choose.

"Glazed. Thanks." He makes a sinful noise when he bites into it, and my dick takes notice. "This is delicious."

I say, "Glad you like it," and go sit on the bed because if he keeps moaning his appreciation for the donut I'm going to have very obvious appreciation of my own.

He moans with every damn bite of the donut, and I'm starting to regret buying them. It's not fair of him to torture the man saving his life.

"You really enjoyed that donut, didn't you?" he asks. Shit, he's looking at my crotch and grinning like a loon. Before I can put together a response, he goes on. "Did you know that you were the one who finally got me to acknowledge to myself that I'm gay?"

"What?"

"It's true," he says, walking to stand in front of

me. "It took me long enough, but I finally figured it out and you had a lot to do with the realization. You're hot, Mal. And I'm getting the distinct impression that you wouldn't mind distracting me from my troubles with a good fucking."

"No." If he's offering, I'm happy to accept. My stupid heart points out that I'd like more than one fuck, but my more sensible brain decides to take what I can get. "I don't have supplies, though."

He pulls a condom and pack of lube from his wallet. "Always be prepared. I'm not sure the Boy Scouts intended for me to interpret that as carrying lube and condoms, but it's good advice anyway."

When he starts to take his glasses off, I recover my ability to speak. "Leave them on."

"Oh? You like the glasses?" He smirks. "Good to know."

"What," I have to swallow before I can continue. Evan is robbing me of my speech, not to mention control. "What do you like?"

"You top. Don't be gentle, I want to feel how strong you are."

I've never believed in heaven, but I might have to reconsider because that's just what I want, too. He takes off his shirt and he's gorgeous, lean, and toned with an intricate Celtic tattoo along the left side of his ribcage, and he's small enough that I can easily overpower him, but not so tiny he'll break.

"Like what you see?" he asks, unnecessarily.

"Hell, yes." I shed my sport coat and start unbuttoning my shirt.

"Any chance you're into dirty talk?" he asks. "Because with your voice that could possibly be the hottest thing ever."

Dirty talk for its own sake doesn't do anything for

me. If Evan gets off on it, though, I'm game. "You like my voice?"

"Are you kidding? You've got that uber-manly, deep voice and I can only imagine what it's like when you're turned on."

"You're about to find out. Dirty talk it is."

He ogles my naked torso. "Have I mentioned how ridiculously hot you are?"

"Yes, but I don't mind hearing it again."

"It's worth repeating anyway."

"You're sexy yourself." I pull him closer by the belt loops on his jeans. "One hundred percent fuckable."

"Well, that's a relief." He runs his fingers through my chest hair and settles in on my lap. "I was afraid I might only have been in the high nineties."

Smart ass. I decide to see if his nipples are sensitive by licking one.

"Mmm," he says, another sexy moan going straight to my dick. At least I don't have to pretend I'm unaffected anymore.

He's frustrated in his attempt to get a similar response out of me, since my nipples have about as much sensitivity as the back of my hand, which is to say not much at all. Meanwhile, his nipple has firmed up nicely, so I move to the other one. This time I gently nibble instead of lick.

"Fuck, Mal."

So, he's not just into hearing dirty talk, he likes to be vocal himself. That presents some very interesting possibilities. "All in good time," I say, nibbling my way back to the first nipple. "Patience is a virtue."

"I don't think either of us cares much about virtue."

He has a point, but I don't want this over with too quickly. Especially not with the little whimpers he makes when I start mouthing his neck. I do enjoy a responsive man, and Evan is amazingly responsive.

"You can leave a mark," he says, causing my cock to harden so much it presses against my zipper. "Give me a reminder for a few days."

Well, shit, I can't refuse an offer like that, can I? I find a nice spot and suck hard. When he looks in the mirror he's going to see that he was mine. When I'm done with his neck there's a beautiful red spot which is a really good look on him. "That's not the only reminder I'm gonna leave," I tell him. "You'll feel it when you sit down."

"God, yes." The words are half-spoken, half-panted.

I lean back and roll us on our sides so I can take off my pants, which have gotten very uncomfortable. Evan takes the opportunity to do the same so we're both naked. His cock isn't remarkable in the size department, but it's a beauty all the same and he's rock-hard for me.

"Damn, Mal, you're packing." He gives my dick an admiring glance. "We're talking porn star material here."

I can't resist the opportunity to tease. "Too big for you?"

"No way. I want that cock."

"Good." Not right away, though. First I want to work him up a little more. To that end I return my attention to his nipples and slowly work my lips south. He's arching his hips, aching for my touch on his dick.

"Come on, Mal."

"Impatient, aren't you?"

"Call me whatever you want, just suck me already."

"You're hot when you're desperate." I barely touch his balls with my fingertips. "I like it."

If I weren't so turned on I'd drag this out a little more. As things stand, I decide he's right, it's time for more, so I lick the underside of his dick from root to tip, then repeat on both sides before taking him in my mouth. His appreciative groans are almost as good as feeling him in my mouth.

It takes me a minute of groping with one hand before I find the lube and condoms. Condom first, because that's easier before my hands are slippery with lube. Once I'm suited up I rip into the packet of lube and take a dab on my finger.

When my finger touches his hole his cock jumps in my mouth. "Like that?" I ask.

"Yes. Give me your finger."

"With pleasure."

My fingers are large but the first one slides in with barely any resistance. "That was easy," I say. "Should I take that to mean you're easy?"

"With the right guy." He's loving it, reveling in the sensation as I work my finger in and out.

Time to ramp up the dirty talk, I think. I hope he likes it, because it's not an area where I have a ton of experience. "You can't wait, can you? You're dying to have my cock fill your ass."

"Yeah." He inhales sharply as I suck down his dick. "Another finger."

That seems a bit hasty, so I work him with the single finger for another minute, getting him good and needy before adding another dollop of lube and the second finger. He hisses a little this time, but the sting has no notable effect on his erection, which stays nicely hard in my mouth. I tongue the head while I stretch him.

I let his cock fall out of my mouth so I can say, "You're even hotter with my fingers in your ass." Then I go back to the blowjob. If Whitmore was bad at giving head, I'm damned well going to remind Evan what a good blowjob feels like, so I relax my throat and take him in deeper.

"Oh, yeah." He's gripping the sheets hard and thrusting into my mouth, then back onto my fingers. I try to take a mental picture to revisit in the future when it's just me and my hand.

When he attempts to change the angle my fingers are reaching, I use my free arm to hold down his hips so he's not getting any stimulation on his prostate. He's not getting that until it's from my dick.

After a couple more minutes, I think he's ready so I pull off his dick. "You ready to take my cock?"

"Yes."

"Roll over. I want to see your ass."

He obliges, and it's a very nice ass, especially since it's on display for me. "So hot with your ass in the air for me," I say, spreading his legs a little further and adding the rest of the lube before lining myself up. "Gonna fill that pretty ass up now."

I go slowly but steadily, focusing on controlling my speed until I'm inside him balls-deep. Evan's a moaner, constantly making these incredibly sexy noises. Once I feel him relax, I start thrusting in earnest, enjoying the view of my cock sliding into his ass.

Oh, right, I'm supposed to be talking dirty, not losing myself in the visual. "You love it, don't you?" I ask. "Being stretched out by my dick."

"Yes. Faster."

I'm happy to oblige and, after I find the right angle, he finally gets the prostate hits he's been looking for.

"Fuck, that's good," he says.

"You're good. Your ass feels amazing around my dick. Can you take it harder?"

"Do it."

He likes harder, if the groans of pleasure are anything to go by. They usually are. A minute or two goes by before I remember to talk again. This dirty talk is harder than I thought, because my brain (or, more likely, my cock) has decided that speaking is a low priority right now.

I lean forward a little so I can get closer to his ear. "So fucking hot, Evan, to see my cock sliding in your ass, to hear how much you love getting fucked. You can't get enough, can you?"

"No."

That's my cue to pick up the pace. What else can I say? "You're gonna feel this all day. When you sit down at your computer, your ass is gonna remind you that it just got reamed."

"Yes. Right there, Mal."

"No touching yourself. We're not done yet."

I want another minute to enjoy this, and I savor that minute before reaching around to take his dick in my hand. "I bet you're ready to come, aren't you?"

"Please."

It only takes a few strokes before he's coming. I hold my own orgasm off as long as I can. There's nothing like the feeling of being inside a guy who's coming around your dick with his muscles going crazy. Inevitably, this sends me over the edge into the best orgasm I've had in a while.

When I return to awareness I slip out of Evan and dispose of the condom before grabbing a fistful of tissues. Not that the tissues are really necessary, since his cum is pretty well contained to the blanket. I think I'll need to run home and do a load of laundry. Despite what my cleaning lady thinks, I do know how to operate the machines. I just prefer to pay her to deal with it.

He pushes away the blanket and we both collapse. "I was right," he says. "Your voice during sex is incredibly hot."

I take that to mean my dirty talk was up to par. "Good to know. For the record, that was great."

"Fan-fucking-tastic," he says in agreement. "Wore me out. I'm going to just lie here and wait for my energy to come back."

"Yeah. Me, too."

That, and try not to think about how amazing we'd be together with a little practice. I have to look away from the bruise that's forming on his neck, because it reminds me that he's not really mine. My brain usually takes a little vacation after a good orgasm, and I wish it would give me some peace now.

****

After we fuck there's a bit of awkwardness, so I leave for work early. It's a good night because a higher than usual percentage of players take loans from me. Sure, I have to send out my guy to break a couple bones, but that's how the business works. People should know that going in, and if they don't, they learn quickly. If you take out a loan, you pay it back with interest as agreed or I'll have my guy give you a painful reminder. I'm not running a charity here.

Evan is asleep when I get back, and I look over at his bed fondly. Maybe the sex was a bad idea, a kind of self-torture to have one taste of what I want. Thing is, I don't just want Evan for sex. It was damn good sex and I'd like more of it, of course, but I want all of him. I want him in my life as well as my bed, and I want him to feel the same way. It's unsettling how much of a soft spot I have for him, because I'm usually good to fuck and part ways. These thoughts keep me awake longer than usual, tossing and turning before I finally manage to get some sleep.

****

I sleep until a more reasonable hour today, and when I get up, Evan is reading the news on his computer. "Good morning," he says without looking away from the screen. "Guess what? Whitmore is getting his very own House Ethics Committee investigation."

"That was fast."

"I found some good stuff linking him to the offshore accounts the Chinese money went to. It's so much easier when you don't have to deal with warrants like the police do."

"CNN must love you."

"I'm sure they love their anonymous friend."

"Any particular reason you chose CNN?"

"Anderson Cooper. He's a hot silver fox. Whitmore's still alive, though." He frowns over the last sentence. "Not that I wanted him dead, but if it's him or me, I pick myself."

I'm just happy Evan and I are past the post-fuck awkwardness. "I assumed he would be alive this morning. Security measures to be considered, routine to learn, and so on. I'd be surprised if he's dead before Friday."

"I'd better text work that I'm still quite sick, then. Did you go with pneumonia?"

I hand over a letter from the doctor. "A very serious case of it."

Evan sets the letter aside. "I'm sure I'd be dead if it weren't for you, Mal. Thank you is terribly inadequate for what you're doing."

I don't need thanks, I just need Evan alive. "You're welcome. I'm glad I can help."

"My knight in shining armor." He winks, sending my heart rate up.

"Nah. Knights had to deal with codes of chivalry and shit. I'm not cut out for that." I'm also sure there was something in those cavalry codes about not fucking someone while saving their life. Knights didn't get to have much fun.

He chuckles. "I'm allergic to horses, so it's just as well you're not an actual knight."

"It must've sucked to be allergic to horses in the days when they were the main source of transportation."

"Allergies are much more prevalent now than in previous generations. Another thing you can take up with our corporate overlords and their desire to sell at any cost."

"I think I'll leave taking it up with corporate overlords to you."

"You don't have to be a hacker. Awareness is the first step. For instance, you should never buy from the big soft drink companies because they're buying up water rights all over the world. They don't give a damn if people go thirsty in Africa as long as their stock goes up."

God help me, he's adorable when he's defending the world. I don't even care about people in Africa, or really most people in general, but I'd avoid buying these products to make him happy. I'm doomed.

"Just don't tell me I can't buy coffee." As soon as I shower, I'm off to get breakfast, including the lifeblood which is coffee.

"Is it fair trade?"

"I have no idea."

"You need to find out. Direct trade is better really, because fair trade isn't the cure-all some people like to think."

So I do find out. When I come back with breakfast sandwiches and coffee, I make sure to let Evan know that I was paying attention. "The place just switched to fair trade coffee a couple months ago. Which, come to think of it, is when the prices went up."

"It's worth paying more to know the farmers are earning a living."

"Is it?" I can't say I ever concerned myself with coffee farmers' lives before.

"Absolutely," he says, nodding with conviction. "That's why direct trade is the way to go."

"I assume if they're halfway decent coffee farmers, they do all right." There's certainly enough demand for their product.

"You'd think, but you underestimate how eager corporations are to screw the little guy in order to further swell their bank accounts."

"I like swelling my bank accounts."

Evan waves away the statement with the hand not holding his breakfast sandwich. "That's different. If people are stupid enough to gamble, that's their own fault."

"Like I said, people come to me looking to be exploited. I make sure they aren't disappointed."

"No," he says. "You're not one to disappoint."

Now, there's something about his expression that suggests we're talking about more than my business. Best guess, he's talking about the sex yesterday, and it's good to know I didn't disappoint there either. Before I can come back with a suggestive reply, his phone buzzes and he starts texting, impressively fast for doing it one-handed.

"My boss hopes I'm feeling better. I guess you don't think that getting Whitmore in trouble over his bribes will end this without anyone dying."

"No. I don't think it's worth betting your life on a guy who's already behind at least one murder. The house always wins, remember?"

He sighs. "Right."

****

Evan comes out of the shower wearing nothing but a towel around his hips. That damned well better be an invitation, because I already watched him go through his calisthenics routine and there's only so much skin I can watch without touching. Nobody's ever accused me of being a saint.

He gives me a sexy little grin. "I thought you might be interested. My ass isn't ready for a repeat of yesterday, but I'm totally up for swapping blowjobs."

Swapping blowjobs sounds great, but the more I have of Evan the more I want all of him. I'm a possessive bastard and don't pretend otherwise.

"If we do this again, you're mine." The words tumble out before I can censor myself, damn it. Since I can't take them back, I might as well make sure he knows exactly what I mean. "And I don't share."

He raises one eyebrow. "I'm not a pet you can claim ownership of, Mal. I'm more than open to the idea, but there are conditions."

"I don't like conditions," I say, crossing my arms to look intimidating and cover the way my heart leaps that he's interested.

"Tough." Evan isn't cowed in the least and damn, he's hot when he's feisty. "Exclusivity is a two-way street."

"That's a condition I can live with."

"Good. Can you live without kids? Because if you're set on procreating there's no future for us."

"I already did the kids thing with Ben and Angie. I don't want to start over with babies." In fact, the idea of a helpless, screaming infant in diapers is fucking terrifying. I think I'd rather get shot. Now, Evan thinking about a future for us, that is a fine and wonderful thing.

"I don't rim."

"Okay." It's nice enough, sure, but there are plenty of other hot things we can do. "That's not a deal breaker."

Evan's shoulder relax with relief, so I get the idea it's been a deal breaker in his past. "Last but not least, don't get caught. Conjugal visits in prison are *not* my idea of a hot date."

"Mine either, so make not getting caught another two-way street. Although a little prison roleplay might be fun." I give him my best suggestive leer. "I could get a prison guard costume and you could trade sexual favors for preferential treatment. Or we could both be inmates and I could make you my bitch."

"You are a dirty, dirty man."

If that's his pressing observation, I guess we're done with conditions, which is a good thing because I can manage the four he already set. "You like me that way, baby, so let's get that damned towel off and your cock in my filthy mouth."

I've never seen a man drop a towel this quickly. Another one for the list of things Evan does to turn me on.

After, when I've demonstrated just how talented I am at giving head and Evan proves he's my equal, he pushes himself up on one elbow and asks, "We're doing this, then? A relationship?"

"I'm no expert, but we've agreed to exclusivity and we're talking about sharing a future. Sounds like a relationship." It also sounds too good to be true, like I'm going to wake up any moment now. Although I've never had a dream close to this.

"It does, doesn't it?" He takes this as license to run his fingers through my chest hair. "I didn't think you'd want more than sex."

"Same here."

"Something good has come out of fearing for my life, then."

"Anyone who messes with you messes with me."

Evan's fingers pause for a moment while that sinks in, then he says, "Hey, if you ever need a little hacking done, you know who to ask."

I'm hoping that doesn't become necessary. "I thought your hacking was to fight corporations."

"I'll make an exception for you."

"I get the special treatment, huh?"

"You're definitely special." He comes in for a kiss that starts sweet and soon adds a nice bit of tongue action. I can't remember the last time I kissed a guy after sex, if I ever have. This thing with Evan is more than sex, so the kissing makes sense. It's good. I like that he wants to kiss me, and that it feels so right to kiss him back.

"You're pretty special yourself," I say when we stop kissing. "And hot."

"You know our sisters are going to tease us mercilessly about this."

He's right, but at least the conversation has moved away from mushy stuff. I'm terrible at mushy stuff. "I don't care what Shelly says about my life. She's the one who sits around feeling sorry for herself and hoping the perfect husband will change her life."

"My sister saw me admiring you at Shelly's wedding and it was months before she shut up about it. God only knows how much mileage she'll get out of this."

"Want me to intimidate her for you?"

He laughs. "Not yet, but I'll let you know if I get that desperate."

"It's an open-ended offer."

"You are good to me."

"Damn right I'm gonna be good to you." I drag him up so he's half-lying across my chest. "I'm not fucking around with you." The words are no sooner out of my mouth than I realize they were not well chosen. This is why I don't do mushy stuff. Why did I even try? "Well, I am, but that's the sex. I mean that this means something."

Evan gets it, I am grateful to see, and he's not much for mushy stuff either. "Keep me sexually satisfied and I won't even miss the dating scene. Or the hookup scene."

"Oh, I'll keep you satisfied, baby, don't worry about that."

My cock is perking up again, but oddly enough, that's the least of the reasons why I feel like the luckiest bastard on the eastern seaboard.

****

We fall into a routine. Evan spends a lot of his time hacking in the name of justice while I attend to my business in the name of making money. We wait, and we distract ourselves from waiting with a generous amount of sex, during which I embark on a personal mission to make up for previous lousy blowjobs he received.

It's three more days before I see the headline we've been waiting for: Congressman Whitmore was killed while walking his dog. Excellent.

Evan is sleeping because it's one-thirty in the morning, so I go upstairs to take care of a loose end or two. My PI charges a fortune, but he delivers every time and has once again come through for me on short notice. This is why he can demand the prices he does.

A quick call from a burner phone later and everything is taken care of. Evan is safe now, as safe as anyone can be in this world. On the strength of that, I get a wonderful night's sleep.

When I wake up, he's already watching the news. "Whitmore is dead."

"I saw when I got back from work."

"And you didn't wake me up to tell me?"

"Didn't see a point. He's no less dead now."

"Authorities have found no trace of the killer," a reporter says on Evan's computer screen, while he rolls his eyes at my comment. "The congressman was embroiled in a scandal stemming from leaked photos appearing to show that he accepted bribes from Chinese state-run media. Right now, we can only speculate as to whether the alleged bribes had anything to do with his murder."

I suppose they did, if only indirectly. "Good. It's over."

"Not entirely over," says Evan.

"They're not going to tie us to his death."

"Probably not, but his aide must know that I know about Olivia Paulson."

Is that only occurring to him now? "O'Donnell's not going to say anything."

Evan gives me a critical eye. "How can you be so sure?"

"I happen to be in possession of some *extremely* compromising audio starring him. I'm sure he won't want his wife to know how much he pays escorts to dominate him, so we made a deal: silence for leaving you alone. Anonymously, of course."

He's called off the hit on Evan, which was my main goal. Right now, O'Donnell is already running scared with the scandal and his boss's death, so throwing in a little panic over his extramarital activities is going to keep him that much more off-balance. Maybe I'll get lucky and he'll off himself without me having to arrange it.

"What if he comes clean to his wife?" Evan wants to know, as though I haven't already planned all of this out.

"He's going to have an accident soon."

"Breaking your deal?" He feigns horror.

"No. My deal was not to give the audio to his wife, which I'm not going to do. We never made a deal about not killing him." Idiot didn't even think to ask.

"I probably don't need to worry about O'Donnell, then." Evan's shoulders slump a little. "However, I'm still homeless."

Another easily solved problem. "Come live with me."

"Don't you think that's moving a bit fast?"

No, I really don't. "I've spent long enough without you."

Evan's eyes widen. "That sounded suspiciously like a declaration of love."

I laugh. "Do you think I'd put out a quarter-million-dollar hit on a congressman for someone I didn't love?"

His response is a searing kiss that goes on for at least a minute before he breaks it to say, "You big romantic, Mal."

"I'm not a hearts and flowers guy, in case you hadn't noticed."

"Oh, I had." Evan gives me a new kiss. "You show your love by taking care of people."

"When you put it that way, it makes sense." I'm not so good at putting emotions into words. Generally, I get around this by not bothering.

"I don't need hearts and flowers, in case you hadn't realized," he says. "Flowers just die within a week anyway, so I've never understood why that's supposed to be romantic. It's corporations commodifying emotions for profit again."

I'm not entirely sure what he means, but since he doesn't have expectations I could never meet, I'll take it.

He pushes his hair to one side, very serious. "All I need is you."

I pull him in for a long kiss. "You've got me, baby."

"Just like that?"

"Yeah. Now, how about I take you home and show you the Jacuzzi?" Evan is going to look fantastic naked with bubbles swirling around his chest.

He laughs and kisses me again. "Take me home, Mal."

I give myself a quick pinch to make sure I'm not dreaming. Nope. This is real, Evan is mine, and I am definitely the luckiest bastard on the east coast. Another decade down the road I might even reconsider my stance on happily ever after.

Best $250,000 I ever spent.

The End

www.evernightpublishing.com/jessie-pinkham

SILENT DEVOTION

Angelique Voisen

Copyright © 2017

Prologue

15 Years Ago

Silent ignored the annoying boy lingering by the door of his hospital room. The brat opened his mouth, but he didn't bother straining to read those lips. Silent glued his eyes to the TV on top of the bed. If he ignored the other boy long enough, the little intruder would get bored and leave.

The effect seemed the opposite. The boy with the bright blue eyes and mess of black hair took it as an invitation to walk in and sit on the side of his bed as if they were pals, not strangers. The brat leaned over, blocking his view. Attempting to shove him proved useless. The blue-eyed boy smiled and Silent wondered if the boy might be a little slow in the head, like his little brother Aaron.

Aaron lay six feet under now, though. His bastard father called it an accident, like he did this time, too, save Silent had been made of tougher stuff.

The boy waved at his face again. This time, Silent caught the words, because he had nothing better to do.

"Hey, are you ignoring me?"

Although roaring quiet made up his world now, Silent could almost imagine the other kid's voice, rushed and excited, like that newborn puppy his father gave Aaron and him last year. No names, he knew. Names meant attachment, weakness. Those two could be used against him, but Aaron had done it nonetheless, and when Ritz got caught in another "accident" Aaron bawled his eyes out.

This kid reminded him of Ritz, kept yapping, lips moving non-stop. Silent wanted to find a pause button. Maybe punching the brat would shut him up. His father always taught him to never speak, to remain invisible unless he had something worthwhile to say.

Silent clenched his fist, the one not attached to the IV drip, but something stopped him. Those blazing blue eyes held shadows, secrets, just like his own, although this brat did his best to pretend he was right as day. This time, he made an effort to read the boy's lips.

"The other kids in the children's ward call you silent, because you don't talk, even though the car accident just affected your hearing. They don't want to be my friends."

That had been Silent's translation. Reading lips still needed getting used to.

The boy looked a little sad now, rubbing his arms. Too thin for his body, Silent saw, studying the boy a little more. Bruises peeked underneath the hospital gown the other boy wore. Broken. Just like him, if not on the outside, then the inside.

However, one difference between them?

Silent stopped pretending to be normal and fine a long time ago, but hope still flickered in those vivid blue eyes, the shade so strange it grabbed his attention. Light blue, like the clear water lapping at his and Aaron's ankles when their parents still took them to the beach, back when his mother had still been alive.

Pure. Clean. This boy might have cracks in his

soul, but they could be fixed, glued back, unlike him.

The boy took a deep breath, extended a hand toward him. "Would you be my friend, Silent? Once you get better, let's go outside together. I can show you the sights and sounds of St. Mary's Hospital."

Sights? Did the boy mean the grim-looking playground with the paint peeling from the monkey bars and rust coating the slide which he could see from his window?

Sometimes Silent would sit up, watch the laughing kids and feel nothing but alienation. Those kids and him, they existed on two different worlds. This strange boy with eyes that had known pain, shared something with him.

The boy patted his arm and he flinched. Silent didn't like being touched, associated it often with violence, but this boy's touch had been gentle, reassuring almost. He tried to make sense of the words again.

"It's okay if you don't want to be." The boy pulled his hand back and Silent didn't like that, didn't know why he gripped the other boy's wrist.

He struggled to form words. No, his vocal cords hadn't been damaged, but after the paramedics extracted him from that car next to his father's corpse, the crash didn't just steal his hearing, but also his voice.

"Wait." The single word felt uncomfortable on his lips, but Silent repeated it, in case the boy didn't catch it.

The older kids laughed at his new disability, came into his room the other day, taunting him. Silent might be deaf now, but he read their body language, the expressions on their face. Rage, a restrained wild animal in him, rose up and he would have lunged at them, answered their jeers with blows, but a nurse walked by and shooed them away.

Even so, he didn't try communicating with another human being until today.

The boy widened his eyes, began babbling excitedly again.

Silent sighed, gave the boy's wrist a warning squeeze. "Slower. Don't speak so fast."

"You don't need to yell." The boy covered his mouth, lowered his gaze. "Sorry, I didn't mean—"

"It's fine. I'll be your friend." *His first friend.* His father never exactly encouraged him to interact with other boys his age, save Aaron. The man had been too focused on his sole genetic legacy to pick up the family business.

"Okay, good. I'm Salvatore Salerno, but people just call me Sal."

The family name rang faint alarm bells in his head, but he didn't pay attention to it. The last thing Silent wanted was to hear his father's voice whispering in his head again. Sal didn't seem to understand the concept of boundaries.

"Scoot over, you're hogging the bed," Sal said, and for some reason he made space.

Sal joined him in the covers, grabbed the remote by the table on the side of the bed, and starting changing channels. At that moment, his annoyance fizzled, because Sal's small, warm body felt nice. The close contact helped ward the icy cold that had settled in his veins—his heart—ever since his mother's death and his father turned from man to monster.

Chapter One

Present

"Are you sure about this, Silent? Retirement at your age? Why, you're at the prime of your life, your career," Frank Santora commented from his desk before exhaling a lungful of smoke.

The desk moved a fraction of an inch, but Silent knew the cause. Every time he came into the boss's office, Frank had a new flavor of the week under his desk, sucking his dick.

He signed an affirmative "yes." Unlike the two other families Silent worked for, Santora bothered to learn his language. That had been one of the factors in why he stayed as a hitman for the Santoras longer than necessary. Despite the family's bloodthirsty reputation, they didn't deal in women or children, one line Silent refused to cross.

"I won't stop you, although I'd sure as hell miss having you around. No one cleans fuck-ups as fast as you, but I'll tell you this. No one leaves this life. They always come back to it. You'll miss it. You know where to reach me or Tony if that happens."

Taking that as a dismissal from the last man Silent would ever serve, he inclined his head, signed, "Thank you for everything." Then he took his leave. Outside Frank's office, he walked past a twisting maze of corridors which led to the main area of the strip club. *Kisses* was one of many profitable businesses owned by the Santoras, but this had been Frank's first and favorite.

Frank's right-hand man Tony barred his path. Hope stirred to life inside his black heart as he spotted the envelope Tony had tucked under his arm. On the outside, Silent's expression remained emotionless, just like his father taught him, defenses airtight.

"I got what you asked for from my source." Tony handed over the envelope, watched him for a couple of seconds.

Aware he had an audience, Silent flicked through the photos with disinterest, before shoving them back in the envelope. He held out a hand. Tony had been wary of bringing him in at first, unable to determine his motives, but Silent proved himself capable and reliable over time.

Trust took time to build. Silent understood that better than anyone. The Santoras took him in even after the other family he'd worked for fell, but his loyalties always remained the same: singular. The Santoras, like the others, had only been stops on the road to his one true goal—retrieve what had been taken from him all those years ago.

"I appreciate it."

"You're really leaving?" Tony asked, surprised. "Can you really expect me to believe a man baptized in violence can fucking retire?"

"I'll keep the secrets of the family," he signed back. In all his years working for the Santoras, no one ever heard him open his mouth. Frank and Tony assumed he'd been mute as well as deaf. His voice he reserved for only one man.

Tony expelled a breath. "That's not what I'm worried about. I'm concerned about you. What will you fucking do? Fish? Open a bed and breakfast?"

For once, Silent told the truth. "Live out my days in peace with someone important."

Tony blinked, as if the notion someone like Silent, someone who only took lives, could care for another human being baffled him. "Well, best of luck, brother."

Brother. He appreciated that, but cutting all ties to

the Santoras had been essential, all part of the plan so no one could trace him back to them, in case he fucked up his last mission. Silent walked past Tony, nodded to the suits he'd worked with, knew the names of. One dancer blew him a kiss as he left.

Cool night air kissed his face once he exited *Kisses*'s doors. Silent walked to his beat-up but trusty black Ford. Once behind the wheel, he could no longer contain the trembling of his fingers. He spread out the photos, each one grimy, taken in haste, but enough. The last one caught his eye. Two fuckers dragging a third man by the armpits—thin, miserable, used-up.

His. Always his.

Fury rippled over him, a crashing, roaring wave. Silent harbored a vicious beast inside of him, rage that had built over years, but he couldn't let that animal take over. One mistake would cost him and all those years spilling blood and gathering information would be for nothing.

Silent had one chance and he couldn't afford to fuck it up. Once the anger settled to cold ice, he started the engine and drove back to his apartment. Within half an hour, he parked his ride by the curb and got out.

A couple of bloodshot-eyed youths smoking pot glanced at him, but soon lost interest—they knew Silent wasn't easy prey. He entered the graffiti-scrawled lobby, walked past the elevator that never worked and took the stairs to his floor. Once back inside his place, Silent took off his shirt, replacing it with a fresh one.

His apartment looked like a temporary space to live in, composed of a bed, a desk with a laptop, and a trunk full of weapons. More knives and guns hung on the wall for easy access, but he'd cleared away the old furniture of the first tenant to build his wall of evidence. A map of names and faces, details hastily scrawled over them, added over time to form an elaborate tree of information that would someday lead Silent to his goal.

Taking out the photos, he added them to the wall, mulled over them for a long time. He had his answer. Silent meant what he said to Frank and Tony. He had one last job to do before hanging up his gun.

He slammed his fist over the top name on the wall, lip curling in distaste. Silent had taken down a number of hard, dangerous men and women during his career. This snake, though, deserved special attention. One death wouldn't be enough to slake his blood lust, the rage that had built over the years.

"I'm coming for you and your entire family, Dom Sabella."

****

Silent pulled the trigger, face unmoving at the spray of blood and brain matter on the side of his face. The second fucker dressed similarly in a cheap suit went down the same way. The third proved more resilient, managed to grab his gun, point it at Silent with shaking hands, but he finished him off, too.

A fourth came running toward him, but in a few steps Silent disarmed him. When the guard opened his mouth to scream, he clamped one hand over his mouth and shot him in the side of the head. After the man ceased to struggle, he lowered the corpse slow and easy.

Silent checked the barbed wire fence. No one rushed out to help the others.

A faded sign was hanging over the fresh corpse he put to rest.

Sabella's Storage Rental. A front for sex trafficking, the Sabella family's main source of income, but they made one vital mistake. Dom Sabella thought by ending the Salernos and keeping one souvenir for himself, no one would come after him. Tonight, Silent would prove to the fucker he'd never been invincible, that he, too, would bleed and beg like any other man.

Past the rusted fence, dim lights illuminated the innocent-looking shipping containers laid side-by-side like colorful dominoes. The interior, Silent knew, had been built with soundproof walls, an added precaution even though few would drive to the city's outskirts and turf owned by the Sabellas.

He debated whether to barrel right through the main gate, but didn't know how many men he'd be up against. Deciding stealth might be the better answer, he found a side gate. One violent tug and the rusted lock over the gate gave.

He slipped in, surprising the guy on duty who'd been stuffing his face with a box of noodles. The amateur dropped the box, spilling food everywhere, fingers tangling into his shoulder holster.

Lax security. Dom Sabella didn't think anyone would dare enter his fortress and make it out alive. Silent put a bullet into the man's chest, cradled the body so it wouldn't make a sound. By the time he made his way further inside, the soles of his shoes turned wet with blood. He wiped them clean on another corpse, this one with a better tailor.

Silent considered it progress, upgraded himself from nameless grunts to actual men who knew how to use their guns.

Silent had no mercy left in him, none for bastards who worked for a monster and inherited Dom Sabella's cruelty. Even the Santoras stayed cleared of the Sabellas, preferring to mind their own business, but Silent hadn't been worried about retribution. Silent would leave no one alive to tell the tale.

Silent checked the silencer on his gun, loaded more bullets in the chambers, before moving in. *For a big bastard, you move so quietly.* Those had been Tony's first words to him during their first job. Silent perfected the art of being invisible, because he knew one way or another he had to make up for his disability.

He narrowed his eyes, stayed put and studied the security detail. Two guards patrolled each section of the facility constantly. Silent picked them off one by one. When his own bullets ran out, he took theirs. By then, he had no need for a silencer. According to the information Tony provided, the Dom Sabella and his top men would be in the main office for their usual poker night.

Dom Sabella had made it too easy for Silent. The boss had killed all of his siblings during his climb to power, had three divorces under his belt, no children. Even Sabella's lieutenants, those in his inner circle, had been made up of nothing but cutthroats who didn't understand the concept of loyalty.

He spotted the lighted office ahead of him, an ugly little single-floor building with harsh lights. Though the windows, various women and young men sat in various states of undress, unmoving, eyes dulled, like lifeless dolls.

Silent clenched his jaw and gripped the handle of his latest revolver hard. He didn't like the unfamiliar feel of the weapon, but had to make do. Some movement inside. One large guy in a suit shouted at his phone before turning to the others. His main target remained seated behind his desk in front of the poker table, eyes narrowed, drumming fat fingers, each one ringed, on his desk.

He tucked the tiny gun away, wiped his sticky hands clean. Silent then swung the rifle he picked off one of the dead from his shoulder and took aim. The man who'd been on the phone he shot first, the kill fast. The fucker died instantly. Lucky piece of shit.

Silent took out the others. A couple managed to rush out the door, but didn't know where he hid.

"I see the sniper. On the roof of that container!" One yelled.

Silent rolled out of the way, dumped the empty rifle, and climbed nimbly down. He emptied his stolen gun on the rest, grabbed another before moving inside the container. Two balding men in expensive suits stood in front of Dom Sabella, smoking a cigar behind the desk. Pale green eyes regarded him. A frown appeared on Sabella's lips.

"You're one of Frank Santora's men," Dom Sabella commented.

"I heard of this freak," one of the baldies muttered. "They call him Silent because he's mute and deaf. You're nothing special, not—"

Silent didn't bother reading his lips. He shot that one in the knee for interrupting this sweet moment, one he'd been dreaming of for years. The second raised his gun at him with trembling fingers. Silent could scent the stink of fear on him, just like the others. Nothing but a sweating pig in a suit. All of Dom Sabella's inner circle had gone soft, lax; all they cared about was greed and excess. Easy prey for Silent.

"Wait," Dom interrupted. The baldy paused, but Silent noted his nervous finger on the trigger. "What do you want?"

Finally, the boss rose behind his desk, put a hand on his last man. Last because the other one tried to reach for his gun and Silent shot him thrice. One bullet took out the noisy bastard's other knee, two rendered his face into a pulp.

He didn't know this one's name, but recognized him from one of the photos, fumbling for his pants, sneer on his face while he stood over Silent's stolen property.

His suffering had been well-deserved. He turned to Dom.

Silent had zero plans to make any deals and wondered if Dom saw that in his eyes.

Dom swallowed. "Look, whatever it is you want, you can have it. Is it cash? I have plenty of that. In fact, you've impressed me so much I'm about to offer you a job."

Silent pulled the trigger. No more bullets. The remaining bald fucker had the gall to laugh, but it hadn't been a mistake on his side. He dropped the useless weapon. In moments, he had the baldie in a choking grip and strangled him in front of Dom Sabella.

The boss staggered backwards as Silent finally broke the asshole's neck. He signed to the filth.

"It's your turn, but you won't go so easily as your men. I gave them mercy, but for you? I have something else in mind."

"I don't understand. I don't sign," Dom blubbered.

Silent smiled in answer.

Chapter Two

He tugged the chain attached to his wrist, the clinking sound the only noise in the room, his prison. It provided him comfort, eased the isolation and loneliness that slowly ate at his soul each day.

Someone put him here for God knew how long, but his memories of the time before his prison eluded him. He'd been part of a family once, had people who cared. One special boy stuck out, one with eyes so pale, like winter frost, but underneath that cold exterior, lay a warm heart, one that boy hid carefully from the world.

Sometimes he wondered if he'd imagined it all, that he began in this cage and would die in it. He flicked the chain again, only to have something heavy ram against the wall he'd huddled up against. He froze, every muscle in his body taut.

Old fears rose up in him, but what hadn't his captors done that they hadn't before? His body still ached from the recent abuse. They'd gotten more and more careless lately, his value dropping as the master, as Dom Sabella liked to style himself, began to lose interest.

Soon enough, he'd simply wither away and die, forgotten and alone. He shivered, dragged his knees to his chest. Maybe that would be better. He didn't mind dying. Maybe he'd wait for that special friend in that other place, one where pain and misery didn't exist.

The wall vibrated again. He paid it no mind. Sometimes, the master's guests came stumbling in his cell, drunk or high. Still, dread coiled in his insides when a thump came from the door. He scuttled further against the wall, hoping it would swallow him whole and make him disappear. Childish hopes, but hope died in him as well as other emotions a long time ago.

The door made a rickety sound when it opened. Heaving, panting noises filled the empty space. Something big and heavy landed on the ground. It took him a second to realize the bleeding and pulverized meat in front of him had once been a human being. The master.

Swallowing, he dared lift his head. Someone blocked the entirety of the doorway, a titan, soaked in splatters of blood—he couldn't quite identify what he wore. Pupils the color of winter frost locked with his. Training made him drop his gaze.

The scary monster stalked over to him. Stalk had been the word, because despite the stranger's size, he made no noise. The stranger hunkered down in front of him. He flinched by instinct, despite knowing he'd be berated for it later on.

Large fingers gripped his chin, made him look up to see a rough profile few would call handsome. He silently took stock. Day-old stubble, a small cut on the bottom lip, fine white lines beneath the man's collar, a broken nose and those eyes. God, but they blazed bright with an emotion he'd been familiar with. Fury so all-consuming it sucked the breath out of him.

It took him a second to realize all that frightening anger hadn't been directed at him, or so he thought. The stranger pulled out something from inside his jacket. Black metal glinted in the harsh lights of his prison.

His breathing grew shallow, but he resisted the urge to fight back. All the fire had gone out of him over the years. Why struggle when it would only lead to more pain? He learned that sometimes, if he was good, it would hurt a lot less.

Still, he flinched when the stranger pulled the trigger. Maybe fate finally sent him an angel of mercy, except he felt no pain. The chain made his favorite sound again, before falling to the floor.

The angel shoved the gun into his crooked fingers and he realized he was being handed a gun. The man made several gestures with his hand. He blinked. The man repeated it.

"I don't understand," he whispered, his voice sounding funny to his ears.

It had been a long time since he last attempted communication with someone else. The master had no use for his words, only took pleasure in his screams.

"Sal." That name jolted him awake although the man whispered it, like a secret between two lovers. Friends.

The fog in his brain cleared a little, making way for memories he kept under lock and key, hoarded like little treasures. That was right. Sal. Salvatore Salerno had been the name given to him at birth, but he only permitted one boy to call him Sal. His heartbeat elevated, hammered like the wings of an erratic bird eager to break free of its prison.

The boy he remembered, one he met in a lonely hospital room, had turned into this lethal, frightening man.

"Silent." The moment he uttered Silent's name, the lock he put in his mind broke. He sucked in a breath, overwhelmed by his life before this, before Dom Sabella. Hatred bubbled up inside him, left to fester like a slow-spreading poison.

Silent shoved the gun in his hand again, rose to his feet, and dragged the screaming thing closer and he understood.

"Not enough time to make him squeal. Cleaners will be here soon," Silent signed. It was slowly coming back to Sal, the language he'd learned so he could talk more with Silent. So many moments, years—what could have been—stolen from them. Anger moved inside of him like a living thing.

Cleaners, Silent mentioned. Professionals. Yes, his family used those, too. Men who cleaned up any evidence of a crime so the local authorities would find nothing but a spotless scene. His old world, his old life, came back slowly to him.

The question of identity, of what he was now that Silent was here, he'd think about later.

"I don't know how," he whispered, looking up at Silent.

No taboos, no judgments between them. Morals didn't, couldn't exist in a world they both grew up in. He'd been the son of a fallen mafia boss and Silent had been raised through violence by a father who honed him to be a human weapon.

Silent showed him how, gripped both his hands over the weapon of murder. He looked into the blood shot eyes of his former master, knew he hadn't been the first. Dom Sabella traded in flesh, he recalled, but sometimes kept souvenirs. Dom's men spoke around him while they played with him, assumed he'd been reduced to a fuck toy, Sal no longer had the capacity to remember.

Dom Sabella was no innocent, would keep doing what he wanted if no one stopped him. The law couldn't touch him. Dom had a few dirty cops on his payroll, even the ear of some senator. Dom deemed himself untouchable, a king, until Silent wrenched his throne from underneath him. Sal had no doubt of that—that Silent hadn't left a trace of Dom's empire behind.

Gripping the gun in both hands, he took a deep breath and aimed the gun at Dom Sabella's head. He didn't know what to expect, something more dramatic maybe, not Dom's face falling flat on the floor, eyes wide open, lacking any sign of life.

"Why was that so easy?" he asked Silent, who shook his head.

Once, at the start of their friendship, he felt awkward around Silent, but as time went on, he understood Silent only spoke when he had something to say. He handed the gun back to Silent, offered it palm up.

Sal would have trusted no one, would kick and fight like a feral animal if it had been anyone but Silent. Silent took the gun, threw it away, offered his hand instead. A choice, Sal decided. No one had ever offered him that in such a long time that he needed to process the situation carefully.

He'd been the son of an important family once. When Dom Sabella extinguished his entire line and those loyal to the Salernos, he became nothing but a hole for men who took pleasure in his pain. Sal realized he was still nothing. What did Silent see when he looked at Sal?

"Come with me." Silent said the words this time, even though Sal knew talking discomforted Silent.

Back when they'd been children at that hospital, the bigger boys made fun of Silent for speaking loudly, still unused to his lack of hearing. Eventually, Silent preferred to learn another language of his own. Sign language had been exclusively theirs, their little secret, because no one in his family knew how to sign.

Pain of a different sort found its way to his heart. His chest felt constricted, as if it were difficult to breathe. He didn't know this hard-eyed man soaked in blood, his fallen angel, but he still saw hints of the boy who'd offered him friendship at a time when he felt lonely.

Unlike his older brothers, his father never considered Sal much of a Salerno, called him soft, wimpy. Like Silent's father, his own thought to toughen him up with fists. Where were they all now? Gone.

Ghosts. Only he was left and he hated the feeling of isolation most.

No. He still had Silent.

"Come. I've searched for you for so long. If you want freedom, it's yours, but we need to go now."

Freedom? That word seemed so alien. A bird kept in captivity for so long and suddenly offered freedom would eagerly spread its wings only to fall to its descent. Sal understood that. Besides, where would he go? The world had gone by during his time in his prison, would be nothing but a cold and unforgiving place for someone who hadn't seen real light in ages.

He closed his dirty fingers over Silent's bigger ones. They looked bent, wrong under the lights, just like him. What would Silent do, once Silent realized that Sal was merely a pathetic shell of his former self? Would Silent discard him then?

Chapter Three

Since his own jacket had been soaked, Silent stripped one off a corpse, decided it would do, and placed it over Sal's thin shoulders. Too thin, he thought when he first laid eyes on the ruin Dom Sabella had made out of his Sal. Not ruined, he decided. He saw the fire light within Sal's eyes when he offered that gun.

It didn't matter what state Silent found Sal in, because while he offered Sal the choice of freedom, Silent would never ever let Sal out of his sight again. Even if Sal spent the rest of his days a broken shell, he'd be right beside Sal, waiting, watching. Any fool stupid enough to take Sal from him, Silent would make an example of.

Until death do us part.

They might not be married. Fuck, Sal might never even see him as a partner, but it didn't matter. The vow held. Silent would stick by Sal until they were both old. He wouldn't stop trying, would never give up hope that someday, Sal would learn to spread his wings and find himself again.

"You made quite a mess, Silent," said Riddle, the crew leader in charge of clean-up.

Riddle and his guys posed as a cleaning company during daylight hours, but at night, they did a different sort of clean-up. Riddle had standards though, wouldn't work with just any member of the mob. Over the years, Silent built this relationship brick by brick, knowing he'd need a professional to help cover his tracks during the most important retrieval of his life.

At the sight of the big redhead, Sal hid behind him, pressed his face into his back and he stilled. Sal clutched at his blood-splattered shirt. Silent wanted to spirit Sal away from the carnage, but he needed to conclude this business first.

"Problem?" he signed to Riddle. Riddle had a deaf sister, knew how to sign and thanks to that, they understood each other perfectly. The cleaner knew what Silent was, but even among monsters, different types existed.

Riddle shook his head. Silent's skin prickled when Riddle gave Sal a once-over, gaze considering. Riddle's men wouldn't be easy prey like Dom's, but he'd persevere, would once again coat himself in blood if need be to ensure Sal's safety.

"Not a problem. After this, there will be no debts between us. You ended the fucker who raped my sister and I made sure no one would find a speck of evidence in this storage facility." Riddle extended a hand, which he shook.

Final business concluded, he steered Sal gently toward the exit. Some of Riddle's men nodded to him, but none of them would sell him out. Riddle prided himself on being a professional. Sal's shoulders started to shake as they exited the barbed wire fence. Sal halted, stared upwards, and lifted his head to see the sun beginning to set.

"My first sunset in I don't know how long," Sal whispered, leaning his head on the curve of his shoulder.

Silent seldom allowed anyone else physical contact; Sal would be the only exception. He reached for Sal's fingers, tentatively at first, and waited for Sal's reaction. These hands of his had been baptized in violence and bloodshed, and yet Sal automatically gave them a squeeze.

"How long," Sal ventured. "Had I been his prisoner?"

Silent gave him the answer, the painful truth. It

still gutted him how long he took to find Sal. Ever since Sal had been taken, his entire family murdered, Silent pooled his resources, his search relentless. Only recently had he found answers. Tony Santora had a source, an ex-bodyguard of Dom Sabella who'd caught a momentary glimpse of Sal.

That same source had planned on going to the police after discovering what his boss really did for a living, but he'd requested first dibs. Silent wasn't worried about the other victims in the containers. Riddle would make sure those men and women would return to their loved ones, either alive or in a coffin.

"You told me you offered me freedom," Sal began and he said nothing, waited.

Sal had to choose for his own, although it would be awhile until Sal managed to walk on his own into the world once more. Plenty of time had passed since Sal's captivity. Thirteen years kept in a cage and suddenly thrust back into a world so changed, so unrecognizable, Sal would undoubtedly have trouble adjusting.

"I want," Sal hesitated, faced him. Those bruised green eyes met his, unflinching, full of resurrected fire.

"What do you want?" he signed.

"To experience freedom with you." Sal let out a breath. "I'm sorry, my sign language is a little rusty."

"Continue talking. I got better at reading lips."

"I don't know anything else, don't want to be with anyone else but you. The thought of seeing you again, that kept me alive, sustained me when my spirit died."

He gripped Sal's thin shoulders. Too many sharp angles. Sal's rib cage peeked from his tattered shirt and his cheekbones were hollow. Sal's skin used to be creamy and smooth, too, he remembered, but Sal was so pale now, his paper-thin flesh stretched over bones and marred with old scars and abrasions.

He planned on changing that, on providing whatever Sal needed to heal, to get better. They'd work on the physical wounds, then to more severe ones on the heart and soul. Silent was no healer, but he'd try.

"You're a survivor, a fighter. Be proud," he said. He spoke because he only allowed his voice to be heard by one person.

A thin line formed on Sal's lips, not quite a smile, but they'd get there eventually.

****

Sal dreamed—the same nightmare that haunted him on the worst nights.

A woman screamed upstairs. Aunt Cecil, but he couldn't help her now, not hiding under the bed. His older brother Sergio shoved him there ever since the security system went off and told him to stay there. Gunfire made him cover his ears.

Phone. Silent. He had to call Silent. His father recently got him the mobile. He fished for it, fingers trembling as the black and green screen powered on. What took so long? Besides, what could Silent do? Silent might be lethal for a fifteen-year-old, but against armed men?

The police. His brain didn't work properly. His father would gut him for contacting the cops. Any member of the family who wailed to the coppers disappeared, never to be seen again, but this was an emergency.

Wood creaked, his door burst open and he stifled a scream. Aunt Cecil's cries turned quiet. More gunfire and shouts outside. He dropped his phone in panic. Huge mistake.

"Who's there?" A face appeared at his eye level and he gasped as the stranger grabbed him by the shirt

and dragged him out. "Only a little brat."

He screamed when the man in the suit pointed the barrel of his gun at his head. Later on, Sal would re-imagine that moment over and over and wished he'd died instead. He hadn't known a worse fate awaited him.

"Fuck, hold on, Bruno. I recognize the brat from the papers. It's Van Salerno's youngest. He's worth more as a hostage. Take him."

He fought, kicked at his captors but they were bigger, stronger. A blow to the side of the head, the ribs rendered him unconscious. The next time he woke up, it would be in the 20-foot shipping container that would be his prison for the next thirteen years. The only thing would be in store for him would be rough hands, harsh voices that told him over and over again that he was no longer Salvatore Salerno, merely a piece of disposable trash. Nothing.

****

Sal jolted awake in the present, shaking, panting, and clutching a handful of comforter.

Wait. Comforter? He touched the silken fabric again. Sal expected the harsh light cast from the single light bulb in his cell, but only natural light flowed inside an airy room. Spartan furniture made up the space, including the king-sized bed he slept on, but wind blew through the wide-open balcony to his left.

Rubbing at his eyes to make sure this wasn't a dream, he flung the comforter away. Someone had taken away his usual rags, replaced it with a giant shirt, some sports logo on the front he didn't recognize, and loose sweatpants. His swung himself off the bed, feet touching a smooth wooden floor, not the ugly orange steel surface he'd stared at for hours at a time.

"This isn't real," he whispered.

He padded to the balcony, wanting to take in as

much of this surreal reality as possible before he woke up back in his dull cell. The view took his breath away, miles and miles of nothing but white sand and beyond that, stretched the endless aquamarine ocean. The sound of waves filled his ears. So much stimulation.

Strange. The white walls, wooden floors, the simple furniture of the beach house and even the view outside, they all seemed familiar, but Sal was pretty certain he'd never been here. He recalled fragments of conversations he had before with Silent.

As boys, he told Silent about owning a house on an island, one isolated from the rest of the world, untouched by the violence and politics that tainted their own reality.

Hungry for more, he looked on, but his attention grew divided as he spotted a more intriguing sight.

Silent wore nothing but a pair of workout shorts, stretched himself on the sand, before starting what looked like a series of martial arts forms.

He gripped the wooden railing of the balcony. No way his mind could construct such an elaborate and vivid illusion. He pinched himself, the pain confirming this might not be a dream.

Sweat dripped down the powerful, inked and tanned muscles of Silent's back. His mouth went dry. Silent reminded him of a sleek and lethal predatory cat. Then Silent turned, as if he knew someone watched him.

He let out a breath. Silent signed for him to come closer. Did Sal dare?

His feet seemed to have a mind of their own. Wind messed up his hair, no longer matted but smelling of shampoo. Silent's shampoo?

It all started coming back to him. He remembered entering Silent's truck. They stopped for food and Silent had an amused look while he chowed down on the burgers and fries only to throw up several hours later. He slept a good long while. His mind came up blank.

He wanted Silent to fill in the blanks. Approaching Silent, he asked, "What happened after we had burgers last night?"

"Two nights ago," Silent gestured. "I drove us to a private airstrip. Flew us here. You've been asleep all this while."

He blushed. "You helped clean me up."

"You stank."

He glared at Silent for that remark, then the words sunk in. He blushed. "You saw me naked?"

Silly of him to worry about a thing like that, but it mattered to him. Sal didn't need a mirror to look at the horror show his body had become. Why would anyone want second-hand goods like him?

Silent regarded him with those eyes that saw far too much. This man possessed the ability to strip all his shields and see him, naked and bare, but Silent had also been his single light in the dark, the anchor he held onto. Seeing Silent again kept him sane. Well, not full crazy at least.

"I plan on seeing more of you eventually. You forget, Sal. You're mine alone. No one else's."

He sucked in a breath at those words. Silent proved his point many times over, had eliminated an entire family to retrieve him and would have climbed over a mountain of bodies at the chance someone took Sal again.

He had nothing else to fear now that all his demons were slain.

Sal wrapped his arms around his body. A chill went down his spine. Weaker men would have shivered, would have run away screaming when facing a man like Silent, but not him. Silent forgot one important thing, so he made that point.

"You're mine, too. Then and now. Forever."

Chapter Four

Mine, too.

Those two little words played repeatedly in Silent's head. Sal didn't look like much, more like a skeleton, a shadow of the defiant fearless boy in the hospital, but he always knew. Peel away skin, unearth bone and he'd find unyielding, unbreakable steel. His Sal had always been the stronger of them when others would have splintered and crumbled living in a 20-foot prison.

Sal lifted his chin. "I'm possessive, too."

Realizing those words had taken too much of Sal, he crossed the distance between them. When Sal hadn't taken a step back, didn't push him away, he wrapped his arms around Sal's slender frame. Silent placed a kiss on Sal's bottom lip, traced the shape with his tongue, pleased Sal hadn't pulled away. He stopped. Sal looked a little disappointed, but Sal hadn't been ready for the next step.

Sal probably associated punishment and pain with sex

Never would Silent take advantage of Sal at his weakest, he'd wait until Sal was ready to be his in every sense of the word, even if it took months, years, decades or an entire lifetime. He'd wait, because they had plenty of time in the world. Silent owned this island getaway, as well as the surrounding smaller ones.

He never spent a cent during his time working for the Santoras and previous employers. Silent had one goal in mind—Sal's extraction and ensuring their disappearance. In a couple of days, news would surface about his death and that of Sal's. True to Riddle's word, a fire had broken out in the storage facility, but the cops had been alerted about rescued and bewildered victims who had no clue who rescued them.

Sal buried his face into his chest, inhaling the scent of him. Then Sal started to shake, tears streaking down his face. Silent held Sal for as long as he needed, until Sal let out all the anger, frustration and feeling of helplessness he'd kept inside of him.

Eventually, Sal wiped at his eyes. "Sorry. You must think I'm a wuss."

"Never that." How could Sal even think that, after everything he'd endured?

Silent licked away the remaining droplets, tasting the salt of Sal's tears. He gestured back to the house. Sal needed some meat on his bones. He released Sal, extended a hand, which Sal automatically grabbed. He led them back to the kitchen, bid Sal to sit at the kitchen counter.

"Wait here."

He grabbed a t-shirt from the bedroom, their bedroom now, although Silent had dragged in the armchair from the living room, in case Sal preferred to sleep alone for the moment. Upon his return, he found Sal curiously examining the touch panel of the hot and cold water dispenser of the fridge. Sal jumped when Silent touched his shoulder.

"You still move so quietly," Sal grumbled, still staring at the panel. "Technology sure has changed, huh?"

Silent pointed to the desktop computer at one corner. "I'll teach you how to use that, and how to surf the web so you can catch up with what's happened over the past few years."

Sal's gaze softened. "Thank you."

"No need to thank me."

In fact, Silent owed Sal, kept wondering if he missed a step. He second-guessed all the decisions he made over the past few years, but this morning, waking up to see Sal tucked in his bed, snores filling the room, he decided on one important thing. The past no longer mattered.

Silent ate, slept, and killed, but he existed, not lived. On the outside, he appeared to be a good watchdog, never questioned orders, developed connections for the sake of fulfilling one goal. Never once did he stray from his search.

Those days were over. He focused on the now. Silent opened the kitchen fridge. Supplies were delivered to him daily by boat by locals he trusted, had created friendships with while he wasn't working.

This way, the foundations had been built for the time Sal returned to this house. Sal's house, for Sal had been the architect, the original dreamer. All Silent needed to do was turn the dreams of a boy into reality.

Sal appeared by the side of the stove again, eyes wide, full of questions. "Silent, this house," Sal began, bit his lower lips. "It's exactly like the one we talked about when we were kids."

"Yes. This is yours."

It had been the least Silent could do. He purchased the islands, the house, established relationships with the locals, formed bonds with an expensive security company to install a fool-proof and state-of-the-art system. All premature actions, Silent knew. Back then, he didn't even know if Sal was still alive. On multiple occasions, he'd nearly given up, but he kept going.

"No," Sal murmured. "Ours. Can I help with something?"

"Sit. I want to make our first breakfast together." At that, Sal obeyed. He made a simple meal—bacon, eggs, and toasted some bread.

After setting their plates down, Sal dug in. Realizing Silent hadn't made a move, Sal stopped and chewed on his piece of toast slowly. "What?"

"I thought you'd need more persuasion to eat, get healthy." He approved immensely that Sal had the initiative to get better.

Sal finished the bread, swallowed.

"I want…" Sal hesitated.

"Speak your mind." Whatever Sal wanted, he'd make it happen.

Sal had held possession of his soul ever since they were kids. After their first meeting at the hospital, he'd been passed among relatives with connections to the mob. An uncle picked up where his father left off, taught Silent the skills he needed for the trade. Only his secret meetings with Sal kept him sane. Sal wasn't just his conscience, but also his heart because Silent lacked one.

Deaths didn't bother him, especially guilty scumbags who preyed on the weak or those who took pleasure in hurting others. Only a monster could end others like him. Silent would have taken his own life a long time ago if not for Sal, who insisted even men like him deserved to live.

"I want to get well," Sal ventured, looked at his plate. Silent didn't like that. He tipped Sal's chin. Wary eyes met his. "I'm second-hand goods, you know?"

A feral growl rumbled out of his chest, making Sal widen his eyes in surprise.

"Don't fucking ever say that again."

Sal frowned. "Are you saying there's nothing wrong with me? Don't lie."

Silent let out a frustrated breath. He anticipated Sal developing self-esteem issues during his time in captivity, but he hadn't realized it might be hard to erase those silly notions out of Sal's head.

"I want you. All of you." Silent let Sal see the hunger in his eyes, one emotion he kept in check for fear for scaring off the only man that mattered. "Strip away this veneer of civility and you'd find a beast. All I want to do is ravish you on this table."

Sal stared at him, fear and wonder in his eyes. "You mean that?"

Silent gritted his teeth in assent, shoveled more food into his mouth. Of course he'd remain celibate if Sal never accepted him to bed. The frustration would continue to brew inside him, like a storm waiting to be unleashed, but he'd wait.

"Every word."

"But you've been careful," Sal eventually said. "Never once took advantage where other men would."

"I'll never force you to do anything you don't want. Your choices are your own."

Sal reached across the table, closed his small hand over Silent's. Silent had noticed Sal's fingers during his retrieval, knew how they'd gotten that way. Old anger simmered inside him even though the fucker Dom Sabella rotted in an unmarked grave along with the men who took similar pleasure in hurting Sal. Dom died too soon. Silent hadn't the chance to get as creative as he wished, his longing to see Sal more important.

"I choose you," Sal simply said, daring to meet his gaze.

"Think carefully." Silent flipped Sal's hand over, spreading out Sal's palm flat on the table, tracing each line on Sal's hand with one callused finger. Sal shivered when he moved it lower, to trace Sal's pulse point. "Once you agree to be mine, there's no going back. You'll be bound forever to a monster."

"You're not a monster, not to me." The sudden vehemence in Sal's voice and those blazing eyes stunned him for a second.

Sal might not understand fully, not yet, that by tying himself to Silent, he'd be dooming himself, but it didn't matter. Sal could still have a normal life if he wished, travel to wherever he wanted and be whoever he wanted. Silent would provide whatever resources Sal needed, watch in the shadows, never taking his eye off his target.

Too bad Silent was one selfish bastard. No material possession interested him, no other person ever held his interest for so long. It had always been Sal.

"Be certain of what you want." Silent extracted his hand, resumed eating breakfast. Sal huffed from his corner and did the same.

They spoke about nothing in particular. No doubt Sal had a thousand questions, about Silent's search, the world that moved on without him, other inconsequential matters. Occasionally, Sal looked out the open balcony, as if he couldn't quite trust what he saw at this moment, that it hadn't been a figment of his imagination.

Silent tapped the table surface, drawing Sal's attention back to him. "Let's take a walk after this," he signed.

Chapter Five

Sal kicked at the heavy fabric weighing his legs down, moaning. He clawed at the floor. *No*. Soft sheets. Heart hammering, he dared open his eyes, breathing harsh. A hand landed on the square of his back, not intrusive or violent hands.

Safe. Someone started to stroke the length of his spine, relaxing all the tense muscles. He turned, lying flat on his back to look at Silent, who sat on the edge of the bed, wearing nothing but boxers. He gripped Silent's hand, relieved Silent hadn't pushed him away, didn't call him childish or needy.

The sight of Silent's solid form, Silent's incredibly warm hand squeezing his, reassured him he'd only been dreaming.

Silent helped him sit up and he took in the familiar details of the room. Their room, not his prison. Sal still found it hard to believe a week had passed since Silent came for him. Wind came from the opened windows, tickling his face.

"Breathe in and out."

Even now, he viewed Silent's voice as a precious gift.

"Why don't you ever talk to other people like you do with me?" His twelve-year-old self asked Silent as they prowled the busy halls of the children's hospital.

"I have nothing to say to them."

Sal grinned, grabbed Silent's hand, ignoring his grunt. "That's okay. It'll be our little secret."

Back in the present, he did as Silent asked, and found it helped.

"Sorry, nightmares," he muttered.

Silent turned on the lamp on the table beside the

bed. "You don't have to apologize for anything."

"I do. I can't imagine you get much sleep on the chair," he muttered.

Silent had been clear about boundaries despite his many attempts to lure the other man to bed. Sal knew he hadn't been ready for sexual contact, not yet, but at the very least, he wanted to feel Silent's body draped over his.

"You know what would help?" he ventured.

"We can leave the light on."

He shook his head. Depending on the mood of his captors, they'd sometimes leave the light on or keep it off. Sal didn't know what had been worse, the swallowing darkness or the harsh light that prevented sleep.

"Join me. Please. If you're next to me," Sal hesitated. "You'll ward off the nightmares."

Silent regarded him for a couple of moments, before joining him in bed. Silent positioned himself behind the curve of his back, wrapped those steel-corded arms around his waist. Heart racing, he snuggled close until his ass pressed against Silent's boxers.

Silent's breathing grew erratic for a couple of moments. He wanted to rip those boxers off, to feel Silent's balls and cock pressed up against the cleft of his ass. Only with Silent would Sal allow intimate skin privileges. He shuddered when Silent nipped at the side of his neck, breath warm against his ear.

"Go to sleep."

Sal slept like the dead.

****

Sal woke up to the smell of frying bacon. He rubbed at his eyes. No morning light. He peered at the closed windows, sucked in a breath to see rain lashing at the glass. Booming thunder startled him. He got off the bed, walked out of the bedroom.

The balcony door remained open as it always did, and he walked towards it, feet bare on the wooden floor. Heavy droplets hit his head. Sal raised his face, enjoyed the feel of the water sliding down his skin. Back in his miserable prison, he always liked it when rain hammered the walls of his container. Any sound apart from his breathing had been welcomed.

He gazed at the angry waves, the storm clouds continuing to gather. Lightning flashed on the horizon, nature at its finest. A moment later, something soft and thick landed on his shoulders, a towel. He turned. Silent didn't look angry, didn't lecture him about getting a cold, merely gestured back inside.

He followed Silent, let the other man dry off his hair.

Silent closed the glass doors of the balcony.

"I always listened for the rain," he told Silent. "I find the sound comforting."

Especially on the worst days, when he'd feel isolation slowly eating its way into his soul. Without another word, Silent pulled him into an embrace. He relaxed in Silent's arms, rested his chin on Silent's broad shoulder. With trembling fingers, he traced the firm lines of Silent's square jaw, thumbing the day-old stubble there. Like an animal denied of touch for so long, he wanted to touch, explore every inch of the glorious male in front of him.

Boundaries. Sal wanted to do away with them. He understood the need for them though, knew Silent kept his distance for a reason. If Sal ever decided to cross that final line and become Silent's, he had to make the choice himself with a rational mind.

Silent taught him how to use the internet. They might be in an isolated corner of the world, but it amazed him they weren't cut off from it. He read about kidnapped victims online, how they had trouble assimilating to normal life, but neither he nor Silent had ever been normal.

Right from the beginning, since they'd been kids, he'd known Silent would be the one steady presence in his life. Even then, as a child who didn't understand desire, he knew two broken boys had forged one unbreakable bond that would last a lifetime.

"It's been two months," he stated, looking up to meet Silent's steady gaze.

Hard to imagine he'd spent two months in paradise with a man he'd never thought he'd see again. Since then, Sal had gained more weight, started going on morning runs with Silent. They explored every inch of the island, took a boat to the mainland so Silent could show him around the main town area where he procured their food and other supplies.

It almost seemed like his captivity hadn't been real, but ugly memories rose up at the oddest moments. Once, he cried silent tears for no reason in a crowded street while they paid a visit to the mainland. He'd been embarrassed by the incident, but Silent steered him to a quiet spot until he calmed down.

Sal could never pretend to be whole, to be the boy Silent knew. His childhood and parts of his adulthood had been taken by force, along with his innocence. Slowly but surely though, his new self began to emerge from its fragile shell. Sal still didn't know whether this new him was better than his old one, but he could think logically now, his state of mind clear, unweighted by old fears and doubts.

"Yes," Silent eventually replied.

"You asked me an important question. Remember?"

Of course Silent did. That question of claim constantly hounded them. He knew Silent held his own desires in check, would have waited for an eternity until he gave his consent. Too much time had been stolen from them already and Sal was sick of waiting.

He took a deep breath. "I'm yours, Silent. Have always been yours."

Only Silent possessed the patience and devotion to continue looking for him when most people presumed him dead. To one person, he mattered, still held value. Rising on tiptoe, he made the first move, kissed Silent for the first time.

Oh, they kissed before on a dare, as boys who couldn't understand the emotions raging inside of them. Those broken boys had grown; Silent to this hard-eyed, deadly man who showed no weakness save for him, and he to this former victim struggling to find his new identity.

Silent tightened his hold, pressed him close until their chests and groins touched. Sal's dick strained against the fabric of his sweatpants. After all he'd been through, he'd never thought he'd find sex enticing, but this was Silent, the only man he'd give his entire surrender without question.

Never in a million years would Silent hurt him. Silent would kill himself first before harming Sal. This man would take a bullet for him, had made a mountain of corpses to get to him. This same man others labeled a killer, a monster, had also built the house of his dreams, had meticulously planned and waited for his return.

Did Silent think he could still look at another man when all he ever needed and wanted stood right in front of him?

He'd read a couple of romance ebooks, knew others could spend an entire lifetime searching for their soul mate. Not them. Fate might have parted them, but they'd found each other again.

Silent angled his head so Sal had better access. He didn't know what the hell he was doing. Then Silent took control, tracing his lower lip with his tongue, nipping at his upper one.

Hunger and need moved him, but so did something else, an emotion he couldn't quite name. Sal loved Silent, even though initially he'd doubted he still possessed the ability to love anyone else after the hell he'd endured.

Silent cupped his cheek, pale eyes intense. He parted his mouth, letting Silent slip his tongue down his throat. His insides melted. Electric jolts traveled down his body and went right to his thickening cock. He sucked on Silent's tongue, deciding they should do this more often.

"More," he uttered once Silent released his mouth.

Silent trailed his hand down the length of his body, slipping it past the waistband of his boxers to hold his shaft captive. He groaned as Silent began to stroke the length of him, callused hand a contrast in texture to the silk of his dick. Silent thumbed away the pre-cum at his tip, gave his balls a tug before resuming stroking him.

No one ever paid attention to his needs. Dom and his men saw him as a convenient hole, one among many, nothing special. Silent looked at him like a treasure beyond price.

The simple contact, the knowledge Silent held his most intimate bits, had been enough for the pressure building inside him to burst. He cried out, seed spilling over Silent's waiting hand.

"I'm so sorry," he whispered, terrified he ended the dance just when they started.

"Why sorry? I enjoyed seeing you climax. Your release, this," Silent gestured to his body, his softening dick. "All mine."

"Yours." Sal had once been disposable property, but Silent picked up the pieces Dom started to think of as trash and built him up again.

He ran his hand up Silent's arm, tracing one old knife wound there. He realized he'd bleed for this man, too, would give his life for Silent without question, too, despite not being a fighter.

"I want to be worthy of you."

Silent took his hand away, still coated with his jizz and to his shock, licked it dry. His Silent reminded him of a large, lazy, and satisfied predator, but ready to strike any second. He didn't mind being Silent's prey, to be at the complete mercy of Silent. His man. Sal had nothing to his name. Everything he once cherished and had known, brutally taken away in a single night, except Silent.

Silent claimed his mouth again, the kiss unexpectedly slow, sweet and tender. When Silent pulled away, he moaned, fisting his fingers into Silent's shirt, a demand for more.

"I'm the one who never deserved you, but I'm one greedy fucker. I'm never giving you up again."

Chapter Six

Silent waited for Sal to pull away at those words, but Sal remained there.

"Good," Sal stated. "At least we're both clear on that."

Hope fluttered inside of him, that emotion his father considered a deadly weakness. However, it had been hope and sheer stubbornness that fueled him, kept him going all these years when others could have given up. He expected to find a shell of the boy he'd known years ago, but this man blew him away. Sal always had it in him, a will made of steel, despite his deceptively slender frame.

"Bed." Silent found himself incapable of forming any other word.

Need roared inside of him, an unstoppable force of nature. The moment Sal granted him consent, full access, he could no longer contain the beast inside of him.

Sal parted from him, grabbed his hand, and tugged him toward their bedroom. Forget breakfast and everything else. Silent had other priorities. He'd been waiting to put his hands, his mouth to good use, to see the expression of bliss on Sal's face after coming undone.

Silent planned on exploring the entire length of Sal's body, familiarize himself with every secret spot, places which made Sal moan and tickle.

In the bedroom now, he edged Sal towards the bed. One gentle push on the chest and Sal landed on his ass, gazing at him with a mixture of excitement and fear, a potent combination.

"Wait," Sal stated, gesturing to his shirt. "Clothes

off."

"You, too."

He peeled off his shirt. Sal did the same, his movements tentative. He noticed with some satisfaction, that Sal's ribs no longer poked out. Sal wasn't just eating more, but also taking steps to get in shape. Silent recalled how out of breath Sal had been during their first run on the beach, but these days, Sal liked challenging him to a race.

In such a short span of time, Sal had come so far and he couldn't put into words how proud he was of him.

Sal wrapped his arms over some old scarring across his stomach, but he gripped Sal's wrists.

"No."

"You changed your mind?" Sal whispered, misunderstanding his meaning.

"No secrets between us."

"But I'm…" Sal murmured. "Imperfect."

He clenched his jaw, wished he had the power of resurrection so he could make Dom Sabella, the monster who stripped away Sal's innocence and confidence, suffer again. Silent didn't give up yet, because over the past few days, he'd seen glimpses of the defiant and fearless boy peeking out.

He spread his fingers over Sal's, moved them to touch his own collection of scars. Silent had a few, considered them reminders, markers which led him a step closer to Sal. Sal's expression relaxed and it took him a second to gather that Sal had let out a nervous little laugh.

When told his hearing would never return, anger festered inside of him. Silent retreated to one corner of his mind, refused to speak to anyone else until Sal. He proved over time that his disability didn't make him flawed, told himself he never cared for the opinions of others anyway, that they had nothing valuable to say to him.

For once, he wished he could hear the sound of Sal's voice, to hear Sal laugh. Never in his wildest imagination did he think Sal could ever come this far so fast.

It didn't matter, he realized a moment later as Sal rose only to wrap his arms around his neck, smiling up at him.

"I get it. We're both alike, suited for each other. I won't mention it again."

"Good." He nipped Sal's bottom lip, because the next time Sal berated himself again, Silent planned on dishing out a creative punishment. Perhaps one that involved Sal at his mercy, circuits so overloaded with pleasure and stimulation that Sal would start begging for his release.

Sal frowned at him. "You have that mischievous look in your eyes, one that says you plan on doing dirty things to me."

"Would you like that?"

"Yes."

"No more interruptions."

They tore at each other's clothes until they both stood fully nude. Another shove sent Sal tumbling onto the bed. Sal showed initiative, scooting further up in bed. He blanketed his body over Sal's, plundered Sal's mouth again, fully enjoying the taste and heat of Sal. Sal kissed back fervently, locking his hand behind the nape of his neck, passion equating his own.

He moved his mouth lower, fisted Sal's hair to bare the smooth graceful skin of Sal's neck. Silent grazed Sal's racing pulse with his teeth, licked at it, liking Sal's shudder.

"Mine," he repeated, establishing his ownership.

"Yes," Sal murmured.

He planted kisses down the cords of Sal's throat, sucked at the hollow of Sal's collarbones. Sal moaned above him, about to touch him, but Silent wrenched Sal's hands above his head.

"Keep them there," he ordered.

Sal nodded, hips rising, the tip of his dick leaving a smear on his abdomen. He firmly held Sal's thighs down, intent on taking his fill.

"You're such a tease, you know that?" Sal signed.

He smirked, took Sal's left nipple in his mouth, sucking on it, before deciding to leave his mark there. Satisfied at the imprint of his teeth there and Sal's wordless cry above him, he continued his task. He traced the scar Sal had been so conscious of earlier, from tip to tip, hoping to show Sal he cherished every part Sal considered an imperfection.

Lowering his body, he eyed Sal's dick, already at half-mast. Sal squirmed, but he planted his hands over Sal's thighs, restricting movement. If Sal wanted to put a stop to this, Sal need only tap him on the shoulder. Silent met Sal's gaze. Sal's expression turned soft, vulnerable, and he drank it up. Only for him Sal would let all his shields down.

He tongued Sal's slit, tasting pre-cum. Silent made a swirling motion over Sal's cockhead, traced every vein, ridge, and bump of Sal's length. Sal speared fingers through his hair, but he didn't mind. Sal's balls, he didn't neglect. Silent took them into his mouth, sucking at them. Then he opened his mouth, and started to take Sal's prick into his mouth.

****

The moment Silent closed his lips over his dick, Sal lost his ability to think. He groaned, one hand tangled in Silent's hair, the other clutching at the sheets as he watched his dick disappear down Silent's throat.

God, the erotic sight only made his dick engorge, close to bursting. Sal couldn't wait to return the favor to Silent one day. Soon, he decided, moaning as Silent bobbed his head. He gave Silent's thick hair a tug. Silent paused.

"I'm close," he mouthed.

Silent pulled his mouth away. He let out a sound of frustration, only for Silent to pull himself back up, sealing his lips for another toe-curling kiss. Silent closed his fingers over his shaft, began to work it again, alternating between a slow and fast rhythm. His breaths hitched and once Silent released his mouth, he came for the second time that day.

Rolling off him, Silent yanked the drawer next to the bed and took out a condom foil and lube. Silent looked to him first for confirmation.

"Stop treating me like I'm going to break any moment."

"You're strong, I know you've always been, but the last thing I want to do is force myself on you."

He laughed, unable to help it. Silent narrowed his eyes. "That'll never happen, seeing I want you as much. Silent, I love you. There will be no one but you."

Sal let the words sink in for a little longer. Silent would never say them back he knew, but only because Silent didn't think himself capable of love. Sal knew better.

"No one else," Silent said, positioning himself at the edge of the bed. "I'm never letting you go, never giving you up."

That sounded like a promise and he knew Silent always kept them. His heart felt like it would burst, his chest constricted. So many words he wanted to say, things he wanted to do with Silent. They had all the time in the world now, he mused, but some part of him still distrusted happiness.

He'd been at a good place, when Dom Sabella painted his family home in red and kept him as a souvenir.

No more doubts or hesitations.

The likelihood all of this newfound happiness would be taken away from him was close to zero. Silent made sure his trail was clean, untraceable. He saw the news through the internet himself. The storage facility had been burned to the ground and the authorities determined the cause as an accident. The sex trafficking victims had been safely gotten out before the flames broke out and were in the process of being returned to their families.

Sal lowered himself until his legs hung off the edge. He let out a squeak when Silent lifted them over his broad shoulders, exposing his dick, balls, and puckered hole.

"I'm not going anywhere," he told the man above him.

Silent uncapped the lube, applied a generous amount on his fingers, before working plenty more into his entrance. His dick pulsed at the contact of Silent sliding his fingers deep in him, rubbing at his inner muscles. He gasped when Silent found his sweet spot, did it again and his dick stirred back to life.

Sal never viewed sex as anything pleasant but with Silent, it felt different. He wanted to make that intimate connection with Silent, who already owned his heart.

"I want you inside of me, Silent. Please." He begged. "Make me forget all the bad memories I have."

Silent made twisting motions with his fingers, making Sal want something bigger inside of him. Finally,

Silent tore open the condom, slipped it over his cock, and angled it towards Sal's slick hole. He gasped when Silent pushed in, well aware Silent wasn't exactly small, probably the largest he'd ever had inside of him, but the bastards who took without asking didn't count.

Only this one man mattered.

"In and out."

Silent's soothing voice. Once Silent passed the thick ring of muscles, it became easier to breathe. Finally, Silent's balls rested against Sal's ass, Silent's cock seemingly stretching him to the limit. It burned, but he knew Silent would render his body boneless, his mind soaring.

He gripped Silent's biceps and without another word, Silent began thrusting in and out of him. The rhythm started slow, steady, but Silent increased the speed. He raised his hips, meeting Silent for every push, his dick brushing against the ridges of Silent's abdomen. Silent gripped him hard, no doubt leaving bruises, but these marks Sal relished wearing. They told who he rightfully belonged to.

"More," he murmured. "Please."

Pleading seemed to help.

Silent moved faster, deeper, breaching his most intimate places and reducing them both to panting messes. He clawed at Silent's shoulders, leaving a red crescent marks of his own, like a cat marking its territory. It appeared it wasn't just Silent who understood possession. When they stepped onto the mainland to get supplies, unwarranted envy hit him whenever someone else looked at his man with appreciation.

Even Sal could have overprotective tendencies, too.

What Silent and he had wasn't obsession or mere lust. He didn't consider his situation similar to victims who'd latch on automatically to their protector, the first face they see after enduring hell. Silent had been his from the start, ever since he intruded on that hospital room many years ago and joined Silent in bed.

Silent didn't seem to mind his little scratches. In fact, Silent appeared more riled up, hammered in and out of him with fast, furious strokes that left him groaning.

"I'm coming." Sal gasped, whimper muffled by another crushing kiss that completely obliterated him from the inside out.

Chapter Seven

Fuck, but Sal's ass felt so tight, inner muscles clamping around his dick. So good. This was even better than the fantasies he'd entertained over the past few nights. Silent had to admit, keeping himself from touching Sal had been the hardest thing he'd ever done. He didn't sleep until he was certain Sal's snores would fill the room. Instead of joining Sal, he'd head to the bathroom and start fucking his hand.

This though, was much better and he planned on rutting with Sal as much as possible.

Silent shifted his hips, must have slammed into Sal's prostate, because Sal arched his back, lips parting to receive another kiss. Their tongues tangled, teeth clashed.

He closed his mouth on the side of Sal's mouth, bit hard enough to bruise. Sal raked his nails down the muscles of his back. Who knew his Sal could be a little hellcat in bed?

Silent aimed for Sal's sweet spot again, felt Silent's ass muscles tightening around his shaft. He let out a snarl. Even though he couldn't hear Sal's cries, he focused on their sweat-slicked skin pressed against each other, Sal's dick rubbing against his body and Sal's expression. Sal gave his left triceps a squeeze and he halted. His balls tightened against his body. Every muscle seemed locked in place.

Fuck.

"Please," Sal mouthed.

"What are you begging me for?"

Silent knew the answer though.

Sal craved release, but he slowed down his pace, prolonging the moment a little longer. He had a feeling the first time they'd come together it would be intense and rough, unraveling years of frustration and pent-up need.

Silent reached between their bodies, found Sal's engorged shaft, leaking pre-cum. He gave the tip of Sal's dick a squeeze. That seemed like the tipping point.

"Fuck."

Sal grew still underneath him, then unraveled, muscles relaxing. Sal bit him back, sinking his teeth into Silent's left pectoral. That spurred him on. Several thrusts into Sal's slick entrance and the pressure inside him burst. The room fell away from his line of sight as he let out a triumphant growl.

Once the haze of bliss cleared, he got off Sal, threw the condom away in the bathroom trash, and returned with a washcloth to clean them both up. That task done, he joined Sal in bed, noticed with approval how Sal automatically scooted back up and settled against him, facing him.

Silent placed a possessive arm over Sal's waist, tugging the other man close.

"I'm glad we did that," Sal said, still looking a little languid. Sal reminded him of a satisfied cat licking the cream off his paws. "We should do that more often."

"I plan on taking you plenty more times," he said, running his fingers over the bruises he left behind during their rough lovemaking. Silent swore the next time he'd take it slower. They had all the time in the world, after all. "How are you feeling?"

"Sore, but the good kind." Sal began to close his eyes, but Silent pinched his cheek. Sal scowled.

"The day's just starting."

"Well," Sal began, resting his head on Silent's chest. "I prefer to spend the earlier part of it rolling around in bed with you. Any arguments?"

Silent considered that proposal. Outside, the storm continued to rage. Staying indoors did sound tempting. "First, a shower, then breakfast."

Sal pouted. "Then bed again?"

"You drive a hard bargain," Silent commented.

Sal grinned. "Of course. Are we squeezing a round two somewhere in there?"

"Are you able to?"

"Not like I plan on doing any other strenuous activity today." Sal untangled himself from him and padded to the bathroom, definitely aware Silent watched him. "Are you going to join me? Showering together would conserve water."

****

Silent beat him to the bathroom by a millisecond. He scowled. Silent turned on the tap. Water filled the tub halfway before Silent entered.

"Where will I fit?" Sal demanded, crossing his arms. "We both can't fit in there."

"That a dare?" Silent signed.

"Challenge accepted," he finished, throwing one leg over the tub.

Sal settled for straddling Silent's lap, water surrounded them both, but Silent proved warmer. He looked down to see Silent's thickening dick. Feeling mischievous, he raised his hips. Silent seemed to know what he planned, because Silent closed his big hands over his waist and helped lower his still-slick hole down onto Silent's cock.

He groaned, taking Silent's prick inch-by-inch, the water helping with the lubrication. This time, there hadn't been a need for a condom.

Call Dom Sabella a monster, but the bastard made sure all his merchandise tested clean.

"I like this," Silent said a moment later as he

groaned and shifted a little, but Silent's shaft completely filled him.

"This?" he managed to grit out, balancing himself by holding onto Silent's biceps.

"You riding me bareback."

He blushed, despite the fact Silent fucked him senseless only moments ago.

Thankfully, his tongue worked. "Me, too. No barriers between us."

He began to move his hips, up and down, side to side, pleased Silent let out a groan and gripped the globes of his ass, eliminating the need for distance between them. This second time proved to be a slow ride. His breathing turned erratic but Silent helped maintain the slow, luxurious pace.

Silent buried fingers into his hair, angled his face for a hot, rough kiss that contrasted sharply with their lovemaking. All fire. Sal decided he liked it both ways, slow and fast, rough and sweet, as long as it was Silent.

"I love you," he murmured. His climax began to build as Silent took over, thrusting in and out of him with relentless strokes.

Silent pressed his lips against the side of his neck, nipped at his earlobe and said those three little words back. It had been enough to push Sal over the edge of oblivion. Once more, he splintered, gripping the solid, hard planes of Silent, his anchor. His heart.

****

The storm clouds cleared by the time noon came around. Tangled in a sea of limbs, Sal shifted to see the bright afternoon sun through the window. With some difficulty, he managed to slip away from the bed, from Silent.

Reaching the window, he opened it, letting natural light in. Sal closed his brown hand into a fist.

He'd acquired a tan over the past two months, among other things. He didn't hear a sound, but knew the moment Silent woke. Unsurprised to feel Silent's arms around him, muscles like corded steel, he leaned against Silent's bare chest.

They stood like that for a few moments, not saying a word. He closed his eyes. Some days still didn't feel entirely real to him. Once, he had a nightmare that all of this had all been a product of his creative imagination and that in reality, Sal was still Dom Sabella's prisoner.

Silent never failed to bring him back, though.

"Want to walk outside?" Silent asked after a while.

He nodded. They dressed and hand-in-hand, walked outside, leaving their footprints on the white sand.

"Have you thought about what you want to do in the future?" Silent asked as they reached the edge of the island.

He could still see their house in the distance, a speck of white and beige, if he looked hard enough. Their house. It still felt odd thinking in those terms. Sal told Silent the truth. No way he planned on living in a city again, or anywhere with too many people around. Visits to the mainland had been enough.

There was no denying Dom Sabella left permanent damage, scars on his heart and soul. He could never be the boy Silent knew, but Silent knew that, too. His kidnapping also irrevocably altered the man next to him. Silent could have chosen to forget him, to pursue another course, but instead, Silent never stopped looking for him.

He told Silent the truth. "I want to stay here with you. I plan on finishing my high school degree online, then maybe take a college course."

"You loved to write," Silent added.

He smiled. Silent remembered all the details, never forgot a single thing. "I did, but my father disapproved, thought he could beat the notion out of my head with his fists."

So much of their lives had been colored by violence. It defined them, altered them. All Sal wanted was peace, to live out the rest of his life, with Silent beside him. He brushed his hand against Silent's. Silent locked their fingers together, an instinctive gesture.

"Maybe someday," he signed. "I'll write our story for the world to know."

Silent frowned at that. "You can do whatever you want, be whoever you want."

"I know." Silent never made him forget that no one would be able to take the freedom of choice from him again.

"My place," he stated, leaning his head against Silent's shoulder, aware Silent's gaze remained fixed on his lips, his face, reading his words. "Would always be with you."

The End

www.evernightpublishing.com/angelique-voisen

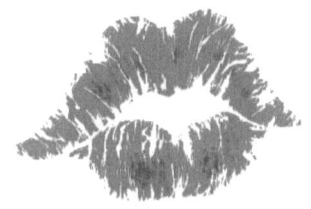

EVERNIGHT PUBLISHING ®

www.evernightpublishing.com